THEATER
IN THE
AMERICAS

A Series from
Southern
Illinois
University
Press
SCOTT
MAGELSSEN
Series Editor

Illustrations

STAGE FOR ACTION

U.S. SOCIAL ACTIVIST THEATRE IN THE 1940s

Chrystyna Dail

Southern Illinois University Press
Carbondale

Southern Illinois University Press
www.siupress.com

Chapter 2 previously appeared as "Radical Economics for the Ordinary
American: Arthur Miller's *That They May Win*," *Journal of American
Drama and Theatre* 23, no. 2 (Spring 2011): 91–107; copyright © 2011 by
the Martin E. Segal Theatre Center Publications, New York, N.Y.

Chapter 3 previously appeared as "Locating Fascism by Dislocating War:
Stage for Action's *Skin Deep*," *Theatre History Studies* 33 (2014): 151–68;
copyright © 2014 by the University of Alabama.

Cover illustration: scene from *Joseph McGinnical, Cynical Pinnacle,
Opus II*. Courtesy of the Tamiment Library and Robert F. Wagner
Labor Archives, New York University

Library of Congress Cataloging-in-Publication Data

Names: Dail, Chrystyna, author.
Title: Stage for Action : U.S. social activist theatre in the 1940s / Chrystyna
    Dail.
Description: Carbondale : Southern Illinois University Press, [2016] | Series:
    Theater in the Americas | Includes bibliographical references and index.
Identifiers: LCCN 2016015720 | ISBN 9780809335428 (paperback) | ISBN
    9780809335435 (e-book)
Subjects: LCSH: Stage for Action (Theater company)—History. | Theatrical
    companies—United States—History—20th century. | Theater and
    society—United States—History—20th century. | Theater—Political
    aspects—United States—History—20th century. | BISAC: PERFORMING
    ARTS / Theater / History & Criticism. | PERFORMING ARTS / Theater /
    General. | HISTORY / United States / 20th Century.
Classification: LCC PN2297.S73 D35 2016 | DDC 792.09730904—dc23 LC
    record available at https://lccn.loc.gov/2016015720

To Stephen

Contents

Acknowledgments

ARCHIVES ARE THE LOCI of discovery for theatre historians. Some archives are available for public consumption and others are accessible solely to those "in the know," demanding the historian engage a combination of analytical and at times seemingly numinous skills. I spent countless hours searching finding aids and combing through other scholars' sources for possible leads while researching this book. I also admit to embarking upon trips to unprocessed collections on a hunch because nothing quite compares to the hand-trembling, heart-palpitating, breath-stopping moment when you realize you have unveiled a crucial artifact. This unparalleled process combining equal parts assiduousness and intuition reminds me of a quote by psychologist Joan Mowat Erikson: "Vital lives are about action. You can't feel warmth unless you create it, can't feel delight until you play, can't know serendipity unless you risk."

My belief in the serendipitous nature of research was uniquely shaped in 2004 while interning at the Library of Congress. Tasked with beginning to catalog Broadway lighting designer Peggy Clark's immense collection, I donned lab coat and cotton gloves to work in the dimly lit, drafty basement storage area that I affectionately designated "The Dungeon." I first came into contact with Stage for Action materials during one of these weekly trips to the bowels of the Library of Congress. The thin file in Clark's papers charmed me like a talisman, and I began researching each of the artists and performers mentioned therein. It wasn't long before this casual research on Stage for Action eclipsed all other scholarly pursuits.

Yet I am keenly aware that this "serendipitous" discovery of Stage for Action, a topic that has manipulated my academic life for the larger part of a decade, is not mine alone. The discovery was preceded by a faculty member (Franklin Hildy) recommending me for the internship at the Library of Congress, whereupon I first met the delightful theater specialist for the Music Division (Walter Zvonchenko), who became my internship coordinator. As the research and writing of this project expanded, so has the list of people to whom I am indebted for readership and support.

Faedra Chatard Carpenter, Jonathan Chambers, James Gilbert, and Catherine Schuler offered invaluable insight on the earliest drafts of this work, and Mark Cosdon, Barry Witham, Elizabeth Mullenix, and J. Ellen Gainor read and generously commented on revisions. The masterful Aaron Tobiason unquestionably deserves my heartfelt gratitude for reading and carefully critiquing (almost) every word, and I am equally indebted to Robert Schanke, Scott Magelssen, Kristine Priddy, Wayne Larsen, Julie Bush, and the editorial staff at Southern Illinois University Press.

A number of individuals personally connected to Stage for Action participated in interviews or responded to queries regarding their own or a family member's involvement with the group. These people include Perry Miller Adato, Laura Frankel, Bunny Kacher, Charles Polacheck, Douglas Clark, Marcia Haufrecht, Marvin Silbersher, and Pete Seeger. Although not all of these interviewees' voices are directly recorded in the book, their presence nonetheless haunts the pages.

Over the past decade I have presented excerpts of this research at the American Society for Theatre Research, the Association for Theatre in Higher Education, the American Literature Association, and the Mid-America Theatre conferences as well as published portions of chapters in the *Journal of American Drama and Theatre* and *Theatre History Studies*. Through feedback received following each conference and publication, the work has improved. I must, however, acknowledge a few individuals connected to these organizations who have consistently supported and heralded my research, specifically Anne Fletcher, Beth Osborne, Henry Bial, Lisa Jackson-Schebetta, Ryan Claycomb, Chris Woodworth, Michelle Granshaw, Jeanmarie Higgins, Jenna Kubly, Lezlie Cross, Tamara Underiner, Harvey Young, and Cheryl Black. Special thanks are extended to Adrienne Macki Braconi and the American Theatre and Drama Society, which awarded this study the 2016 Publication Subvention Award.

I am rewarded daily by the opportunity to work with talented and ardent colleagues in the Department of Theatre Arts at Ithaca College, though I would be remiss not to mention the support and encouragement received from people outside of my department, including Michael Richardson, Danette Johnson, Stacia Zabusky, Yvonne Rogalski, MaryAnn Taylor, and Wade Pickren. I received a summer research grant from the Center for Faculty Excellence at Ithaca College as well as travel and subvention funding from the provost's office; both aided greatly in the completion of this book. I drew daily inspiration from the passion, courage, and commitment of students enrolled in my course on U.S. social activist theatre and performance over the past several years. Wendy Dann, Jennifer Tennant, and Claire Gleitman deserve special thanks for making Ithaca feel like home. Across the hill at Cornell University, Sara Warner has given graciously of her time, exemplifying the true meaning of collegiality by helping me transition to living in "ten square miles surrounded by reality."

Individuals at a multitude of libraries assisted my research and provided access to cataloged as well as to unprocessed collections. I am especially indebted to curators and specialists at institutions where I did the bulk of my onsite research: the Billy Rose Theatre Division of the New York Public Library for the Performing Arts, Tamiment Library and Robert F. Wagner Labor Archives of New York University, Spingarn Library of Howard University, Industrial Relations and Labor Library of Cornell University, and the Library of Congress. I additionally received assistance from specialists at the University of Arkansas, Southern Illinois University Carbondale, Schomburg Center for Research in Black Culture, Stanford University, the University of Iowa, Radcliffe Institute for Advanced Study at Harvard University, Duke University, and Northwestern University.

Continuing appreciation is extended to the people who have bolstered this project and my spirit as I transitioned from theatre artist to theatre historian. Heather Nathans has been a singular influence over the years. Her constructive criticism and enduring mentorship have shepherded me through this process. Eleasha Gamble and Jessica Morgan have long been guiding lights to the soul. My extended family—especially Sharon, Mark, Bill, and Barbara—offered support and graciously gave of their time when requiring childcare during research trips. Much gratitude goes to Marisa Andrews, Bethany Holmstrom, Amy Hughes, Jenn-Scott Mobley, Naomi Stubbs, and Joanne Zerdy for being trusted peers. My siblings, Stephen, Julianna, and Kathryn, are constant sources of inspiration in my life. Thanks and adoration go to my parents, E. Michael Dail and Orysia Mochnacz Dail, for modeling devotion to occupation, education, and service, as well as for encouraging an appetite for passionate discourse in all of their children. I am blessed by the presence of my daughters, Lelia and Emma, and marvel at their boundless curiosity; they are my joy. Finally, this book is dedicated to my best friend, Stephen Andrew Shaffer, because love never fails.

STAGE FOR ACTION

INTRODUCTION

"ART IS A WEAPON!" announced playwright Friedrich Wolf before the Workers' Theatre League of Germany in 1928.[1] This militant slogan echoed across time and nations, delivered by artists such as Pablo Picasso, Diego Rivera, Charles Seeger, Paul Robeson, and Nina Simone. Although the phrase "Art is a weapon" is inextricably linked to Marxism, its core significance is not restricted to any one theoretical or political system but is grounded in the philosophical perspective that art is an exemplary tool for addressing social problems. Since theatre is a union of the arts and operates as a means by which culture reflects on itself, it is not surprising that Wolf, a theatre practitioner, sounded a call to action that invoked performance as an instrument for radical change.

Fast-forward nineteen years to April 6, 1947. A house attendant posted the "Standing Room Only" sign outside the patron entrance at the Knickerbocker Music Hall on Second Avenue in New York City. Those waiting outside in the blazing midday heat wondered if they would be some of the lucky few gaining entry into the now sold-out theatre. It was the hottest Easter on record in the city, and the audience already seated inside and those standing on queue anxiously awaited the opening performance of a series of one-acts produced by the progressive theatre company Stage for Action (SFA). The performance, publicized as "an afternoon of social theatre," featured *All Aboard* by Ben Bengal, *The General and the Goats* by Mike Stratton and Saul Arons and that ubiquitous social protest play *Waiting for Lefty* by Clifford Odets. The day after SFA's performance at the Old Knick, Rudolf Hoess, the former commandant of Auschwitz, was hanged inside the infamous camp.[2] The cultural backdrop of SFA's prodigious New York season in the spring of 1947 must be acknowledged. As SFA raised funds and brought attention to regional and national social issues by means of theatrical performance, throughout Europe war criminals were

1

tried and punished, the rebuilding effort surged, and the Soviet Union expanded its iron curtain.

SFA's two-weekend run in April at the Knickerbocker succeeded its mid-February drive for five thousand new members in the New York City metropolitan region, which had included a sold-out performance at the Theatre Des Artistes. Additionally in February, it was a featured group involved with Negro History Week (an annual celebration in the city since 1926), producing three separate plays for the New York City community on racial discrimination. The Knickerbocker performances in April over-lapped the opening of SFA's acting school at 430 Sixth Avenue and were followed by its latest incarnation of *Headline Cabaret*, "an afternoon of satire, song and dance" starring current Broadway artists, emceed by per-formers such as Ralph Burton, and sponsored by Sam Wanamaker, Ella Logan, Groucho Marx, Norman Corwin, and many others well known in theatre, radio, and film circles.[3] The performances featured comedi-ans, prominent jazz artists like Mary Lou Williams and Pops Foster, and pithy songs and dances bringing focus to national social issues via wit and derision.[4] One song, "Atom and Evil" by Hy Zaret and Lou Singer, had its debut at the inaugural *Headline Cabaret* before being recorded by the Golden Gate Quartet. Addressing the potential misuse of atomic weapons in four-part harmony, the song features the lyrics

> I'm talkin' 'bout Atom and Evil
> Atom and Evil
> If you don't break up that romance soon
> We'll all fall down and go boom, boom, boom![5]

So in the spring of 1947, while the U.S. government was still trying to decide "what to do about the Gadget"[6] and Secretary of State George C. Marshall prepared to implement the economic aid program that would ultimately bear his name, SFA was producing a string of sold-out performances and continuing to pursue a national theatre organization, with headquarters and an acting school in New York City, dedicated to addressing social concerns. Within a year and a half, however, the triumphs of SFA's 1947 spring season dissolved, revealing the ultimately quixotic nature of the group. Yet despite its many misguided choices, the significance of SFA is not easily dismissed. This work introduces SFA to the historical record and traces its successes and failures in a time when citizens blacked out windows and hid in basements during air raid tests, neighborhood rumors ended careers and sometimes even lives, and civil liberties were regularly trammeled. For it was in the midst of the Second World War that SFA embraced the axiom originating during the 1920s that art is a weapon but imagined its purpose anew. Theatre in the hands of SFA would promote neither violence nor destruction but instead would serve as a powerful progressive instrument working for global solidarity and peace.

Stage for Action acknowledged from its very inception that its artists would engage specific social and political issues. Heightened anxiety regarding Spain's inability to achieve democracy during the Spanish Civil War, the attack on Pearl Harbor, and rising global and native fascism inspired Perry Miller, a young stage and radio actress, to initiate the group in December 1943.[7] Sensing an intense desire in the performing arts community to connect the home front and the war front, Miller, in association with stage and radio personnel Berilla Kerr, Peggy Clark, and Donna Keath, launched SFA in New York City to bolster morale and simultaneously raise awareness about pressing social issues. Funding originally came from private donations and a large benefit performance on April 19, 1944, at the Henry Hudson Hotel, where Eleanor Roosevelt was the guest of honor. Following the benefit, SFA's major funding sources outside of private sponsors were labor unions and the National Citizens Political Action Committee.

SFA's performances informed audiences about what could be done to help the war effort on the home front, which its members believed would impact international politics over time. SFA advocated for wartime issues at a national level not seen since the demise of the Federal Theatre Project in 1939. The group soon expanded from New York City to major metropolitan areas across the United States including Chicago, Washington, Philadelphia, Detroit, San Francisco, and Los Angeles. A few of the better-known playwrights and performers involved with SFA during its five-year existence included Arthur Miller, Philip Loeb, Abram Hill, Sandra Michael, Edward Chodorov, Norman Corwin, Will Geer, Paul Robeson, Studs Terkel, Thelma Schnee, and Sam Wanamaker. The group broadened throughout the 1940s, both in membership and the social problems it addressed, but its basic mission during and after the war remained the same. SFA performances were free or very reasonably priced, were topical, and inspired personal responsibility from audiences by focusing on realizable post-show actions. In this way, SFA was a direct descendant of Friedrich Wolf's message that art is indeed a powerful tool for change.

The modern historical period embracing art as a weapon emerged during the rapid rise in size and power of the Socialist movement (1880–1917), due in part to the pivot toward Marxist philosophy among European intelligentsia. Social activist theatre in the United States developed in response to the rise of the Popular Front and was subsequently influenced, but never wholly dominated, by policy changes in the Communist Party. The Popular Front bloc (1929–59) spanned a period encompassing the Great Depression and the New Deal policies it spawned, the Spanish Civil War, World War II, the advent of the Cold War, the Korean War, and significant progress in the civil rights movement. Many of the noncommercial theatrical performances created during the Popular Front were lumped under the term "Theatre of the Left." These performances embraced a vast range of techniques, genres, and levels of theatrical expertise on the part of both creative artists and audiences. They also covered a panoply of social agendas. Just as scholars today struggle with defining political performances, historian Morgan Y. Himelstein asserts that "Theatre of the Left" became a catchall phrase during the 1930s for "liberal dramas . . . Marxist plays that explained the Depression problems by the philosophy of economic determinism. There were liberal plays with Marxist overtones. And, finally, there were Communist dramas that not only followed the Marxist analysis of American society but also called for the violent 'transition' to a Soviet America."[8] Indeed, the 1930s witnessed what is customarily acknowledged as the heyday of social activist theatre in the United States. This was the decade in which performances were delivered to audiences through artistic outlets such as the Workers' Laboratory Theatre, Theatre Union, New Playwrights Theatre, Group Theatre, New Theatre League, and Federal Theatre Project (among many others).

This study is dedicated to revealing and recuperating Stage for Action, calling attention to a previously unexamined yet important moment in U.S. theatre history. Drawing on both underexplored and only recently available archives, it contextualizes and analyzes a vital social activist theatre group of the 1940s, unearthing yet another volume in the long-hidden canon of social activist theatre that existed during the early years of the Cold War. I argue that SFA is the theatrical reflection of Progressivism and a pro-labor theatrical aesthetic during the 1940s—the political ideal expressed first in the New Deal and subsequently in Progressive Party rhetoric—an organization that saw performance as *the* solution, the ideal weapon for combating native fascism, unemployment, atomic warfare, and other serious social problems. What sharply differentiates the group from earlier radical social activist collectives of the 1930s, however, was its high level of professionalism and, following the end of World War II, adoption of theatre as a propaganda tool for promoting global peace and equality, a project informed by presidential candidate Henry Wallace's Progressive Party platform.

Despite exhaustive research by scholars focusing on the first decade of the Popular Front, there remains a paucity of scholarship on theatre created for working-class audiences during the period between the disbanding of the Federal Theatre Project in 1939 and the emerging impact of well-known social activist groups during the New Left movement of the late 1950s and early 1960s—groups such as the San Francisco Mime Troupe, Free Southern Theater, and El Teatro Campesino. Perhaps this is because the years between 1940 and 1955 are often considered a time when the commercial theatre community succumbed to social and political apathy. This study is not addressing the presence (or absence) of social activism in commercial theatre during the 1940s. Instead, it is uniquely focused on theatre for working-class audiences and their advocates during and immediately following World War II. The argument that social activist performance for working-class audiences vaporized in the aftermath of the atomic bomb (or even a decade earlier) but returned during the late 1950s and early 1960s is supported in a number of otherwise excellent studies, including Colette A. Hyman's *Staging Strikes: Workers' Theatre and the American Labor Movement*, Himelstein's *Drama Was a Weapon: The Left-Wing Theatre in New York, 1929–1941*, and Bruce A. McConachie and Daniel Friedman's edited work *Theatre for Working-Class Audiences in the United States, 1830–1980*. This final study does not include a single performance or group from the World War II or postwar era, and the final chapter, written by Friedman, opens with the sentence, "Theatre for work-ing-class audiences in the United States, for all practical purposes, ceased to exist in the 1940s."[9] Cultural historian Alan M. Wald acknowledges that the 1940s and early 1950s are "relatively neglected decades for the study of Left writing," despite their significance as the "bridge between the 1930s and the 1960s."[10] This study is deeply indebted to Wald's scholarship. I am, like Wald, attempting to "return to memory" the talents of 1940s artists "who have 'disappeared' from cultural history, while reassessing scores of others who have been appraised out of context . . . due to the still existing secrecy about activities of the Literary Left during the Cold War."[11] Although the hysteria of McCarthyism and the Cold War may seem equivocal to current generations, maintaining silence regarding so-called questionable activities (as perceived by the U.S. government) during the 1940s remains significant to those who lived through it.

Thankfully, when the living archive demands silence, the paper archive howls for attention. Much archival evidence was closed to the public or classified until the twenty-first century, and the lack of exploration of such evidence potentially accounts for gaps in earlier scholarship and substantiates the alternative narrative for the 1940s forwarded in this study. One need only read the illustrious John Gassner's criticism of the 1940s to perceive a downward spiral in socially relevant plays at midcentury. Bemoaning a departure from the theatrical innovation and social consciousness of the 1930s, Gassner wrote, "Zeal for any drastic transformation of American society was virtually absent from the theatre of a period of economic well-being and of revived disenchantment with Russia after the war-time enthusiasm for an ally."[12] Six years prior to Gassner's assessment of the desperate state of commercial theatre, however, he was so convinced that SFA was a promising successor to 1930s socially conscious forms that he agreed to serve on its advisory council. A host of other critics from the period—including Harry Taylor, Samuel Selden, Arnaud d'Usseau, Samuel Sillen, and Burton Lindheim—also saw merit in SFA's work. In articles and reviews, critics acknowledged the dramatic and social potential of SFA productions by playwrights such as Arthur Miller, Jean Karsavina, Charles Polacheck, Sidney Alexander, Anita Short, and Arnold Perl. These playwrights focused on vital issues, such as childcare for working mothers, popular notions of racial difference, the effects of the House Un-American Activities Committee, and ways to achieve full, postwar employment. If the majority of these artists and plays are now forgotten, it is because two primary factors have helped silence SFA and its members for over half a century: inaccurate beliefs that the early Cold War was a period of political apathy in the theatre, and the branding of SFA as a Communist front, instigating the lifelong silence of many of its members and supporters. This study is committed to ensuring that canonized narratives of the postwar period do not continue eclipsing the vital work of SFA and other like-minded groups of the 1940s.

In the years immediately following World War II, which were far from idyllic for the majority of Americans, pockets of resistance and activism existed and continued operating at a wholly grassroots level across the United States. For example, in his pivotal text on race and class in postwar Detroit, Thomas Sugrue explains that his work intentionally highlights the ability of people seemingly without sociopolitical clout to effect social change. He writes persuasively about Detroit residents with "little access to political power [who] survive, resist, adapt, and gain access to power."[13]

Likewise, my research reveals that the majority of artists involved with SFA and other 1940s social activist theatres had limited political influence yet continued fighting with some success against these seemingly insurmountable odds. Upon closer examination, I find that the late 1940s did not suffer from any absence of activism; rather, activists' voices were often drowned out by the stentorian shouts of Dixiecrats and red-baiters. Perhaps it is fitting, then, that one year after the dissolution of SFA, its first and most prolific playwright, Arthur Miller, penned the prophetic line in *Death of a Salesman* that has also echoed down the years: "So attention must be paid."[14]

Assessing the political or social impact of a group or a performance can be difficult, depending on whether one considers the artist or the audience. While some artists allow the reception of a performance to define its political stance, others deny any social relevance or political commentary in their performances. W. E. B. Du Bois, an advocate of SFA's work, was an early supporter of the politicization of performance in the United States and wrote in 1926, "Thus all Art is propaganda and ever must be, despite the wailing of the purists."[15] Contemporary playwright Tony Kushner responds to this ongoing debate, stating, "All art of every sort changes the world. Perhaps an artist aims at less direct, precise, immediate an effect than a president or legislator or general or banker or activist will have; but more effect, more potency, more agency than the ordinary is inevitably an artist's inspiration, and artists who choose to deny that are simply kidding themselves."[16] Nonetheless, Kushner concedes that despite all art's potential for social change, a simple or single formula for politically efficacious theatre does not exist. Be that as it may, if "all art of every sort changes the world," then how do we separate performances explicitly advocating immediate change from those interested in a long-term ideological shift? "Political performance" has a multitude of definitions, serving as an expansive umbrella for any work challenging the current hegemonic structure. Should academics, however, insist on developing a hierarchical schema that parses the political attributes of party conventions, street demonstrations, community-based performance, and, say, commercial musical theatre productions like *Urinetown*? What seems most important is acknowledging that each may prove effective in challenging audience members or participants to think differently about the world and their place in it, despite sometimes radically different performance methodologies. Yet because labels like "socially relevant" or "political" are used to classify such a vast array of performances and performers as different as *A Doll House* and Pussy Riot, some clarification is necessary.

I appreciate the comprehensive model of political performance delineated by theatre historian Douglas McDermott. McDermott proposes a political performance continuum, with commercial theatre at one end and mass participatory performance at the other. Commercial theatre "avoids political comment and effectively denies the significance of political structures."[17] Although I would suggest that very few plays fall neatly under the commercial label, there are certainly productions where the goal is purely financial or focused on entertainment without patently advocating any type of social change. At the opposite extreme of commercial theatre is mass participatory theatre, in which there is little to no separation of audience and performer; the performance event itself functions as a political act. Neither of these extremes—the commercial and the mass participatory—leave much room for introspection or awareness during a performance or necessitate immediate social action once the performance has concluded. Balancing between these extremes is theatre of social significance, residing closer on the continuum to commercial theatre while still offering discussion and debate of social issues. The other distinctive marker on the broad spectrum of political performance is what McDermott calls "explicitly political theatre" or what is more commonly referred to today as theatre for social change or social activist theatre, which is what SFA practiced. Explicitly political theatre is "typified by the agitprop play, which not only identifies problems in the society but proposes specific political strategies for their solution. The work of art concludes the social discussion and agitates for direct action by the audience."[18] Pedagogically, McDermott's broad spectrum is appreciatively utilitarian, suggesting that what ultimately separates politically relevant performances from one another are not the techniques in use, the economics of a performance, or even the aesthetic quality of a production but whether or not demands are placed on the audience for immediate social action and change.

This is not a question of efficacy, which is frequently subjective and often impossible to assess from a historical perspective; it is rather a question of expectations. Some performances intimate a need for change, but only social activist theatre demands it of its audience (and, therefore, of the society in which that audience lives). Social activist theatre is pressingly relevant, carefully tailored for its intended audience, and pointed in its goals. It is anticipatory as well as transformative and at times, therefore, naively optimistic. SFA's repertory, the majority of which is discussed for the first time in this study, illustrates the group's belief that audiences of the 1940s would enlist in the progressive fight for peace and join performers in striving to end fascism, racism, and war. This expectation is indicative both of the progressive liberal sensibility still in existence during the postwar period and of the unwavering optimism often permeating social activist theatre.

Yet this ambitious optimism did not prevent SFA, or its social activist theatre offspring, from creating professionally produced art dedicated to remedying a social problem through immediate action. What separates social activist theatre from the often overlapping genres of community-based and applied theatre is that these latter forms often involve the far end of McDermott's spectrum in order to produce social change. They allow, and often encourage, the viewer to become a performer (Augusto Boal's concept of the "spect-actor"), providing everyone "the opportunity through an engagement with the aesthetic object of performance to develop their critical consciousness and to rehearse options toward action."[19] This method of community engagement reaps clear rewards for its administrators, spect-actors, and audience members, but the creative approach or development of a piece and even of a potential audience is quite different from that of social activist theatre. Social activist theatre, as SFA practiced it,

- comprises trained theatre artists,
- creates performances in direct response to a specific social problem,
- is intended for an audience that the problem personally affects, and
- desires and expects immediate change.

Like mass participatory theatre, social activist theatre focuses on addressing social inequities. However, the artists involved are all professionals and conscious of aesthetics as well as audience reaction. They are creating informative and entertaining performances intentionally interested in local and immediate influence rather than in expansive universality. More than any other type of theatre practitioner, social activist theatre artists use their skills to craft live performances that function as a tool for social change, often focusing on neo-Marxist issues of labor, race, sex, and gender inequities.

Beginning with an analysis of how SFA followed the trajectory of what has, at different points in history, been referred to as "Theatre of the People,"

"Workers' Theatre," and "Theatre of the Left," the first chapter positions SFA as a bridge between 1930s groups and the socially relevant performances of labor unions and off-Broadway groups during the 1950s (with whom SFA had direct connections). This chapter additionally introduces the women responsible for initiating SFA and transitioning the group from a New York City operation to a national one in eight metropolitan regions. By situating SFA in its cultural and political context, chapter 1—indeed, the book as a whole—begins the vital work of filling in the lacunae created by conventional narratives of post–World War II U.S. theatre history. In doing so, this study reveals how many of the performance techniques and grassroots methods prevalent in sociopolitically minded performances today are the inheritors of a rich history of theatre activism.

A rupture occurred in the Democratic Party following the end of World War II, driven by differing opinions regarding postwar social inequalities, fear of subversive forces within the United States, and increased distrust of the USSR. As the Democratic Party split and competition for votes increased, Progressives joined forces with labor unions and began forming political action committees, a relatively new idea in the 1940s. Chapter 2 addresses how SFA's involvement with various political action committees influenced both a pivot in production focus as well as subsequent support of what conservative politicians considered radical social agendas. It also highlights SFA's involvement with the emergence of the Progressive Party and Henry A. Wallace's failed 1948 presidential campaign. In doing so, I analyze two significant scripts in SFA's catalog: Arthur Miller's *That They May Win* and Les Pine and Anita Short's *Joseph McGinnical, Cynical Pinnacle, Opus II*. By examining multiple iterations of *That They May Win* (including a performance Eleanor Roosevelt attended), I reveal how interconnected Miller was with progressive social activist theatre in the immediate postwar period. *Joseph McGinnical, Cynical Pinnacle, Opus II* coincides with SFA's involvement in the inaugural School for Political Action Techniques, a conference dedicated to "get out the vote" training in Washington, D.C., sponsored by the National Citizens Political Action Committee in 1946. Secretary of Commerce Henry A. Wallace spoke several times at this unprecedented national event when the possibility of forming a third political party to contest the 1948 presidential election was first publicly discussed.

The third chapter addresses what is perhaps SFA's most significant legacy: its commitment to civil rights and racial integration. SFA responded to pressing issues concerning civil rights as evidenced through my analysis of *Skin Deep, All Aboard, Dream Job,* and *Talk in Darkness.* Race riots and segregation were pervasive in the late 1940s, and SFA used performance to vigorously pursue equality for all U.S. citizens, both on the mainland and in Puerto Rico. SFA's focus on civil rights was connected to its involvement with labor unions as well as with Wallace's Progressive Party, which crafted the most robust civil rights–minded platform of the 1940s. Historian Mark L. Kleinman states that Wallace's presidential campaign was unprecedented, as across the southern states Wallace "spoke before integrated crowds and stayed in African-American homes. . . . In some instances he was actually driven from a platform without getting to deliver a speech as he became the focus of a powerful southern conflation of segregationism and anticommunism."[20] Many historians argue that President Harry Truman would not have adopted the sturdy civil rights platform he did during his 1948 campaign had Wallace and his party's actions not pushed Truman in that direction. SFA's 1946–48 performances supported the Progressive Party's drive to educate labor audiences about civil rights and to activate those audiences. The plays addressed in this chapter warrant a reevaluation in terms of how race work was considered during this period in theatre history.

A host of factors led the U.S. government to treat SFA as a subversive organization. Perhaps most important were the group's active endorsement of Wallace's presidential bid, assumed Communist ties, and support of racial equality. But SFA also intentionally provoked government officials and politicians in ways many found unforgivable during the early years of the Cold War. The fourth chapter introduces plays that directly confront what SFA members (and many other Americans) considered controversial government policies. These plays—*The Investigators, You're Next!,* and *Salem Story*—highlight affronts to civil liberties and the flagrant misuse of citizens' trust perpetuated by the U.S. government during the late 1940s. *The Investigators,* by Lewis Allan, envisions an American population replaced by government-controlled robots. It was performed at pro-Wallace rallies in Chicago during the summer of 1948. *You're Next!* is a piece written by Arthur Miller about the social ramifications of the House Un-American Activities Committee for small-town business owners. Finally, Sidney Alexander's award-winning 1948 one-act *Salem Story* draws upon the same source material as Miller's 1953 production *The Crucible,* dramatizing the powerful conflict between a man's responsibility to society and to himself.

There exists no single or simple reason for SFA's failure to endure into the 1950s and beyond. Despite having a projected repertory for the 1949 season, including the pro–Puerto Rican independence play *Who Are the Weavers*, all of the SFA branches shut down within a few months of Wallace's loss in November 1948. But this was not the end of its story, as the government continued investigating—and in some cases prosecuting— radicals and subversives well into the next decade, with many SFA members falling victim to the political crossfire. The final chapter of this study examines this issue and provides analysis of two plays in SFA's repertory addressing U.S. social issues that have yet to achieve significant change since the 1940s, namely the eradication of atomic weapons worldwide (which was debated through performances of *Open Secret*) and the independence of Puerto Rico (the focus of *Who Are the Weavers*). I conclude by addressing SFA's legacy, connecting SFA writers, performers, and directors to People's Drama Inc. and the emergence of the off-Broadway movement.

Despite its brief existence, Stage for Action was the firebrand of the 1940s, keeping alive and fostering new flames of radical social activist theatre in the United States. Perpetuating its continued absence from the historical record would be a great injustice, not only to the multitude of artists involved with the group but also, more importantly, to the social causes they served. SFA's performances and participants provide theatre historians an intriguing glimpse at the social activist offerings of a moment rife with political tensions, as well as a significant collection of virtually unstudied dramatic literature. It stands proudly as a twentieth-century national theatre group functioning as the theatrical voice for a political party. Many of the issues addressed in its performances are reminiscent of earlier social activist theatres: combating racism, union regulation, housing shortages, and the treatment of immigrants. But SFA also embraced topics not previously explored, including debunking myths about the biological differences between races, advocating for the rights of Puerto Ricans, calling attention to the lack of childcare for working mothers, and demanding the cessation of all nuclear warfare.

What ultimately differentiates SFA from the workers' theatre groups of the 1930s, as well as from other activist theatre groups operating during the 1940s, was its professionalism and advocacy of Progressivism: "In every department . . . it tries to avoid doing what a pamphlet or a speaker could do better, striving to get its message across strictly in terms of theater entertainment values . . . and it is a child of this particular period."[21] SFA's confrontations with the government were directly connected to its involvement in promoting pressing social issues in ways that made audiences take notice. Addressing social agendas such as civil rights and

Soviet-American relations was considered at best liberal and at worst subversive (and therefore un-American in the early Cold War climate). Additionally, SFA's choice of performance venues—including union halls, churches, high schools, town halls, and YMCAs and even at labor strikes— combined with its radical message and support of Henry Wallace's agenda ruffled the feathers of many local, state, and federal government officials intent on clamping down on anything or anyone challenging "peacetime" prosperity. This study serves as the inaugural step in throwing back the curtain on Stage for Action, a fascinating theatrical and social endeavor using performance to impact U.S. society by encouraging direct action and personal responsibility for change.

1. THEATRE AS A WEAPON

MARXIST THEATRE CRITICS DUBBED Arthur Miller a talented play-wright three years before the commercial world acknowledged his prowess. Harry Taylor of the *New Masses* and the *Daily Worker*'s Samuel Sillen recognized Stage for Action's first play, Miller's *That They May Win*, as "the sturdiest" in the group's repertory and noted that "after a year, it is still going strong."[1] Sillen went so far as to admit that Miller's piece and his subsequent offering to SFA, *You're Next!*, were successful examples of how the group was moving progressive theatre away from the type of social activist performance produced during the 1930s. Reflecting on SFA's three-year existence in the summer of 1946, Sillen wrote, "While Stage for Action wants to hit hard at major themes, it wants to avoid being an agit-prop theater in the old sense. The audiences are not satisfied with crude presentations, and the actors in turn want scripts that will give them a creative opportunity."[2] Sillen was correct in his assessment of SFA. The talent of its original playwrights such as Miller, Edward Chodorov, Norman Corwin, and Ben Hecht drew other progressive-minded writers as well as some of the finest mid-twentieth-century theatre artists to the group. A few examples from the thousands who worked with SFA over its five-year existence include Will Geer, Zero Mostel, Pert Kelton, John Randolph, Studs Terkel, Gordon Heath, Sam Wanamaker, and Gertrude Berg.[3] Marvin Silbersher performed with SFA for two years while studying under Erwin Piscator at the Dramatic Workshop with close friend and fellow SFA performer Walter Matthau. Silbersher recalls rehearsing until the "wee hours of the morning" with SFA and that the "production values were scant but the performances impassioned."[4] Although Silbersher asserts that *Open Secret* was his favorite SFA play, he has clear memories about performing in a series of one-acts at the Old Knick with the group in April 1947. The plays included Ben Bengal's *All Aboard*, Mike Stratton and Saul Arons's *The General and the Goats*, and a revival of Clifford Odets's *Waiting for Lefty*. When asked what it was like to be onstage in this particular SFA production, Silbersher responded, "Very exciting. The cast and the production were at a high temperature. Everything was important. We had been rehearsing like crazy. When we got onstage it was like an explosion, but not in the wrong sense. Very exciting theatre. The actors were involved in a very deep way, like they wanted the audience to remember the play."[5]

The audience's ability to "remember the play" is arguably a goal of all theatre; however, it is critical to social activist performance where the response of the audience following a production is equal to, if not more important than, the performance itself. Silbersher's memories of his time spent onstage with SFA and the intended impact of the group's performances on the audience are confirmed in Harry Taylor's 1945 evaluation of the group:

> Without more fuss than lights out at the back of the hall, a troupe of actors takes over the small platform—and suddenly the tired men and women [in the audience] sit up; they laugh, they feel, they identify themselves in the playlet so that they grow angry or are gratified, or as sometimes happens, forget themselves sufficiently to enter the argument before them. In any case, the skit makes them *think* and it makes them *do*.[6]

SFA entreated both audiences and performers alike to "remember the play." But this style of motivational performance did not originate with SFA. Nothing of significance in theatre history occurs without precedence, and SFA is no exception as it was undeniably an outgrowth of the 1930s Workers' Theatre movement, New Theatre League, and living newspapers of the Federal Theatre Project (FTP). Yet the work of SFA is marked by significant innovation as well. By uncovering and tracing some of its artists and sponsors, expansion into a national organization, and eventual status as theatrical "spokesgroup" for the Progressive Party, SFA emerged as a reimagining of progressive performance, both during the war and after, and as an underappreciated model for social activist theatre in the United States. In order to assess the significance of SFA's impact on the history of social activist theatre, it is imperative to situate the group in its historical context, which includes placing it in discourse with the various European and U.S. theatrical and ideological movements from which it drew inspiration.

SFA's performances were created by artists who focused on particular social problems with the intent of producing immediate changes in society. They created explicitly political theatre by reinventing performance methods popular with groups of the 1930s, especially the New Theatre League. As reviewed by Eugene Gordon in 1945, "Stage for Action has taken the old concept of education and turned it inside out. It has shaken the stuffiness and dust of formalism out of it and filled it completely with new meaning. It has then taken this new product directly to the people who want it—not waited for the people to come and get it."[7] The particular styles of political performance most commonly produced by SFA, living newspapers and agitprop, emerged amid the Socialist movement's rapid expansion, in both size and power, during the period of the Second International (1889–1916).[8] Philosophically, the movement was directly inspired by the theories of Karl Marx and Friedrich Engels. In the compelling *Introduction to the Critique of Political Economy*, which Marx composed between 1857 and 1859, he ponders, through discussions of Greek art and Shakespeare, the eternal value of art despite its historicity.[9] Countless early twentieth-century theatrical theories emerged in response to Marx's provocative—albeit incomplete—proposal of a civically minded theory of aesthetics. Some of the more influential works addressing the social value of art were Romain Rolland's *The Theatre of the People* (1902), the writings of Alexander Bogdanov and Platon Kerzhentsev that emerged from the Proletarian Culture Movement (or "Proletcult," 1919), and Erwin Piscator's *The Political Theatre* (1929). These writings and the aesthetic forms they supported or inspired—such as socially conscious drama, living newspapers, and agitprop—traveled slowly across the ocean in the texts and practices of European immigrants. Many of these immigrants were content with staying theatrically isolated within their own ethnic communities, while others joined intercultural workers' groups combining what theatre scholar Ilka Saal refers to as the "classic humanist" and "iconoclastic" European methods into hybrid forms on U.S. soil.[10] Additional discoveries of new theatrical practices were made by artists studying these imported forms in the United States or by Americans touring Europe during the first half of the twentieth century.

In one of the many well-constructed histories of early twentieth-century social activist theatre in the United States, Raphael Samuel argues that performances prior to the Russian Revolution of 1917 tended to emphasize the promotion of "equal rights in the cultural sphere" rather than theatre for social change.[11] The focus of these early productions was on broad audience appeal more than on the political implications of a piece. A focus on recreation that exalted the soul and provided "guiding light to the intelligence" marked the formative years of social activist theatre in the United States.[12] These goals were hardly original, deriving their ambitions directly from the pages of Rolland. Thus early U.S. political theatre groups produced dramas of social significance in the vein of Henrik Ibsen or George Bernard Shaw rather than propaganda-driven works engaging problems of immediate relevance to workers' lives or actively promoting social or political change.

The impact of Marxist theory, revolution in Russia, and the end of World War I fundamentally altered the production focus of U.S. workers' theatre. It transitioned from primarily producing theatre of social significance or discussion-based works, where the audience was separated by the fourth wall, to producing social activist theatre, works directly addressing audiences and challenging them to remedy a specific social problem. Social activist theatre in the United States owed its next phase (1917–35) to the transforming influence of Russian artists, such as the pro-Soviet Blue Blouses, and to Piscator's ongoing development of epic theatre in Germany. The cynosure of class revolution in Europe directly affected the emergence of social activist theatre in the United States. Almost overnight, the pre-1917 belief that performances for working-class audiences must be aesthetically beautiful and spiritually uplifting was supplanted by the inspiring call to use theatre as a weapon for social change.

Identifying the contours of social activist theatre in the United States is not the overarching intention of this study. Rather, my central concern is establishing that the rich and prolific social activist theatre movement that existed in the United States during the 1930s did not, as has been assumed, disappear for almost two decades before reemerging phoenix-like during the late 1950s with the New Left movement. As Raphael Samuel attests, noncommercial theatre operates not in unbroken progression but as a "succession of moments separated by rupture."[13] Therefore, it is essential when addressing significant periods of social activist theatre to search for fissuring in the cultural landscape. One need look no further than the United States' entry into World War II for this moment; indeed, a great chasm was forming in American society based on contrasting ideas of war, religion, race, class, sex, and gender, and SFA formed in direct response to this rift.

In July 1942, actor Philip Huston wrote in *Equity*, the Actors' Equity Association magazine, that "the theatre can be important only where the need for it is important. And some three million khaki-clad arms point to where that need is."[14] The following summer, President Franklin D. Roosevelt bolstered Huston's statement in a telegram reprinted in *Billboard* magazine: "Entertainment is always a national asset; invaluable in time of peace, it is indispensable in wartime."[15] SFA was in good company when theatre professionals and government organizations across the country answered the presidential call. The USO (United Service Organizations), the Department of the Treasury play program, and the American Stage Wing (with its Stage Door Canteens) all rallied to bolster the troops. But SFA was not simply another flag-waving cheerleader for the industrial war complex. It should instead be considered an integral player in the Popular Front movement for four reasons:

- SFA involved some of the leading radical and artistic minds of the day on its executive board, including Howard Fast, Elizabeth Hawes, Paul Robeson, Norman Corwin, Edward Chodorov, Abram Hill, and Dorothy Parker.
- It operated as one of the earliest racially integrated pro-civil rights theatre groups in the United States.
- SFA became the theatrical voice for a generation of progressives by advocating for labor unions, civil liberties, equality, and Soviet-American friendship.
- It served as a propaganda outlet for Henry Wallace and the 1948 Progressive Party campaign.

In only a few short years, SFA rose from beginning as a small New York–based volunteer theatre company working on a shoestring budget to becoming an instrumental force in the creation of a Political Action School in Washington, D.C.; supporting theatrical training in New York City; establishing branch companies in D.C., Los Angeles, San Francisco, Cleveland, Detroit, Philadelphia, and Chicago; and performing at Wallace campaign rallies throughout the country in 1948. Once the group became a national organization in the spring of 1946, it sustained a national executive committee (also referred to as its board of directors) as well as a national advisory council, many of whose members were the group's major nonunion sponsors. The affiliated branches also included advisory councils, sponsors, and executive committees overseeing daily operations of specific units. National sponsors of SFA, as listed in the majority of publicity materials as well as letterhead for the group, included Howard Bay,

Gertrude Berg, Edward Chodorov, Norman Corwin, Howard Fast, James H. Fay, Elizabeth Hawes, Felix Knight, Canada Lee, Sandra Michael, Fredric March, Dorothy Parker, Paul Robeson, Oscar Serlin, Herman Shumlin, and James Thurber.[16] In most (but not all—Washington, D.C., being the primary exception) of the regional branches, performers were members of the professional theatre community working on a volunteer basis with Stage for Action. Although it was a nonprofit organization, SFA aimed at being self-sustaining, and so "a very nominal booking fee" (fifteen dollars in 1947) was charged for each performance.[17]

Unlike its entertainment-focused USO and Stage Door Canteen counterparts, SFA's mission during the war was to transform society through theatre. As a review of the group in the *People's Voice* touted, SFA was "determined that they should apply their art and devote themselves to the cause of a better America."[18] The New York City and Chicago branches of the group were even influential enough to warrant televised productions of two of their plays. Arthur Miller's *That They May Win* was broadcast by WBKB of Chicago on December 15, 1944, and reviewed by *Billboard*'s Cy Wagner as "the best television show of the year."[19] Another SFA script, Arthur Laurents's *Walk with Me*, played on the same network on January 24, 1946. A review stated that "the play is probably one of the best to emerge from the local tele-station. . . . Of such stuff is good propaganda fashioned."[20] In the aftermath of World War II, however, many government officials perceived Communist propaganda in SFA's efforts, in both live and recorded performances, to create a "better America." The political climate shifted rapidly following the death of Franklin D. Roosevelt. Henry Wallace, the last of FDR's New Deal cabinet members remaining under the Truman administration and the inspiration for many SFA performances following the war, was removed from his secretary of commerce post in 1946 because he did not support the direction Truman was taking the country. Due to their presumed radicalism, SFA members faced relentless red-baiting and blacklisting by the Truman administration, and when Wallace was soundly defeated in the 1948 presidential election, the group officially disbanded.

But prior to its demise, SFA was critical in creating performances about social issues—such as a lack of adequate childcare for working mothers, voting rights, price gouging, labor laws, unemployment, inadequate housing opportunities, nuclear weapons control, and civil liberties violations— for millions of audience members across the United States. SFA was far from the first successful social activist theatre in the United States; it drew inspiration from a number of groups operating between the late 1920s and early 1940s, such as the New Playwrights Theatre, traveling units of the New Theatre League, and the Living Newspaper Unit of the FTP. SFA adopted the most successful qualities of each of these groups—including production mobility, fluidity of form, message-centered performances, a membership-driven funding structure, and a strong network of like-minded artists—developing into a nationwide network of social activist theatre artists intent on shaping the future of the United States.

Another influential 1930s predecessor of SFA was the Workers' Laboratory Theatre (WLT), formed in 1930 under the artistic direction of Jack and Hiram Shapiro, Alfred Saxe, Harry Elion, Will Lee, and Ben Blake. In its four years of operation, the WLT was "primarily an amateur group producing agit-props dealing with the Depression, the New Deal, the New York City political scene, and foreign affairs."[21] Most significant to SFA's development was the WLT's Shock Troupe and its practice of responding directly to current events. The Shock Troupe staged agitprops about current events for workers on docks and at factories. Evening courses in performance were offered to workers in order to expand the WLT's membership and to provide cultural education. SFA's promotional pamphlets and articles echoed the mission of the WLT Shock Troupers, who were "ready to bring their revolutionary agit-props to the public at a moment's notice."[22] In all of its publicity, SFA stressed that it would travel and perform anywhere accessible by public transportation. In a 1944 *New York Times* article on SFA, Burton Lindheim wrote cheekily, "To reach the people Stage for Action troupers journey to the hinterlands of the Bronx, trek through the wilds of Canarsie or even cross the waves to Hoboken."[23] Likewise, in a Chicago SFA pamphlet, the group publicized that members would perform at "Unions, Women's Clubs, PTA and other Educational Groups, Non-Partisan Political Action Meetings, Churches, Philanthropic organizations, Community Conferences, Conventions, Civic Rallies, Club, Lodge and Social Organizations. . . . In fact, wherever people gather together for meetings, Stage for Action is ready to present a timely, to-the-point production."[24] Mobility, flexibility, and easily transportable costumes and props were advocated by the WLT Shock Troupe, and SFA followed its lead.

When the WLT disbanded in 1934, the newly formed Theatre of Action (an offshoot of the WLT's Shock Troupe) "reorganized on a full professional basis for the indoor presentation of realistic plays," utilizing a writing technique that demanded "Marxist ideas [woven] into a realistic plot."[25] The Theatre of Action's shift in forms correlated directly to the dramatic literature directives of the Communist International (Comintern or Third International). Established in 1919 by Vladimir Lenin, the Comintern was dedicated to combating the international bourgeoisie. Under the Comintern's mandate, theatres and playwrights were to convert their style from formalist (and therefore bourgeois) styles such as agitprop to social realism. Following the rise of Joseph Stalin and the influence of the Association of Proletarian Writers beginning in 1928, all theatre in Russia (all of cultural life, actually) was expected to clearly support the Soviet state and agenda. Artists whose creative output conformed to these specific political directives drove the heated "Art as a Weapon" debate swirling in progressive and Communist circles in the United States during the 1940s. The debate reached its apex in 1946, within months of SFA restructuring as a national group.

Unlike many of its predecessors, SFA never fully embraced any specific literary or scenographic style, nor did it achieve anything close to the "New Theatre technique" suggested in *Theatre Workshop* or the New Theatre League performances and publications during the late 1930s. Instead, SFA created pieces that were hybrids of many forms—specifically expressionism, realism, and agitprop—due largely to the many playwrights involved with the group, the different style(s) each playwright embraced, the ever-shifting beliefs of what social activist theatre should be and how best to achieve it during the 1940s, and variations in commitment to political doctrines. In terms of scenography, although SFA relied primarily on audience imagination to fill in the technical aspects of its productions, a few benefit performances and nontouring productions included set designs. For example, Peggy Clark designed the cartoonish circus sideshow backdrop for Ben Hecht's *The Common Man* at the group's first benefit performance in April 1944.

Two years later, in the fall of 1946, Puerto Rican muralist and set designer Rafael Ríos-Rey was hired to design the settings for SFA's *Keynotes of Unity* at the Fraternal Clubhouse Theater on West Forty-Eighth Street in New York. Ríos-Rey met members of SFA, including the creators of *Keynotes of Unity*, Robert Adler, George Bellak, and Elmer Bernstein, at Camp Unity in Wingdale, New York, where he was participating in a collective painting exhibition and they were workshopping their production.[26] *Keynotes of Unity*, which is not mentioned anywhere in biographies of the Tony Award–nominated and Academy Award–winning Elmer Bernstein, was described by the composer as "a hell of a lot more militant than any review seen for a long time."[27] But a critique in the *Daily Worker* of the first (and final) performance evaluated the production differently, stating,

Scene from Ben Hecht's *The Common Man* at Stage for Action's Henry
Hudson Hotel benefit performance in April 1944. Set and costume
design by founding member Peggy Clark. Actors pictured (*left to right*):
Ronnie Gibson, Adele Jerome, Robert Davis, Arthur Elmer, and Will
Geer. *Courtesy of the Tamiment Library and Robert F. Wagner Labor
Archives, New York University.*

"There are pretty legs and bright faces and alert talents and an eager, young
energy to nourish, to refresh an unhappily jaded progressive audience
and to win support and sympathy from middle-of-the-roaders. It speaks
a hearty, indigenous and non-sectarian lingo."[28] The review highlighted
the performances of Jerry Jaraslov, Ruth Tarson, Laura Duncan, Seymour
Mandel, and Janie Martin but ultimately called the production amateur,
noting, "It needs to be tied together with the continuity of a tangible theme,
so that it will be less a grab-bag variety show. It needs to be better lit, better
costumed, better rehearsed."[29]

A theatrical "grab-bag" is perhaps appropriate when describing the
variety of scripts produced by Stage for Action branches over its five-year
existence. The hybridity of forms practiced by SFA did not result in any
single performance technique unique to the company; rather, by firing a
range of styles at its audiences in order to see which "landed" and earned
the desired response (or, in the case of *Keynotes of Unity*, clearly did not), it
was diligently involved in theatrical praxis. At times SFA's artistic choices

adopted the political valences of New Deal Democrats, the American Communist Party, or Wallace Progressives, and therefore certain artistic choices were tantamount to specific political expressions. However, the majority of artists involved with SFA were not primarily responding to theories and practices espoused by politics but rather were interested in creating theatre that thoroughly engaged their audiences and motivated them to take part in a current social struggle. Harry Taylor wrote in 1945 that SFA's "presentations have included farce, drama, living newspaper, comedy and fantasy. And every one of them has been designed to make people *think, feel,* and *do* something on the issues of the day."[30] Full commitment to a specific political agenda did not occur in SFA performances until the emergence of Wallace's Progressive Party, and even then the stylistic preferences of playwrights dictated how the political content of a script was delivered.[31]

SFA built upon established 1930s social activist theatre aesthetics, especially those found in the FTP living newspaper productions and workers' theatre outfits. When analyzing performances of the 1930s, however, it is important to recognize that scholars and critics do not always agree on the definition and boundaries of "social activist theatre." Many question whether the performances were simple propaganda or a new form of theatre. John Gassner, one of the most influential American theatre critics of the twentieth century, stated in 1938 that either approach—calling the performances "brutally realistic" and "unmitigated propaganda" or, alternatively, "an absolutely new phenomenon in the theatre"—was reductive and only partially true. Instead, he saw in the performances of the 1930s, as I do of SFA, a combination of forms based on individual playwrights' intentions and preferences. Some of the performances of the 1930s were agitprop, yet an equal number were not; some adopted social realism, while a great many others were expressionistic. All, according to Gassner, were "intended to inculcate a lesson, agitate for the elimination of abuses, and indict a social order that tolerated them. . . . Theirs was the drama of dynamic processes affecting society and its individuals."[32] Although Gassner wrote in 1938 that the previous season signaled the end of what he then termed "sociological drama" in the United States, in 1946 he saw in SFA a promising resurgence of these earlier forms, writing about the group in the preface to his Best Plays series and serving on the group's advisory council.

The forms incorporated by many SFA playwrights also drew inspiration from performances staged under the auspices of the New Theatre League, which emerged from the League of Workers' Theatres in 1935. Gassner described the New Theatre League's exact purpose as the "development of the American theatre to its highest artistic and social level" and to serve as "a theatre dedicated to the struggle against war, fascism, and censorship."[33] This struggle, which Lynn Mally asserts resulted in the New Theatre League being "a vibrant force in American theatrical life," was originally funded directly by the Comintern and later by the Communist Party of the United States of America (CPUSA).[34] Yet while the league served a foreign political agenda, it also directly affected U.S. theatre development through the accomplishments of its individual companies, lectures by theatrical luminaries of the 1930s, discovery of burgeoning playwrights, and "new plays with a strong social message," as well as through its publications.[35] *Theatre Workshop*, the league's quarterly journal of theatre and film arts, contained writing by most of the theatrical heavyweights of the day, including Lee Strasberg, John Howard Lawson, Marc Blitzstein, Alice Evans, Mordecai Gorelik, Irwin Shaw, Hallie Flanagan, and many others. The publication announced important social activist productions, sponsored playwriting competitions, advertised classes in the performing arts, printed translated texts of vital theatre theorists, and published plays. It was also the source for increasing membership in the New Theatre League. The April–July 1937 edition of *Theatre Workshop* announced that year's national membership drive by stating,

> The theatre isn't dead yet! Some people think it is, but take our word! The commercial theatre may have entangled itself in a mesh of profit and loss statements—but the new theatres have a way of surviving and growing in spite of all their troubles. . . . The NEW THEATRE LEAGUE . . . [is] the only national cultural organization of the theatre striving to build a genuine, progressive people's theatre movement.[36]

Annual membership in the New Theatre League for 1937 cost one dollar and included discounts on all league publications and delegate representation at regional and national conferences. The memberships were advertised to both professional and nonprofessional theatre groups, as well as to anyone involved in the Federal Theatre Project. SFA adopted similar practices when it transitioned in 1946 from a New York–based group to a national organization. Beginning in the spring of 1946, the national office of SFA, located in New York City, started charging branches fifty dollars a year to affiliate and use the name Stage for Action. For this fee, affiliates were offered a "service of scripts, and other advisory services on technical questions from time to time."[37] Established groups choosing not to affiliate with the national organization beginning in 1947 were able to purchase scripts for the cost of five dollars, paying one dollar in rights per performance; however, they were no longer able to use the name Stage for Action. Following the 1946 announcement, the Washington, D.C., Philadelphia, and Chicago branches decided to affiliate with SFA's national organization, while the Detroit branch did not.[38] SFA also offered individual audience memberships in its regional branches. New York City metropolitan area audience membership cost five dollars annually, granting members a "20% discount on classes in acting, directing, designing, and playwriting as well as to all Stage for Action performances for which admission is charged."[39] Membership in the Washington, D.C., branch of SFA cost two dollars annually for a regular membership and six dollars for a sustaining membership.

Although inspired by the organizational structure, theatrical output and activities, and professionalism of the New Theatre League, it cannot be stated with certainty that SFA was also directly funded by the CPUSA. It would, however, be naive not to consider this a possibility. As Mally indicates regarding Soviet influence on the New Theatre League, "Even though direct oversight from Moscow became more attenuated [beginning in 1936], the New Theatre League continued to serve as a conduit for Soviet dramatic theories" such as "realistic acting techniques" inspired by the teachings of Konstantin Stanislavsky and adopted a repertoire of "plays with social relevance, a clear and positive message, and a broad appeal."[40] Ultimately it must be acknowledged that the New Theatre League was a Communist front, but as Mally so aptly argues, the theatre it produced and ideas it forwarded (often completely separated from its political roots) "have become an integral part of our nation's heritage" and continue to be taught at every higher learning theatrical institution in the United States.[41] There is no smoking gun evidence from materials produced by Stage for Action directly linking it to the Comintern or the CPUSA; however, there are many congressional testimonies and red-baiting materials suggesting that the group was influenced by the party. Yet it must also be stated that just as with many of the artists involved in the New Theatre League, numerous artists joined and financially supported SFA not because of any specific knowledge of its political affiliation but because they believed in the messages of the plays and wanted to participate in a meaningful theatrical experience. Ultimately, it is the intention of this work to bring focus upon the productions of Stage for Action and not upon the group's political affiliations.

As influential as the New Theatre League clearly was on SFA, it is the Federal Theatre Project that offers the strongest thread connecting it to social activist theatre of the 1930s. SFA founder Perry Miller admits the FTP was her direct artistic inspiration for the group, and Marvin Silbersher, an actor with the New York branch of SFA in 1946 and 1947, stated that it was "the grand canvas that all this [SFA] came from."[42] Newspaper articles of the 1940s analyzing SFA observed that the group embraced the living newspaper technique, which was based on a Soviet form made popular in the United States by the FTP. Upon closer investigation, however, it appears the more important connection between the FTP and SFA was their shared participants; many artists who first made names for themselves in FTP productions continued their social activist theatre work with SFA. One example is Morris Watson, who cowrote the stage adaptation of the Albert Kahn and Michael Sayers book *The Great Conspiracy against Russia* (1946). SFA performed *The Great Conspiracy* at Carnegie Hall on September 22, 1947. The cast included one hundred SFA artists led by Paul Robeson and Paul Draper, with financial support provided by the *New Masses* magazine. Morris Watson had been supervisor and contributing writer of three 1930s performances produced by the Living Newspaper Unit of the FTP: *Triple-A Plowed Under* (1936), *1935* (1936), and *Power* (1937). Brett Warren, Watson's cowriter and director for *The Great Conspiracy against Russia*, had previously directed *Power* for the FTP. Warren was involved with social activist theatre prior to his FTP experience as a director with the Collective Theatre of New York. Additionally, Will Geer, Ben Hecht, Arthur Miller, and a host of other artists vital to SFA had performance or playwriting ties to the FTP.

Without question, SFA's tactic of recruiting members of prominent 1930s social activist theatre groups played a significant role in its five-year success. While many were members of previously discussed companies (such as the WLT or the FTP), others were associated with the New York Harlem Suitcase Theatre, Union Theatre, and Group Theatre. These artists included Paul Peters, Mike Gold, Langston Hughes, John Gassner, Peter Frye, Freda Altman, Cheryl Crawford, Harold Clurman, Ben Bengal, Howard Da Silva, Michael Gordon, Howard Bay, Robert Steck, John Wexley, Earl Robinson, Mitchell Grayson, and Philip Loeb; they served in various capacities with SFA, among them playwriting, performing, designing, and directing for the group, as well as sponsoring events.

Furthermore, SFA had direct ties with the League of American Writers (LAW), which disbanded the year before SFA's formation. At its height, the LAW included more than eight hundred members; among them were some of the early twentieth century's most important novelists, poets, and playwrights, such as Theodore Dreiser, Lillian Hellman, Langston Hughes, Richard Wright, and John Steinbeck. The LAW was determined to use its prestige to combat global and native fascism while simultaneously improving the development of American literary arts through the establishment of writers' schools and organization of national writers' congresses. The LAW dissolved under government pressure in 1942, resulting from perceived Communist ties, but this did not dissuade a number of its members from joining the ranks of (or contributing plays to) SFA over the next few years.[43]

The overlap in membership and production techniques between vital activist theatre and literary groups of the 1930s is central to understanding SFA, though perhaps more important is these groups' shared commitment to social change. John Gassner maintained that during the 1930s, social activist theatre was necessarily relevant to a working-class mentality, stating, "Authors implement[ed] their social sympathies with revolutionary Marxist visions of the overthrow of the capitalistic system in the course of an apocalyptic 'final' conflict between capital and labor."[44] While revolutionary, pro-Marxist discourse was acceptable during the Great Depression, social activist theatre companies had to temper this radicalism during the 1940s if they wished to continue working.

The shifting cultural conditions between the 1930s and 1940s concerning radicalism are reflected in a transformation of CPUSA rhetoric. In June 1941, CPUSA national chairman William Z. Foster encouraged breaking with the methods of the previous era and emphasized developing "the broadest united front and People's Front activities. . . . We must especially avoid short-cut slogans, radical sounding appeals, in our eagerness to defend the Soviet Union and to fight Hitler. We must know how to work out practical slogans calculated to really mobilize the masses, rather than merely to give forth revolutionary sounds."[45] A number of points relevant to the shift in U.S. radicalism between the 1930s and 1940s appear in Foster's speech, delivered at a meeting of the Communist Party national committee on June 28, 1941 (less than a week after Hitler violated the Nazi-Soviet Nonaggression Pact). Foster admitted that the methods of the 1930s were not applicable to a country facing imminent war and suggested that, in order to reach the broadest possible audiences, new approaches must be applied, including forgoing theory in favor of practice or action. Foster argued that mobilization of the masses would occur only through the development of "the broadest united front and People's Front activities." Some of these activities included traditional meetings and lectures on Marxist ideology, but music groups, dance clubs, theatre training, and performances aimed at achieving social change were also developed during this time. There exist voluminous records of CPUSA supporters (but not necessarily members) who found their most significant political and social motivation through the arts. Performer Jackie Gibson Alper, for example, stated that she "always enjoyed participating in musical, theatrical, and dance activities and had the feeling that people who could not be reached in other ways would attend a cultural function and be moved to thought and possibly even action enough to become involved in [the Communist Party's] struggles."[46] Historian Robbie Lieberman suggests that utilizing the arts for political purposes implies that "cultural products [are] important in shaping peoples' world views; that people had to be affected emotionally as well as intellectually in order to change their political outlook; and that participation rather than passive consumption was critical to the process of changing consciousness and acting on that changed point of view."[47]

Increasingly active participation in cultural events intent on promoting political or social change was the focus of many Popular Fronters during the 1940s. The transitional year in SFA's existence, 1946, was also the year in which the national debate on the political influence of the arts in U.S. culture (or as *PM* journalist Charles Norman originally presented it, "the whole pressing, fascinating question of the artist's place in society") reached its apex.[48] The conversation began in late 1945, initially in response to the question of whether poet Ezra Pound's Fascist political views and actions (he supported Benito Mussolini during the war and was anti-Semitic) should outweigh public appreciation of his poetry.[49] The dialogue originated in literary circles among writers such as e. e. cummings, William Carlos Williams, Karl Shapiro, and Louis Untermeyer but quickly spread to leftist papers and inspired debate among artists in various mediums on whether one can separate a person's politics from his or her art. This question haunted many theatre artists throughout their lives, as the House Un-American Activities Committee (HUAC) made it clear that a person and his or her political affiliations were considered one and the same. Journalist Max Lerner, concluding his article in *PM*, expressed how many artists of the 1940s felt regarding the interconnectedness of politics and art:

The relationship between art and life is a two-way street. We have always recognized that life nourishes art. But it is also true that art nourishes life. I don't want to cut my culture off from anything valid or beautiful in art, even though I might consider the man who did it a fool or a barbarian. Nor do I want to cut myself or my culture off from the great tradition of reason, on which depends the long-run war against the forces of unreason.[50]

The debate about art's purpose in society continued into 1946, spurring the "Art as a Weapon" conversation in the United States and inspiring a series of articles in the *Worker* discussing social art. As Marion Summers writes,

Anything which deals with humanity and therefore, of necessity with society may be said to be social art. . . . It has been applied to art which recognizes the existence of poverty, inequality, strikes, lynchings, war, exploitation or the myriad other problems of contemporary life. It is an art which is aware that the world is not one big musical comedy in Technicolor. Social art, as we understand it, is unequivocal and outspoken propaganda for social progress.[51]

Summers's comments occurred in the same month as Foster's call for increased activity by Communists in cultural endeavors. Foster stated, "The Communists must, above all others, be the ones to understand the true significance of art as a weapon in the class struggle, and to know how to combat all reactionary capitalistic hindrances to the development of the new people's democratic art."[52]

Although the "Art as a Weapon" debate inspired much-needed public discourse on the function of art in contemporary culture, the increasingly red-tinged and often underhanded rhetoric adopted by leaders of the debate also drove apart long-standing relationships and tarnished many careers. The controversy reached its breaking point following the Art as a Weapon Symposium conducted on April 18, 1946, with thirty-five hundred in attendance at the Manhattan Center in New York City. The event included speeches by Arnaud d'Usseau, Howard Fast, William Z. Foster, Joseph North, Elizabeth Catlett, and Samuel Sillen. Additional greetings from the absent Albert Maltz, John Howard Lawson, and Alvah Bessie were read aloud. Lawson hailed the event as a call to arms: "Let us appeal to all writers and artists and scholars to fulfill the responsibilities that life imposes upon us, to dedicate our skill and talent to the cause of labor, to use our art and knowledge as weapons in the struggle for peace, freedom and security."[53] Maltz was more concerned with the economic future of the arts in the United States, declaring, "It is the ironic truth that where culture is limited—where it is the privilege of the purse rather than the automatic possession of citizenship—there, even for the purse, it is a twisted thing, a stunted culture."[54] It is somewhat surprising that Maltz was allowed any voice at the symposium at all, as he had recently become the whipping boy of the CPUSA for publicly questioning the "Art as a Weapon" slogan. Cultural historian Alan Wald states that *New Masses* literary editor Samuel Sillen's ganging up on Maltz in a series of reviews published in the *Daily Worker* was "repugnant" and "astounded even [Sillen's] closest friends," earning him "a place in U.S. literary history as a loathsome hatchet man."[55] A decade later Sillen would deeply regret his treatment of Maltz (as well as many other choices he made as a top-ranking CPUSA leader).

In 1946, however, Sillen's leadership in Communist circles as well as in the "Art as a Weapon" movement advantaged SFA. Sillen not only favorably reviewed SFA performances in the *Daily Worker* but invited the group's artists and board members to events that showcased their work and perspectives. For example, d'Usseau, SFA board member and co-playwright of *Deep Are the Roots* (a Broadway production featuring SFA members Gordon Heath and Barbara Bel Geddes), spoke at the 1946 Art as a Weapon Symposium and wrote soon after in *New Masses* about the movement. D'Usseau noted that some playwrights were abandoning the concept of "Art as a Weapon"; however, he recommended staying the course and emphasized that playwrights have to "go back, understand more fully our sources of inspiration, and draw from them every possible idea and insight that will serve us. We must become utilitarians, not in a narrow sense, but broadly—dialectically, if you will."[56] D'Usseau and his *Deep Are the Roots* writing partner, James Gow (also on the SFA board), wrote an article for the *New York Times* five months after the symposium, toning down their message for a more centrist-leaning audience. They were responding directly to Lawrence Langner's alarm at the prevalence of "social themes" plays being written and produced on Broadway. D'Usseau and Gow defended such plays, suggesting that "they have helped open the way to wider, more exciting and more varied content in the commercial theatre. . . . The theatre is a good place indeed for the sharpest kind of comment on the manners and morals of America, 1946."[57] Not wanting to offend their anticapitalist comrades at the *Daily Worker*, the two playwrights suggested that audiences who found Broadway tickets too costly should support neighborhood and grassroots groups. They proclaimed that "theatre is breaking out all over" and promoted companies such as the American Repertory Company, the American Negro Theatre (which shared many SFA members including Gordon Heath, Peggy Clark, and Abram Hill), SFA, and the proposed experimental unit of the American Stage Wing school.

It is important to note that d'Usseau's statements in his symposium speech and his perspectives in the *New York Times* article, as well as the opinions of several other writers quoted above, supported Popular Front thinking of the period and recognizably Marxist rhetoric. Lenin's writings on the need for developing intelligent and accessible arts for the people (specifically workers) were quoted quite often during this debate on the purpose of the arts in people's lives. Lenin wrote, "Art belongs to the people. It must have its deepest roots in the broad mass of the workers. It must be understood and loved by them. It must be rooted in and grow with their feelings, thoughts and desires. It must arouse and develop the artist in them."[58] The concept of produced results—of emotions, action, and intellect stimulated and changed in audiences (that is, effect)—and the best method(s) by which to achieve them (that is, form) is the preoccupation of most theoretical treatises on theatre over its long history, not just Communist or Marxist ones. What separates the questioning of the 1940s from many previous theories, however, is the infrastructural role of economics in artistic creation. The Art as a Weapon Symposium's focus on how economics influences creative output introduced Marxist theory to a new generation. Marx, keenly aware of limitations on equal access to art, endeavored to theorize the ideal relationship between content and form. He was conflicted—as were many in the 1940s debates—as to whether artists as creators should be allowed a "false consciousness" or an extreme subjectivism that might grant them authority to write about aspects of humanity outside of their own class, or whether they should adhere to "a strict dependence on the proletariat."[59]

The relationship between form, content, and economics would be reexamined yet again in 1956 with Arthur Miller's review for the *International Theatre Annual* of the then-current Broadway season. The commentary, much more guarded than the polemical tone found in 1940s papers such as the *New Masses* or the *Daily Worker*, questioned the purpose and future of commercial (specifically Broadway) theatre. Though by the end Miller was cautiously optimistic, it is clear he still held out hope for a change and, perhaps, for a resurgence of social activist theatre. The article appeared in response to a newspaper editorial calling 1956 "the most exciting Broadway season in many years, as well as the most successful financially."[60] By contrast, Miller found the season to be "the usual trendless jumble."[61] Asserting that Broadway audiences and theatre critics had no capacity for judging what they saw, he asserted the same audiences who raved about *Cat on a Hot Tin Roof* would be shocked to discover it is truly a commentary about the bourgeois, or "on nearly everyone who watches it."[62] In his article Miller dissected Broadway theatre and its monotony without offering any solutions, though he intimated a revolution in theatre, inspired by as-yet-unknown playwrights, waited just around the corner: "There seems to be a genuine dissatisfaction with the uncourageous play or the ill-made, meandering work whose only justification is its spontaneity and its departure from living room realism. There is an as yet half-conscious but nevertheless growing awareness of the larger social mission of theatre among these people which was not there even two years ago, in my estimation."[63]

Miller's "Concerning the Boom" article hailed the theatrical work he and fellow playwrights, directors, designers, and performers did with SFA as significant to "the larger social mission of theatre" and signaled a coming change. Perhaps it was written in self-defense, since 1956 was the year he was called before the HUAC for being (in his words) "a disloyal lefty."[64] Yet Miller saw the Broadway stage as truly void of any work resembling social activism. I believe Miller understood he was already too involved in Broadway's maelstrom to return to the kind of grassroots theatre he explored in the mid-1940s, but he also felt the need to champion a new cadre of social activist playwrights willing to question the economics, politics, and purpose of theatre in society. As the rapidly approaching 1960s exploded with social activist theatre groups intent on taking the theatre to the people (and to the streets, factories, neighborhoods, schools, and fields), as SFA had so bravely done, the hopes of Miller and many others for an activist future were rewarded.

Although SFA was continuing the tradition of 1930s workers' theatre by responding directly to the social problems of the day, it broke new ground for women's involvement in U.S. social activist theatre. In her work on the women's movement, Kate Weigand states that radical leftist women, whom she refers to as "Old Leftists," contributed some of their "most valuable feminist work" during the years 1945–56 and "built an ideological and organizational base for a much more visible and successful women's movement twenty years later."[65] SFA substantiates Weigand's argument in that the majority of its branches were initiated and managed by women with direct ties to, or passion for, both politics and the arts. Perry Miller, the founder of SFA, was a twenty-three-year-old radio actress when she developed the idea for organizing a theatre group that would support home front war causes and "bring to public attention the menace of native fascism."[66] She soon invited fellow radio actress Donna Keath, stage performer Berilla Kerr, and lighting designer Peggy Clark to join her in forming the group.

At two years of age, Miller lost her father, a dentist, to a heart attack. Miller's mother became the sole provider for three children under the age of five and encouraged her children's academic and extracurricular activities. Performing from an early age at camp and in Yonkers community theatre, Miller's first professional work was in summer stock at Lake Champlain in Essex. She was an acting apprentice but went on in *Goodbye Again* when the lead did not arrive in time for curtain. Miller worked in modeling and commercials before being cast in the Theatre Guild's production of *Madame Bovary,* which opened on November 16, 1937, at the Broadhurst Theatre in New York City. Miller was still in high school when she performed as one of the "Girls in the Balcony." She left school for six months to participate in the production but still graduated on time as salutatorian of her class. Through this production she became a member of Actors' Equity.

Miller has identified the work of Hallie Flanagan and the living newspapers of the FTP as her inspiration for forming SFA. Miller was very political in the sense that she understood that change had to come by political action, though not through lectures but rather through entertainment.[67] As vital as Miller was to the founding of SFA, however—she led the group during its first three years of existence as it transitioned from a New York City–based collective to a nationally recognized group—her career in theatre was relatively brief, as she soon became a documentary filmmaker. Her shift from theatre to film was instigated by a growing disillusionment with the limitations of live performance. She began searching for a different medium in which she could more effectively communicate her ideas. One afternoon she attended a screening of a film in the *Why We Fight* series, directed by Frank Capra, at the Museum of Modern Art in New York. Miller recalled, "The emotional effect of this film was so powerful that if there had been a recruiter that signed you up, and I was such an intense pacifist until Fascism[,] . . . I would have signed up."[68] What drew Miller to the films was Capra's underlying message in each of the documentaries, which was "insuring against the recurrence of world war" by "showing the necessity for better understanding between nations and peoples, showing the necessity for outlawing conquest and exploitation by the few, and showing the necessity for eliminating economic evils."[69]

Miller alludes to an epiphany while watching one of the fifty-minute *Why We Fight* films, suggesting she instantaneously understood that documentary filmmaking was the best way to treat significant topics for a broad audience. Miller's change of career led her to a series of jobs in the independent and documentary film community before she began directing her own films. She archived a collection of social welfare films for the United Nations, cofounded the Film Advisory Center in Manhattan, and worked for CBS in Europe as a film consultant before landing a position with National Educational Television—the predecessor to PBS—in 1964. Although her initial job at the network was that of a film researcher, she quickly worked her way up to directing and producing her own documentary television programs and films.

Although Perry Miller, better known after 1955 under her married name of Perry Miller Adato, ultimately left the live performance world for an extremely successful career in television and film, what undoubtedly makes much of her work stand out is her training as an actress and experience with dramaturgical analysis. Filmmakers as renowned as Ken Burns name her a major influence on their work. Miller was the first U.S. documentary film director to master the art of merging documentary film and drama and consequently changed the field. Her career in film has spanned over forty years, garnering numerous Emmy nominations as well as a win for her film *Dylan Thomas: The World I Breathe*. She was the first woman to win a Directors Guild of America Award when her film *Georgia O'Keeffe: A Life in Art* was honored in 1977 (she would win the award three more times). Her 1970 documentary, *Gertrude Stein: When You See This, Remember Me*, is considered "one of the key works of the historical documentary genre."[70] Along with her work on Thomas and O'Keeffe, Miller directed works about radio comedians of the 1930s and 1940s as well as films on Mary Cassatt, Charles and Ray Eames, Helen Frankenthaler, Pablo Picasso, Carl Sandburg, and Eugene O'Neill. In 2010, long after the age most people have retired from their profession, Miller released a two-hour documentary about Parisian cultural life titled *Paris, the Luminous Years: Towards the Making of the Modern*.

It was a fervid desire to change society through theatre that drove Perry Miller's founding of SFA in the late fall of 1943. FDR had charged the nation with supporting the war effort in every way possible, and Miller quickly convinced an impressive list of theatre and radio artists to join her ranks. Immediate recruits were Peggy Clark, who would go on to design lights for the Broadway productions of *No Time for Sergeants, Auntie Mame, Brigadoon, Gentlemen Prefer Blondes, Wonderful Town, Kismet, Peter Pan, Flower Drum Song,* and a host of others from 1946 to 1980; Berilla Kerr, an actress and Circle Repertory Theatre resident playwright who participated in SFA from 1943 to 1948 as a board member and sponsor; and Donna Keath, a radio actress who served as chairman of SFA and was a commanding presence in the American Federation of Radio Artists.

Of these four founding members, Walter S. Steele named Perry Miller as associated with Stage for Action in his testimony on Communist activities in the United States before the HUAC in 1947, but only Keath would eventually be named to the infamous *Red Channels* list.[71] Of the people listed in the first major *New York Times* article detailing SFA's work, four of the seven—Edward Chodorov, Norman Corwin, Arthur Miller, and Sam Wanamaker—faced HUAC inquests. These supporting members are all male and better known to the average theatre historian than are the founding women. This speaks not only to the ongoing marginalization of women in theatre history but also to the intense level of interest the HUAC showed in SFA once the group included, and was run, by men renowned in their artistic fields and who also had a considerable history of involvement in leftist theatre.

During the first few years of its existence, SFA supported a number of agendas important to women in the United States subsequently taken up postwar by the Congress of American Women (CAW), especially the Commission on Child-Care and Education and the Commission for Action on Peace and Democracy, positioning SFA at the forefront of women's rights during the 1940s.[72] By the time Elizabeth Gurley Flynn's 1947 pamphlet *Woman's Place in the Fight for a Better World* appeared advocating eleven demands for American women, including "adequate childcare facilities with federal and state support for nurseries, recreation centers and schools with hot lunches," Arthur Miller's *That They May Win* (calling for the exact same support for working mothers) had been performed for more than three years by almost every national SFA unit and proved continuously to be one of its most popular pieces.[73]

From its inception in December 1943 until the summer of 1946, SFA was exceptionally supportive of women's rights. Founded and run by women during its first years of existence and openly supported by Eleanor

Roosevelt, the group rallied around issues significant to the CAW and other leftist women's groups of this period. Perhaps this is because many of the members and affiliates of the CAW were also sponsors, family members of sponsors, or members of SFA. SFA's political connections outside the realm of theatre show how interconnected politics and performance could be during the 1940s. For example, when the CAW and its board came under attack from the Justice Department in 1950, its lawyer was longtime SFA sponsor John Abt. Muriel Draper, the executive vice president of the CAW and the founding member of the Women's Committee of the National Council of American-Soviet Friendship (NCASF), may have entreated her nephew Paul Draper, the famous dancer, to perform in *The Great Conspiracy* for SFA. Paul Draper was well connected with Arthur Miller and Paul Robeson (both members of the NCASF), as well as with Robeson's wife, Eslande, who also served on the CAW board. In addition to his participation in *The Great Conspiracy*, Paul Draper served as co-host with Zero Mostel of SFA's inaugural *Satire Matinee* at the Café Society on November 17, 1946. Other women of influence who involved themselves with both SFA and CAW-sponsored commissions were department store heiress and leftist activist Elinor Gimbel (also the vice chairman of the Women's Committee of the NCASF); fashion designer and radical feminist author Elizabeth Hawes; Joyce Borden Balokovic, actress and heiress wife of Zlatko Balokovic, a Croatian-born violinist (and SFA board of directors member); Katherine Earnshaw (also involved with the NCASF); and actress Jean Muir (named as vice president of a CAW chapter in her 1949 congressional hearings), who was eventually blacklisted and lost her television series due in part to suspected involvement with SFA.

Though the female leadership structure of the New York City branch of SFA seems to have been largely displaced by 1946, I suggest that the early affiliations between the female sponsors and advisory board members of the organization, as well as the protofeminist politics of the immediate postwar period, inevitably shaped the early development of SFA. Almost immediately on the heels of V-J Day, women in every profession across the United States were finding themselves less welcome than they had been during the war years. The government issued an unprecedented number of advertisements suggesting that a woman's proper place was in the home. Many women who enjoyed the work they had done during the war and wanted to continue in their professions, or who desperately needed the income their jobs provided, were informed they were losing their positions to returning GIs. SFA shares the same history as many other female-run operations

Since attendance is by invitation, please return this reservation promptly to Stage for Action, 130 W. 42 St., N.Y.C. (Bryant 9-1425). Tickets are available at $2.00 each.

Please reserve (   ) tickets.

Enclosed please find check for.............................

Name...

Address...

Stage For Action, Inc.

invites you to its premiere presentation of
"Satire Matinee"

PROGRAM:

★ **ZERO MOSTEL**   ★ **RALPH CUMMINGS**

★ **PAUL DRAPER**   ★ **LAURA DUNCAN**

★ **DIANE ADRIAN**   ★ **THE SKEPTICS**

★ **TALLEY BEATTY & CO.**

NEW SONGS: Hy Zaret and Lou Singer, Irma Jurist and Leonard Gershe

Ticket reservation form for the premier performance of SFA's *Satire Matinee. Courtesy of the Tamiment Library and Robert F. Wagner Labor Archives, New York University.*

during the war. Started by women in December 1943, the New York City unit remained a female-run operation for three years, though letterhead dated December 12, 1946, indicates that Mildred Linsley, originally elected executive director in January 1945, had been replaced by Alex Leith. Leith would remain in the position for only a few months, as letterhead dated February 18, 1947, lists Gene Frankel as acting executive director. Frankel served in the position until the New York group's disbanding in 1948.

In some ways, however, the female grasp on the New York chapter of SFA began slipping as early as January 1945 when playwright, screenwriter, and producer Edward Chodorov was elected chairman of the board, replacing Perry Miller in that position. Lillie Mayer, the wife of movie producer Arthur L. Mayer, performed the duties of vice chairman for a few months following Chodorov's election, but by April 1945 she was no longer a member of SFA's executive leadership and Abram Hill, director of the American Negro Theatre, assumed the role. Beginning the following year and for the remainder of its existence, the executive branch of the board of directors for SFA—chairman, vice chairman, and treasurer—was filled by men. What is important to note here is that while the board of directors was all male after 1946, the person in charge of daily operations for SFA during its formative period (a role Alex Leith in his August 1950 HUAC hearing described as "in charge of the over-all functioning of the organization") was always a woman.[74] Women provided all of the foundational work for SFA, from its inception through its disbanding. In particular, Mildred Linsley deserves much of the credit for transitioning SFA from a grassroots theatrical operation in New York City to a national group with units in at least eight other metropolitan cities. The initial executive directors of many of the subsidiary regional units were also women. In Washington, D.C., for example, the chairman was Hilda Worthington Smith, and she remained in this position from the launch of the unit in 1945 through the end of the group's activities in 1948. The Chicago SFA unit was also originally run by a woman; Virginia Payne was the chairman of the Chicago executive committee during its first three years (1944 through 1946). In 1947, Benjamin J. Green was listed as chairman of the group, though the executive director was Lucille Colbert. Although very few records of the Philadelphia SFA unit list its executive committee, it appears that as late as June 28, 1947, Ruth Deacon was the head of that city's SFA unit. Deacon's paying job was bookkeeper at an assumed Communist hub, the Locust Bookshop in Philadelphia.[75]

Linsley was also one of the incorporators and employees of another assumed Communist book and cultural operation, the Bookshop Association, located in Baltimore. According to HUAC testimony, the Bookshop Association "was a local shop where people would join for one dollar a year and take advantage of the cultural programs [offered] at reduced prices, or get books at twenty percent discount."[76] Some of the cultural programs presented during the association's existence included concerts by Laura Duncan, Ray Lev, and the Jefferson String Quartet, dance programs by Lili Mann, and lectures by leading scholars and artists such as Vladimir Kazekevitch and Rockwell Kent. The Bookshop Association closed its storefront in 1943 but remained active through mail orders until 1946. Louis Ginsberg was treasurer of the Bookshop Association and in his subpoenaed testimony to the HUAC named Linsley as an employee of the store for twenty-five dollars a week. He did not specify the dates she worked at the store, nor did he admit that the association or Linsley was connected to the Communist Party. Prior to working for the Bookshop Association, in her function as publicity and educational director of the United Cannery, Agricultural, Packing, and Allied Workers of America, Linsley was instrumental in garnering national support for a wrongly accused black labor organizer named Willie Joe Hart in Tallapoosa County, Alabama, and also served as conference secretary for the Maryland Labor League.[77]

Despite several years of work in various labor organizations in the Washington, D.C., metropolitan area in the late 1930s and early 1940s, it is clear that by January 1945 Linsley was living in New York City and working, most likely full-time, for SFA. In a February 1946 *Daily Worker* article featuring her position with SFA, Linsley stated that working for the group was "the best job she's had in her life" and that she "always yearned for a setup that would enable professional people to give their talents for more than just entertainment," continuing, "We figure we're doing our part to help make America a good place for workers and artists and all the rest of the people too."[78] Linsley insisted that Broadway producers were also in support of the work SFA was doing and encouraged actors and designers to get involved with the group in order "to keep in trim."[79] It was in this feature article that the *Daily Worker* revealed Stage for Action had plans for a permanent national theatre organization, which would be announced publicly at its *Theatre Parade* variety show at Carnegie Hall the following month.

Mildred Linsley, SFA executive director, 1946. *Reproduced, with permission of the Communist Party USA, from the Daily Worker, February 6, 1946, 6.*

Linsley remains the most elusive of the SFA executive committee members. It is perplexing that Linsley, apparently not directly involved in professional theatre prior to SFA but employed in public relations and responsible for arranging some of the cultural programs at the Bookshop Association, was appointed executive director of a theatre company with so many other prominent stage, radio, and film artists working in its ranks. Linsley does not appear in any promotional materials (programs, pamphlets, and the like) until the January 1945 *New York Times* announcement of recent election results for the group. Additionally, in February 1946 Linsley was listed as a member of the advisory council of People's Songs. People's Songs, which was led by Pete Seeger and shared many of the same members and sponsors as well as offices with the New York unit of SFA, was formed "to make and send songs of labor and the American people through the land," and quite often the two groups performed together at strikes and pickets.[80]

Mildred Linsley's appointment to SFA coincides with a clear change in the organization's mission. Two of the group's founding members, Perry Miller and Peggy Clark, retired from the project within a year of Linsley's appointment. More important, perhaps, in terms of external perceptions of the group, the involvement of members such as Linsley (who had no clear connection to the theatre but who did have distinct ties to various political organizations) suggested that SFA was gearing up to position itself anew. The year 1945 was one of transition in U.S. politics as the country took a collective breath from the fallout of the war and regrouped for the 1946 midterm elections. SFA's appointment of Linsley seems to signal a deliberate choice to change direction and tactics: within a year, SFA shifted rapidly from a mobile theatre company operating with a minuscule budget to an established national people's theatre headquartered in New York City with branches across the country. Its message had also changed; it was no longer necessary to support the war, but it was vital to fight for peace. The group's postwar marketing clearly expressed its future vision: "The war is over—but the need for action continues. Rumors of war . . . atomic energy . . . inflation . . . native fascist movements . . . veterans' problems . . . are the stuff of today's drama and Stage for Action will dramatize the answers as progressives see the answers."[81] SFA turned a political corner and fully embraced a progressive agenda, growing ever more adamant in its support of the fight for global peace and equality as the 1948 election inched closer.

Although Mildred Linsley had more than eight hundred actors on file willing to perform with Stage for Action in 1946, the list of executive committee members for the New York City unit of SFA during its five-year existence is relatively short, containing only thirteen people in the important roles of executive director, chairman, vice chairman, and treasurer during this period. The list includes the original four: Perry Miller, Donna Keath, Berilla Kerr, and Peggy Clark, with Elias Goldin stepping in as treasurer in early 1944. Goldin was an accountant by profession who became a financial general manager and producer of hundreds of Broadway shows. He remained SFA's treasurer until 1946, when he was replaced by Milton Baron, another Broadway general manager and producer. The remaining seven executive committee members—Edward Chodorov, Lillie Mayer, Mildred Linsley, Abram Hill, Art Smith, Alex Leith, and Gene Frankel—were all connected to the performing arts in some way (except, of course, for Linsley).

The *New York Times* ran eight promotions, including two major stories, for SFA from March to December 1944. The first article detailing the work of SFA in a primarily leftist or labor-supported paper occurred on January 2, 1945, in the *New Masses*. This two-and-a-half-page article, written by Harry Taylor, occurred within days of the annual meeting when Mildred Linsley became executive director of the group. The *Daily Worker* published a feature article on SFA three months later and began regularly covering SFA's performances in January 1946. This date coincides with the formation of the National Citizens Political Action Committee, emerging out of the Congress of Industrial Organizations Political Action Committee, which in early 1946 solidified plans for a Political Action School. Several executive committee and advisory board members participated in the school as faculty. By January 22, 1946, SFA had become so intimately connected with labor unions and other workers' rights groups that it received its own calendar of events in the *Daily Worker*. What is notable about the differences between the coverage in the *New York Times* and the workers' newspapers during 1945 and 1946 is that most of the articles in the former address the playwrights involved or summarize a specific performance, while those in the latter tend to focus on Linsley, major union sponsors of SFA, operational procedures, and target audiences. This suggests that the labor newspapers were less interested in the aesthetics of the work and more concerned with how workers' rights were being supported through the performances. There is a disappointing lack of focus on the actual production values of SFA performances in either the leftist or centrist newspapers of the 1940s.

Under Linsley's tenure as executive director, SFA formed strong connections with many different unions and expanded into a national organization. When she was replaced (or resigned) as executive director in the summer of 1946, more than one thousand people were registered members with the New York branch of SFA alone. The New York City outfit boasted nine touring companies, each consisting of approximately eight members from the professional acting community. Still, very little information is available on Linsley, either prior to her joining SFA or after her tenure with the group ended. What is evident, though, is that she continued her commitment to social issues, as during the early 1950s she was the director of volunteers for the Brooklyn Jewish Hospital, responsible for recruiting, training, and managing a staff of three hundred volunteers.[82]

Ultimately, Mildred Linsley remains one of the many silent or silenced bodies in SFA's history despite influential members and supporters on every rung of the social and political ladder. Records indicate that audiences numbered in the millions across the eight metropolitan markets by the end of the group's five-year existence, yet because of the political climate of the period, many of SFA's performances and artists remain unknown. In a decade when select members of the government executed extreme measures to silence "radicalism," it was the so-called radicals, people such as those involved with SFA, who were promoting world peace and equality for all Americans. If they conspired, it was to educate audiences about important social issues, not to overthrow the country. Although some members of SFA were assuredly CPUSA supporters, the majority were Democrats, Progressives, and independents (there were likely very few Republicans in their ranks); they were dedicated social activists, if a bit politically naive. McCarthy-era historian Ellen Schrecker argues that the "American Communist Party was, above all, an organization of activists." The CPUSA expected members to dedicate "every evening to party work" and to "attend meetings, read party literature, and become active in labor unions and other so-called mass organizations [CP term] or front groups [CP opponent term]."[83] Although many members and supporters of the CPUSA ultimately left the group because of boredom or burnout, others stayed for long periods of time because of the camaraderie that came from belonging to a passionate activist group whose members shared a deep-seated belief that their actions meant something. The ambiguous political nature of the Popular Front bloc is augmented by SFA sponsor Arnaud d'Usseau's reflection of the period: "But for all the confusion whether they professed themselves liberals or humanists or Marxists, a majority of our artists in the theater began consciously to develop this idea of the theater as a weapon."[84] SFA members were the recipients of this consciousness as they actively used their theatre as a weapon for equality and peace.

2. **PROGRESSIVE INSURGENCY**

IMMEDIATELY FOLLOWING THE END of World War II and in preparation for the 1946 election season, liberals began changing their rhetoric when articulating the purpose of theatre. Much of this change was driven by increased factionalism in the Democratic Party between pro- and anticommunist progressives, groups that political historian Mark L. Kleinman delineates as Cold War and Popular Front liberals.[1] In order to drive particular policies to the center of political debate—such as full employment, racial equality, Soviet-American friendship, and an end to all nuclear warfare—Popular Front liberals joined forces with labor unions. Although Congress of Industrial Organizations (CIO) union leadership during and immediately following the war shared many of the same political and social goals of Popular Front liberals, their collaboration increased in late 1946 and early 1947 when rallying support against the much-maligned Taft-Hartley Act. This act, arguably the strongest political action of the Eightieth Congress, was designed to significantly amend the Wagner Act and break down other pro-union policies implemented during the New Deal. A few of the many aspects of the legislation that proved especially unsavory to labor and its liberal supporters included forbidding financial contributions by unions in national elections, barring federal employees from striking, and, perhaps most significant for many Popular Fronters, prohibiting Communist Party membership. It was this final mandate of Taft-Hartley that led directly to an increase in labor union red-baiting and, assuming he was at one point a viable candidate, cost Henry Wallace the presidency.

One major result of the unification between Popular Front liberals and labor union leadership, which continues to impact current politics, was the formation of political action committees (PACs), a relatively new entity in the 1940s. Disillusioned by both Republicans and Democrats following the end of World War II, many Popular Fronters and their representative

PACs supported forming a third party to contest the 1948 presidential election. Their chosen candidate for this new Progressive Party was Henry A. Wallace, President Truman's recently ousted secretary of commerce who had formerly served as secretary of agriculture and vice president under Franklin D. Roosevelt. This chapter explicates the relationship between Stage for Action and labor unions during and following World War II, emphasizing the impact the decidedly anti-union Taft-Hartley Act had on progressive politics and the Wallace campaign. It also examines SFA's transition from a New York City–based theatre company supporting home-front issues during the war to a nationally organized propaganda vehicle for the Progressive Party following the war's end.

Involvement with the Congress of Industrial Organizations Political Action Committee (CIO-PAC) and the National Citizens Political Action Committee (NC-PAC) influenced SFA's pivot in agenda. Three significant events in SFA's history highlight this shift: a major benefit evening at the Henry Hudson Hotel in April 1944, its involvement in the first-ever School for Political Action Techniques in June 1946, and President Truman's veto of the Taft-Hartley Act in June 1947. These events are particularly signifi-cant because they brought national attention to the group while revealing SFA's political and labor affiliation following the war. Although SFA per-formed the work of numerous theatrical and radio luminaries during the time span covered in this chapter (December 1943 to June 1947)—including Edward Chodorov, Norman Corwin, Anita Grannis, Raphael Hayes, Ben Hecht, Jean Karsavina, Sandra Michael, Paul Peters, and others—I pay particular attention to Arthur Miller's *That They May Win* and Les Pine and Anita Short's *Joseph McGinnical, Cynical Pinnacle, Opus II*, given that they were favored productions of the CIO-PAC and NC-PAC. Further-more, although stylistically disparate, both pieces were adopted as Wallace election propaganda because they discuss vital Progressive Party policies.

That They May Win

In April 1944, First Lady Eleanor Roosevelt wrote the following about Stage for Action in her "My Day" column: "This group decided some time ago that we have a real need for informed and active citizens in this country, and that one way to give people information is to do it painlessly, through the drama."[2] Between the years 1935 and 1962 Eleanor Roosevelt wrote a syndicated newspaper column read by millions six days a week. Her "My Day" column covered everything that she accomplished in her seemingly endless days and offered up opinions on child-rearing, shopping, cultural events, and politics. As Martha Gellhorn aptly acknowledges, "[Mrs. Roosevelt] could not escape a certain fuss in public events but in her personal life she ignored pomp and trimmings."[3] A mother of six by age thirty-one, Eleanor Roosevelt was passionately invested in social issues, her husband's political career, and the future of the United States. She had neither time nor inclination for frivolities, as her "My Day" column illustrates. It is straightforward and devoid of any flowery rhetoric or jargon, which is precisely what made it one of the most respected columns produced by the United Feature Syndicate during its twenty-six-year run.

In addition, the people, events, and issues Mrs. Roosevelt addressed inspired the interest of the American public. It is therefore not surprising that within weeks of her mention of SFA in her column, the group acquired an office space and began receiving requests for performances from a growing number of women's groups, labor unions, and advisory councils. Roosevelt spent part of her five-hundred-word column describing the performance techniques of SFA and subtly advocated their need for funding:

> They do not receive salaries, but they would like to be able to have an office of their own and a couple of people on salary who could devote all their time to spreading this activity throughout the nation and establishing it on a firm basis in headquarters in New York City. They raised some money last night, but I hope many more people will be willing to help them.[4]

The First Lady was commenting on an SFA benefit event (more than likely its first) at the Henry Hudson Hotel on April 19, 1944. Roosevelt was the guest of honor and sat with other distinguished guests, including husband-and-wife performers Fredric March and Florence Eldridge, playwright Edward Chodorov, boxer-turned-actor Canada Lee, and vice president of the New York State AFL-CIO Betty Hawley Donnelly. The audience that evening was entertained by three short plays, choral numbers, and speeches by significant liberal literati and artists such as John Gassner and Norman Corwin, as well as by prominent members of the labor union community like William Feinberg (secretary of the American Federation of Musicians) and Saul Mills (secretary-treasurer of the Greater New York Industrial Council). Roosevelt made no mention of the speeches in her column, instead emphasizing the performances and how they "use a little of the technique of the 'Living Newspaper,'" wherein the audience "is made to feel very much a part of the show because its members speak up and take part in the discussion of what is going on on the stage."[5] Although clearly inspired by the living newspaper productions of the Federal Theatre Project and relying on topics ripped directly from the headlines, SFA did not employ multimedia techniques, fully realized music and light scores, or "panoramic, historical presentation" embraced by the New York City productions of the FTP in works such as *Triple-A Plowed Under.*[6] Rather, scripts written expressly for SFA were a hybrid of literary techniques adopted from their 1930s workers' theatre predecessors and productions on Broadway but without much, if any, technical design elements. What reviews indicate separated SFA productions from commercial theatre occurring during the 1940s was their dedication to professionalism, cultural relevance, and impact on social change despite impoverished production values. Barnard Rubin reviewed one production as "handicapped by inadequate facilities" but still a production "that for pace, intensity and sincerity makes most of the Broadway stuff look amateurish."[7] Guests at the Henry Hudson Hotel in April 1944 were entertained by one of these intense, sincere pieces written expressly for the group, Arthur Miller's *That They May Win.* It was Miller's play that Eleanor Roosevelt praised in her column as being particularly timely.

Due to SFA's not-for-profit economic structure, as well as its suspect political ties and funding platform, the group operated in a somewhat transient nature. Thousands of participants could be found in its eight regional locales, and ascertaining the duration of participation for any one person involved with the group is difficult. One of the few participants with a traceable paper trail and extensive influence on the group is Arthur Miller. Miller produced *That They May Win, You're Next!,* and *Hiccupping Mr. Higgins* with SFA.[8] Alan Wald refers to the years 1945–46 as Miller's "missing chapter" because Miller disappeared from Broadway during that time. It is true that between the failure of *The Man Who Had All the Luck* in 1944 and the success of *All My Sons* in 1947, Miller poured himself into revolutionary work and leftist theatrical criticism with the *New Masses.*[9] But Miller did not turn his back on playwriting. Instead he became the resident playwright of SFA, though he did more than write for the group, directing at least one of its productions. Even after the Broadway opening of *All My Sons* catapulted Miller into the national spotlight, he continued working with SFA, using plays he wrote for it to serve Wallace's Progressive Party platform. Additionally, he sponsored "a meeting of writers, playwrights, composers and lyricists. . . in connection with the National Council of American-Soviet Friendship's membership drive" at

Zero Mostel's home "to discuss a projected series of performances which Stage for Action will produce for the National Council. . . . Special material, such as plays, sketches and songs, will be written on American-Soviet friendship."[10] Attendees at the meeting included Irving Wexler, George Scudder, Leslie Stevens, Paul Kent, Lou Kleinman, Joe Darion, Paul Sekon, Dave Schreiber, and George Kleinsinger, many of whom already had prolific Broadway and Hollywood writing careers.[11]

It could be argued that this meeting did more to hurt the Progressive Party's campaign than to assist it, though Henry Wallace chose never to alienate himself from groups that he believed were in service of his "One World" agenda. The National Council of American-Soviet Friendship was the successor to the National Council on Soviet Relations, which had been founded in 1941 to serve a radical pro-Soviet and Socialist movement. During the 1940s, the purpose of the NCASF was emphasizing cultural interchange and education to strengthen the "bonds of understanding between the American and Soviet people."[12] Despite Wallace's tireless efforts to bolster American-Soviet relations after the war, his published memoirs indicate he politely declined the NCASF's invitation to speak at a November 16, 1945, meeting in Chicago.[13] Wallace was acutely aware of the political quicksand that awaited him if he spoke at a pro-Soviet, radical rally while a member of Truman's cabinet (although he participated in a number of its rallies following his removal from government service). NCASF came under formal investigation by the House Un-American Activities Committee in 1947, the same year that Miller held a pro-NCASF meeting at Mostel's home, and the group was indicted for failure to register with the Subversive Activities Control Board. The executive director of the NCASF, Reverend Richard Morton, was eventually charged with contempt of Congress and spent three months in prison.[14] The fact that Miller organized an SFA meeting on such a politically sensitive topic and that his invitation aroused the interest of prominent members of the entertainment writing community effectively illustrates that by 1947, Miller was a leader in SFA and comfortably situated in leftist culture (as well as on Broadway). The plays written and produced during the "missing chapter" of his career, such as *That They May Win*, demand a closer reading based on their cultural context, even if they are not necessarily laudable for their literary qualities.

That They May Win comments on most of the economic issues facing American families during the war, including unemployment, food shortages, housing, and childcare. The play was both the first performance and one of the final performances in SFA's repertory, as well as one of its most popular. In a letter to committee members in early December 1943, SFA founder Perry Miller explained that "our first script on the need for child care centers for the children of working mothers, written by Arthur Miller, is being directed by Sam Wanamaker, and has been cast in triplicate with prominent actors of radio and stage."[15] This letter confirmed the published edition of Miller's play. According to Margaret Mayorga's introduction to the play in her Best One-Act Plays series, the piece was "originally produced for the Victory Committee of Welfare Center at Albemarle Road, Brooklyn, New York, on December 21, 1943."[16]

The play was first published in *The Best One-Act Plays of 1944*, though two additional versions exist. One is undated, though likely written while the war was still going on (probably in 1944); there is also a much-revised third version of the play dated June 1948. The three scripts rely on the same characters and most of the same dialogue and ultimately share the same goals of rousing audiences to demand change from their local and national politicians. The first two versions of *That They May Win* are focused on obtaining suitable childcare so that both parents can work, while the third—revised specifically for the Chicago Arts Committee for Wallace— suggests that voting the Progressive Party into the White House would fix both the lack of jobs and sky-high rent and food costs. The iterations and chronology of *That They May Win* are especially significant to SFA because this script's journey embodies the group's transition from a New York–based social activist theatre group made up primarily of Popular Front liberals supporting home front issues into a political propaganda vehicle for Henry Wallace and the Progressive Party.

That They May Win's initial focus on childcare for women working outside the home offers intriguing insights into how SFA situated its work in the larger economic, political, and social debates raging in the 1940s. In his 1944 work *The First Round: The Story of the CIO Political Action Committee*, Joseph Gaer writes that the "War Manpower Commission has listed 370 community problems affecting the utilization of manpower—most of them affecting womanpower more. The most prominent of all these vexing problems is Child Care."[17] By July 1944, one-third of the civilian workforce was women; this means that between July 1937 and July 1944, 7.5 million women entered the workforce. This brought the total to 17.7 million, with an estimated 33 percent of these women being mothers of children under the age of sixteen.[18]

Demand for improved childcare for mothers working in wartime industries did not become a national issue until late in January 1942, when the Department of Labor issued emergency dispensations for longer work hours by women. All over the nation, the need for childcare rose "many hundred percent with the war program's gain in momentum."[19] The government responded by providing approximately twenty-five hundred nursery schools and childcare centers and upwards of $20 million in childcare funding for the fiscal year stretching between July 1944 and July 1945.[20] The immediate and ever-increasing workforce demands on women during the war made adequate planning impossible, given the significant effort required to design and implement the daycare facilities, a process that included identifying and staffing appropriate locations, many of which operated seven days a week. Additionally, funding by the Lanham Act was provided only in areas determined to be centers of wartime industry. Cities such as New York, with its significant demand for childcare, did not receive proper government support because it was not considered part of the industrial war machine.[21]

The first two versions of *That They May Win* explore in part the problems of those families *not* covered by the government's action, particularly the challenges faced by women dealing with their husbands' absences, high living costs, and inadequate military wages. Indeed, during World War II, women were responsible for most aspects of a household's finances, including purchasing food and sundries, paying rent or mortgages, making home and automobile repairs, and deciding how much to spend or save each month. Women's rising fiscal responsibility directly affected government policies. New York State named thirteen women as Office of Price Administration (OPA) rationing board advisers in May 1944. This change in OPA policy occurred one month after the Henry Hudson Hotel benefit, whose audience included some of these future OPA advisers.[22] *That They May Win*'s message that women should involve themselves with causes like the OPA and the Consumers' Council in order to combat political oppression was an important strategy for promoting wartime political and economic change.

That They May Win focuses on a married couple, Delia and Danny, who live in tenement housing with their small child. The third main character in the play is their best friend, Ina. Ina is unmarried and the only character with a stable job. The 1943 and 1944 versions of the script begin a week after Danny has returned home from combat a hero but with a serious war wound. While he was overseas (serving in Italy in the 1943 script, Africa in the 1944 version, and Germany in the 1948 version), Delia had lied to him in her letters about how she and the baby were surviving on his military allotment. In truth, she had been forced to move to the slums because she could not afford rent and food with the high inflation of the war years. At one point in the play she admits to Danny,

> I didn't move to this place temporarily, like I told you. I moved here because I can't pay a decent rent and eat right, too. Danny, you got no idea what it is to buy anything today. They cut your throat for a bunch of carrots. I go out and I spend five dollars and I come back with a bag full of nothing. I walked a mile and a half last week to save twenty cents on vegetables. I'm dealing in nickels and dimes and pennies. We can't live on that money.[23]

This speech is replicated in all three versions of *That They May Win*. Each version also includes two figures planted in the audience ("Distressed Man" and "Man Who Knows") who vociferate at the characters onstage, at each other, and at other audience members, debating potential solutions to the economic problems faced by Delia and Danny (and therefore society). In the 1943 version of the script the two men advocate government-funded childcare centers. They also encourage female audience members to obtain training through and volunteer with the OPA, which was established in 1941 to regulate domestic prices. By the 1948 version of the script—where, unlike in the two previous versions, Danny is first seen in his wife's apron washing and drying dishes at the kitchen sink, rather than recovering from a battle wound—the call for childcare centers and cooperation with labor unions and the OPA have yielded to calls to vote the Progressive Party ticket. The significant shift in political directives in the 1948 script dramatize three pressing social issues: President Truman's decision to allow price-control laws to expire in June 1946, despite protests by many leading conservative and liberal economists; labor unions' rejection of Wallace; and the forma-tion of a third party following Truman's 1947 veto of the Taft-Hartley Act.[24] Furthermore, Danny's physical transition from injured to apron-wearing operates as a potent visual metaphor for his inability to find consistent work outside of the home and serves as a reminder that full employment, a major campaign focus of Wallace, was not being achieved under Truman.

In the 1943 and 1944 versions of *That They May Win*, Delia suggests that Danny might stay home with their daughter while he recovers from his war wounds. But Danny, who has secretly secured a part-time job, offers an alternative that he has read about both in the British soldier papers and at home. The following exchange between Delia and Danny illustrates the dire situation facing working parents:

> DANNY. Ain't there some nursery or something? I was reading about in London how they got nurseries. . . . The kids get the best of everything. And come to think of it, didn't I read that our government was granting money for these things?
>
> DELIA. It's in the newspapers, darling. They're not here, though. And the ones that are, are either too full or they cost too much.
>
> DANNY. Well, what are all the women in the factories doing with their kids, throwing them in the sewer?
>
> DELIA. They put a key around the kid's neck and let him run loose, or they got relatives or something . . . I don't know. I looked all over; there's no place to leave her. So if you'd stay home . . .

The exchange leads to the climax of the play when Danny, exasperated, yells at Delia, "What's the matter with you? They knock you down; they walk all over you; you get up, brush yourself off and say it's workin' out great. What do you pay taxes for; what do you vote for?"[25] In his tirade and through the denouement of the short piece, Danny suggests changes for women and presents attitudes toward them that are enlightened for the period: women should have the right to work if they want to and should have access to adequate childcare; women should educate themselves on their legal rights; and women can become a powerful lobbying group if they work together for change.

The 1943 version ends with a speech by the Man Who Knows, who defends the intellect and power of women before the Distressed Man, stating:

> [Women] aren't dumb, my friend; look what they learned to do in this war. They learned how to weld, how to run a drill press, how to build a P-47, how to hold a home together while their husbands are away fighting to win the war, how to vote. And they're learning that women can fight in this war too, right here on the home front. Their army is the Consumers' Council and their machineguns are market baskets, and some day, when Johnny comes marching home, they'll be able to say to him, "Okay, soldier, I was a soldier, too!"[26]

The rhetoric is filled with empowering justifications for female engagement in politics during the war, suggesting that women's first military front should be an economic one. The text reads as a Marxist, albeit mildly paternalistic, critique of American society. Intriguingly, the message changes substantively in the 1944 version when the raisonneur is played by a woman. The Woman Who Knows concludes the short play by stating,

It's up to women like us who are the wives of our fighting soldiers, the mothers of their children, to get together to fight conditions like that. They're holding the prices down in Canada and England because the people there won't stand for them going up. Even in China they've got nurseries; they've got no shoes but they've made a place for their children. What can we do about it here? Why aren't the unions, the housewives, the church clubs all working together more closely? Why aren't all the groups who want the same things getting together about it? The President can't do it alone. He needs your help. Let our congressmen know that we're dead serious about keeping our people on the home front happy and well. Organizations are like microphones. Turn on the juice and speak up, and when our boys come home you'll be able to face them and say, "I also fought. Yes, and I also won."[27]

It is not surprising that Eleanor Roosevelt's "My Day" column would mention a play that simultaneously highlighted the good works of her husband and rallied audience members together, though the 1944 version of the play serves as much more than a simple FDR campaigning tool. It attempts to fundamentally alter the gender dynamic, consciousness, and behavior of political participation. By changing the sex of the audience member who stands up in her seat and vehemently disagrees with what is happening on the stage (and therefore in society), SFA declared that women had the right to take political action to rectify injustices in the United States. *That They May Win* also offers parallels between union labor, "housewife" labor, and grassroots community organizations, suggesting that each can mobilize to effect change. Marguerite Higgins, covering a May 1944 performance held in the auditorium of Public School 104 in the Bronx, reported that "the applause that filled the hall attested once more to the effectiveness of Stage for Action. . . . Half of the 150 United Parents' Association in that Bronx audience announced they were going home and write their Congressmen, for the first time in their lives, urging them to back up the O.P.A.'s price-control program."[28] The persuasive power of *That They May Win* rests in its ability to produce dialogue in its audiences and a sense of personal responsibility for the national economy. As one audience member in attendance at the United Parents' Association performance responded, "I had heard this [*That They May Win*] talked about by some consumer groups, but I hadn't realized how good it was. It shows the importance of doing something now. It makes you feel that you can do something, must do something."[29]

By 1946 many of the wartime advances for women, including equal pay, maternity leave, and most of the government funding for daycare centers, had been terminated, which was another social issue Henry Wallace wanted the Progressive Party to rectify.[30] For SFA audiences, Miller's play illustrates the obstacles facing American families and challenges progressive males to engage in domestic responsibilities. A perfect example of the shift in postwar domestic structure occurs in the following exchange at the beginning of the unpublished 1948 version of the play:

> INA. What's wrong?
>
> DANNY. No more than usual. Kid didn't sleep all night's all. He don't sleep, we don't sleep—who sleeps? They're taking a nap now. (*Kicks a chair toward Ina*) Relax a minute. She'll be up soon. (*A little guiltily*) Helping with the dishes. (*Indicates apron, laughs a little*)
>
> INA. On you it's got class. If more men put on more aprons more times, things might be a little better.[31]

Ina, who I interpret as a stereotypical Rosie the Riveter in the 1944 version of the play, assumes an even more significant role in the final revision of *That They May Win*.[32] She has a job and can earn money to buy food (specifically meat). More important, she is the one who "knows history" and takes Danny to task for not trying to find a job and for not paying attention to what is happening to his family and society around them. The message of the postwar version of the script is not that Danny is "less of a man" for helping with domestic responsibilities or that Delia is wrong for wanting to work outside the home but rather that they are both cogs in an enormous economic and political machine. Their only "failure" is not attempting to change any of the social problems that placed them in their economic predicament.

An additional message of the piece is found in the strength of the two leading female characters, Ina and Delia. Neither Truman nor FDR were staunch advocates of women's rights, but this was something at which the Progressive Party excelled. Female leadership was a clear focus of Progressives, and as political historian Richard J. Walton argues, "Henry Wallace was ahead, well ahead, of his time. . . . At a time when women were usually relegated in political campaigns to stamping envelopes and other such 'women's work,' the Progressive Party gave women important substantive jobs and campaigned for broader women's rights."[33] Wallace, for example, included policies on women in the workforce in his campaign platform. And Ina and Delia, in their desire and ability to work both inside and outside of the home, provide the "ideal" images of progressive women as evoked by the Wallace campaign.

Several new issues appear in the postwar script of *That They May Win*, including the lack of available jobs for the working class, the suggestion that another war is on the horizon (as indeed it was), dwindling support of the unions, and the idea that a unified people (both men and women) are required to produce change in the country. Whereas in the 1943 and 1944 versions of *That They May Win* the Man (or Woman) Who Knows calls on women to make economic changes in the United States, in the 1948 version this character asks,

> Where are the people? . . . To be people, you gotta start acting like people. You gotta be people. This is a government of the people, by the people, and for the people. Get the dame [Ina] who knows history . . . she'll tell you. The government is you, and you gotta do something about it. We, the people, gotta go into politics. And don't get me wrong. Politics isn't something way off in the clouds. Politics is just another way of saying how much bread and chopped meat and milk your dollar's going to buy, and what you'll have to pay for Junior's new shoes. You have to go to those Senators and Congressmen you elected . . . and that President you got in on a default . . . and you gotta say to them: "Listen here for a minute, mister. We're your boss, and you have to work for us. You get right in there and give us a little price control, a little housing, a little efficiency, or by God, you're on your way out!"[34]

This speech by the Man Who Knows, a response to the Distressed Man calling him "a Henry Wallace," emphasizes two significant points: economic problems are political problems (and vice versa), and citizens ultimately change economic issues and society by voting.[35] In his final speech of the 1948 version, the Man Who Knows declares,

> Vote 'em in, vote 'em out. They gotta bring prices down, these Republicans and Democrats. They gotta feed the people and clothe the people and give the people a place to work and a place to live. They gotta do this, these Republicans and Democrats . . . or else they just gotta stand aside and let somebody else have a try at it. If the first two teams can't carry the ball, . . . then by God, let's put in a third team![36]

Since this iteration of *That They May Win* was sponsored by the Chicago Arts Committee for Wallace, voting for the "third team" clearly meant that a vote for Wallace and the Progressive Party ticket in the 1948 election was necessary to produce social and economic change.

One additional element that all three versions of *That They May Win* share is adherence to the twelve propositions set forth by the CIO-PAC. SFA had sponsorship from a variety of CIO unions, and Wallace was at one time referred to as the CIO-PAC's "darling."[37] Several CIO-PAC leaders were also individual sponsors of or served on the board of SFA. The CIO-PAC was formed out of a delegation of CIO members on July 7, 1943, in order to educate labor union members and provide "effective labor action on the political front."[38] Clearly there were early connections between SFA and the CIO-PAC, as evidenced by Betty Hawley Donnelly's position as a guest of honor at the Henry Hudson Hotel benefit performance and the fact that leaders from various labor unions were invited to speak that evening.

That They May Win espouses sentiments strengthening the relationship between the CIO-PAC and SFA. Miller's play, for example, directly refers to numbers 1, 6, 7, 8, and 12 of the "One Dozen Simple Propositions" of the PAC, which state, "America belongs to Americans," "Earning and spending are political matters," "The government should serve the people," "All the people should elect their governments," and "Education for political action requires organization."[39] These simple propositions are drawn distinctly from Marxist economic theory. At the core of Marxist theory are ideas about class conflict, commodity and the division of labor, and human fetishism of "articles of utility" or more so our obsession with things and how this reifies social relations. Certainly Miller is pondering these ideas in *All My Sons* and *Death of a Salesman* (and arguably even earlier in *The Man Who Had All the Luck*), but these basic Marxist principles were present already in *That They May Win*. The major difference is that while Willy Loman's fetish for a variety of articles of utility leads to his demise, *That They May Win*'s characters are clearly blaming the government for blocking their access to basic needs such as food, housing, and jobs. This was a message espoused by the majority of liberals during the 1940s. However, it gained a more prominent position in U.S. politics due to the formation and power of the CIO-PAC and its subsidiary, the NC-PAC.

Joseph McGinnical, Cynical Pinnacle, Opus II

The first political campaign in which labor unions invested significant funds and energy was the general election of 1936. This was due in no small part to the formation of the Committee of Industrial Organizations the previous year.[40] Eight years later, in July 1943, the CIO created the first modern political action committee, the CIO-PAC, "to collect and disburse the voluntary political contributions of union members."[41] In order to broaden its financial support and voter canvassing strength, in June 1944 (only two short months after SFA's benefit performance and Mrs. Roosevelt's subsequent "My Day" call for a more active citizenry) the NC-PAC formed as an outgrowth of the political action committee of the CIO. According to its secretary, Clark Foreman, the NC-PAC "was the product of demands by non-trade union progressives for an organization which could effectively express their views and collaborate with the progressive trade unions in a program of practical politics."[42] The connections between the CIO and the NC-PAC cannot be overstated, and CIO-affiliated unions were prodigious financial supporters of SFA. Performers were often invited to union rallies, strikes, sit-ins, and political events in order to wage theatrical war against antilabor groups and officials, educate union members about a specific political or social issue, or bolster morale. A relatively common sentiment regarding the group, espoused early on by the *New York CIO News*, illustrates the relationship succinctly: "A Stage for Action skit brought the issue home more dramatically than any resolution or discussion."[43]

In December 1945 Edward Chodorov, a successful Broadway playwright and chairman of the New York SFA unit, sent out a national call for scripts running twenty to thirty-five minutes that used experimental forms of any kind, minimal props, and fewer than seven characters. Chodorov was relaying an "urgent" request from "the National Board of the YWCA, the Farmers' Union, the Federation of Women's Clubs," and the "United Automobile Workers of America," which was the largest union in the country by this time. Requested subject matter included "Veterans' Problems, the OPA Program, International Unity, Women's Contribution to the Trade Union Movement and Native Fascism," and scripts were to be sent to Mildred Linsley, executive director of SFA.[44]

Chodorov's call for scripts, printed in newspapers across the country at the end of 1945, suggests the changes that occurred in the year and a half since the Henry Hudson Hotel benefit performance. SFA had incorporated, and organization letterhead no longer included the four founding female members on the executive board (although, as noted, they all remained active with the group for at least the following year). PACs and labor unions were now driving subject matter and requesting scripts directly from the group. SFA and labor were so integrated that Dr. Frank Kingdon, the

chairman of the NC-PAC and a progressive radio commentator, served as an advisory board member of SFA.

Due directly to SFA's involvement with the CIO-PAC and the NC-PAC, the group was invited to participate in the inaugural School for Political Action Techniques sponsored by the NC-PAC, which took place June 26–29, 1946, at the Willard Hotel in Washington, D.C. Touted as the "first school of practical political instruction," five hundred students from thirty-six states descended on the nation's capital and attended a range of classes. Content spanned the political consciousness–raising gamut, from organizing citizens' committees to establishing rights for public radio use. Significant to this study was a course occurring on the final day of the event, when SFA hosted a three-hour workshop on using the theatre for political action. Promotional materials for the School for Political Action Techniques described SFA's course as including "discussion and demonstrations of living newspaper techniques [and] discussion of available scripts and services."[45] The "faculty" for the SFA course included Perry Miller (also teaching a course that weekend on using film for political action), Alex Leith, and Art Smith. They were joined by SFA actors who performed scenes from plays addressing how to organize and prepare canvassers for public discussion of political candidates' records. Newspapers across the country published coverage of the NC-PAC school, but only the *Baltimore Sun* printed a two-page article dedicated to the SFA course. Reporter Joseph Short wrote that "the drama—or something along that line—was introduced today in NCPAC's politics school as a new competitor of doorbell ringing and rabble-rousing speeches."[46]

Playwright Jerome Bayer wrote a script titled *Ballot Box Ballad* specifically for the school and enlisted five students (two women and three men) to perform the script along with him "before a hundred embryo politicians."[47] The playlet, which could easily be compared to contemporary "Rock the Vote" campaigns, is simplistic; its aim was getting people to register and vote; and for reasons of performance flexibility and applicability to a variety of elections, it did not address social issues specific to voters in the mid-1940s. The piece is full of gags and catchy one-liners such as "That one on the *left* is so *right* he's always *wrong*."[48] The brief play concludes triumphantly with the character "Miss You" stepping downstage and stating directly to the audience, "I guess that's all for the moment. But just for the moment. There are big things ahead. I'll be seeing you!"[49] Banal as the script reads, it is significant that a full 20 percent of the students in attendance at the NC-PAC school chose to attend a course on how to use theatre for political advantage. Based on Bayer's experience with the event, he wrote another voter canvassing script for SFA later that summer titled *Dress Rehearsal*. This script did inform citizens about issues significant to the midterm elections, including the OPA and Fair Employment Practices Committee. While neither of the Bayer scripts can be considered excellent dramatic literature, they are effective forms of agitprop and significant to social activist theatre history because they address a relevant issue (voter registration) for a specific audience (nonregistered voters) in an amusing, decidedly middlebrow manner.

More advanced dramaturgically, and discussed by SFA faculty during the NC-PAC school course, was Les Pine and Anita Short's musical satire *Joseph McGinnical, Cynical Pinnacle, Opus II*. SFA originally acquired *Joseph McGinnical* and began casting it in June 1945, but the debut of Pine and Short's offering did not occur in front of press and trade union officials until March 1946. SFA continued revising and performing the piece up until the 1948 elections in support of the Progressive Party.[50] Reviewing the performance for the *New Masses*, Jane Lawson called *Joseph McGinnical* a "pocket musical" with "catchy lyrics. . . . Its theme is the danger of public apathy as represented by a citizen who sleeps between elections."[51] Although combating citizen apathy between biennial elections was the foundational premise of the NC-PAC's formation, its second reason for forming was "to bring out the real issues of our time, issues on which the decisions will be of vast historical significance."[52] In less than twenty minutes, *Joseph McGinnical* succinctly summarizes all of the ideals and concerns of Popular Front liberals (what conservatives in both the Republican and Democratic Parties would soon define as the Progressive Party's radical agenda): full employment, antifascism, the end of racial discrimination, and global solidarity.

While it is tempting to view it as prophetic, it was rather for political reasons that *Joseph McGinnical* was included in the School for Political Action Techniques events in the summer of 1946. During the first six months of the year, Popular Front liberals debated and ultimately decided that making any significant changes in the country would require running a third-party candidate. C. B. Baldwin (or "Beanie," as he was called by most of his friends), vice chairman of the NC-PAC and eventual Wallace campaign coordinator, threw down the gauntlet at the four-day training event, stating, "A people's machine [is] needed to liberalize both parties, but if party leadership is not responsive to the needs of the people this same machinery can be used for a third party."[53] This statement is clearly reminiscent of the Man Who Knows in Miller's 1948 version of *That They*

May Win, but it was also Baldwin's open challenge to Wallace. This was a dangerous move, because in the summer of 1946, Henry Wallace was still a Truman cabinet member, albeit one greatly disillusioned by his commander in chief. Wallace's political position, however, did not prevent him from making a speech before the five hundred students at the School for Political Action Techniques. By the third week of September 1946, Wallace had made one speech too many questioning Truman's foreign policy, and he was out of a job. *Joseph McGinnical*, ridiculous though its title may be, was deadly serious in its support of radical political change, as were SFA members. Once the School for Political Action Techniques ended, SFA participants devoted themselves full-time to national expansion, and they now had a focus for all of their productions: promoting progressive politics, convincing their man Henry A. Wallace to run for president as a Progressive, and voting him into the White House.

Joseph McGinnical, Cynical Pinnacle, Opus II was only one of many SFA scripts aimed at stimulating votes for the Progressive Party. It was, however, one of the most effective because it was exceptionally entertaining and the least heavy-handed or didactic of the group's scripts. Also, like its Arthur Miller–penned partner *That They May Win*, multiple versions of the script were developed. The extant version used for this study was updated to support Wallace's presidential bid. Only six actors are required, playing the roles of Joseph McGinnical, John Q, Union, Young, Farmer, and Business. John Q (as in John Q. Public) serves both as narrator of the play and spokesperson for the average progressive American. The rest of the characters portray hyperbolized, metonymic realizations of their cultural counterparts aimed at waking Joe McGinnical from the literal and figurative torpor he has been living in since the last election.

The first time the ensemble is able to waken Joe, he introduces himself to the audience, stating,

> Up until last November, if you will remember, the mud was flung
>   most energetically.
> But I was McGinnical, cynical pinnacle, and viewed it all quite
>   apathetically.
> Contented to cower in my ivory tower, my politics were at a
>   minimum.
> I tried to abstain from the recent campaign and from votes and
>   platforms ad infinitum.[54]

He explains that he was awakened from his political slumber by a group of young activists who got him:

> So, worked up to a fever, I slaved like a beaver with vim and with
>   verve and vitality
> To help the boys win who will make the world into a global
>   municipality.[55]

Joe falls asleep again, content with the officials who won the last election and with his pivotal role as a canvasser. But he quickly falls into a nightmare and is visited by Senators Arthur H. Vandenberg and Burton K. Wheeler, as well as by Congressman John E. Rankin.

The quasi-Dickensian scene that follows marks the moment in which the piece changes stylistically from musical comedy (Joe has already sung a parody of "Little Man, You've Had a Busy Day," a song made popular by SFA-sponsor Paul Robeson) to what cultural historian Michael Denning has aptly characterized as "proletarian grotesque." In his *Cultural Front*, a landmark history of the arts and literature during the Popular Front, Denning argues that the grotesque is "an attempt to wrench us out of the repose and distance of the 'aesthetic.'" He defines the proletarian grotesque genre as "a plebeian appropriation of the avant-garde hostility to 'art,' the anti-aesthetic to dada and surrealism . . . an unstable, transitional modernism."[56] The play's portrayal of current politicians as hunched-over fiends who abruptly morph into mad doctors and attempt to disembowel an American in order to protect their "Fascist" ideals clearly indicates that *Joseph McGinnical* is neither social realism nor simple agitprop but rather a hybrid form, a dramaturgical chimera. (Such characters and actions also suggest that Jane Lawson's description of a "pocket musical with catchy tunes" fails to hit its mark.) The multi-casting intensifies the grotesque nature of the play. For example, the actor who plays the character Union is also expected to play John Rankin, the "head surgeon" of the mad doctors, as well as an idealized member of Congress.

Although audiences in the late 1940s would have been well versed in both the political jargon and public servants parodied in *Joseph McGinnical*, contemporary audiences may require a bit more context to "get the joke." For example, the character Union, introduced by John Q as "Miss Cio-Affel," states,

> Our soldiers and gobs, they're all gonna need jobs because
>   freedom from work isn't freedom.
> And we'll need quite a few. Sixty million will do.
> That might seem like a lot but we'll need 'em.[57]

Union packs a significant number of political references into these brief introductory lines, evoking FDR's Four Freedoms as well as Wallace's outspoken support of the need for sixty million postwar American jobs. In his 1945 treatise *Sixty Million Jobs*, Wallace argued that sixty million was largely a symbolic figure because the real goal was full employment with a $200 billion national production.[58] Wallace contended that if the nation could achieve full employment by 1950, the "much-vaunted American standard of living [would become] a reality for *all* of our people."[59]

Far from the economic fantasies of a leftist dreamer, Wallace's treatise demonstrates the astute entrepreneurial knowledge of a self-made farming millionaire. Although *Sixty Million Jobs* is only a little over eighty pages in length, it ultimately establishes ten essential actions for achieving full employment, including these: reduce taxes in a balanced manner to stimulate private initiative and increase consumption; maintain wages in order to protect take-home pay; establish a government housing agency; promote educational equality through federal grants-in-aid; and eliminate trade barriers by opposing "monopolistic practices whether applied by a foreign cartel, a domestic trust, a trade union, or a farm organization."[60] Wallace's economic plan in 1945 was largely in keeping with the prescription for a mixed economy shared by a majority of U.S. economists. The significant difference between Wallace's plan and the fiscal outlines of other government or academic economists was that Wallace truly believed that if the United States could achieve full employment by 1950, the nation—and perhaps even the world—would be closer to peace.

Each of the characters in *Joseph McGinnical, Cynical Pinnacle, Opus II* represents either a specific Progressive Party platform issue or—in the case of Vandenberg, Rankin, and Wheeler—actual politicians whom Progressives advocated voting out of office. Arthur Vandenberg was a Michigan Republican who switched from isolationism to internationalism and gave a major speech to the Senate in support of a successful "new world organization" on January 10, 1945.[61] Yet, while it appears that Progressives might have agreed with Vandenberg's political objectives, he was also the chairman of the Senate Foreign Relations Committee and responsible for encouraging the development of the European Recovery Program (better known as the Marshall Plan) by the State Department. Wallace and his Progressive Party followers believed that both the Truman Doctrine and its economic partner, the Marshall Plan, were unilateralist and that these programs undermined the strength of the United Nations and the possibility for world peace. Furthermore, according to Wallace, the two international programs were intentionally and unnecessarily adversarial toward the Soviets. Wallace spoke out publicly against the Truman Doctrine during a spring 1947 trip to Europe, and Vandenberg repaid these actions by leading a bipartisan attack against him. According to Mark L. Kleinman, "Many senators condemned Wallace as a virtual traitor. Several of Vandenberg's colleagues even called for Wallace's prosecution under the Logan Act of 1799 (which made it a crime for an American citizen to deal with a foreign government regarding a matter in dispute between the two nations or 'to defeat the measures' of the U.S. government)."[62] Vandenberg's change of heart from isolationism to internationalism did not negate his clear dislike of Wallace and distrust of the United Nations.

As for the other two politicians denigrated in *Joseph McGinnical*, Congressman John E. Rankin of Mississippi was openly segregationist and pivotal in defeating a 1944 bill for the establishment of a bipartisan War Ballot Commission. The commission would have sent ballots to all military service people in advance of elections.[63] Many pro-segregation politicians felt that granting open voting rights to all servicepeople, regardless of race or congressional districting, would adversely affect campaigns. Rankin was also one of the most vocal members of the Dies Committee (the predecessor to the standing House Un-American Activities Committee that was led by Martin Dies Jr. from 1938 to 1944) and retained his seat, and position of power, on the HUAC throughout its existence.

Finally, Democratic senator Burton K. Wheeler, who had in 1924 been the vice presidential candidate for Robert La Follette's Progressive Party, had grown increasingly isolationist to the degree that he held "rancorous objections to even the mildest proposals for American postwar participation in any international association."[64] Wallace stated about Wheeler, who had apparently become quite outspoken in his dislike for FDR, that it was "very unfortunate when any person becomes completely dominated by his hatreds." Wallace continued by observing that "it is a mistake to pay any man the compliment of hating him because in the process of hating him, you give that man power over you."[65]

These three politicians—Vandenberg, Rankin, and Wheeler—approach reprobate status in *Joseph McGinnical*. Labeled as native fascists by Progressives, the play represents them as book-burning, antilabor red-baiters who care only for big business and the "cauterizing" of American civil liberties. At one point during the titular character's nightmare, the three chant the following lines invoking the specter of lynching, which was ominously present during the immediate postwar period:

> So just sleep, people, sleep. You can trust us to keep you all safe from subversive forces.
> We've a date in the woods. Martin, hand us our hoods,
> For we're riding tonight—where's the horses?[66]

These grotesque characters are eradicated only when John Q and his gang spray them with the following ingredients from a Flit can: unity, CIO, AFL, PAC, Hollywood Democratic Committee, and GIs.[67] Some of the spray also hits Joe McGinnical, sending him into a utopian postelection dream in which the Congress, Senate, Supreme Court, and cabinet are all in agreement regarding reconversion, full employment for people of all races and ethnicities, wage increases, and postwar production equal to wartime production. Joe wakes up from this idyllic dream full of energy and, in a Gilbert and Sullivan–style patter song highlighting the Progressive Party platform, sings of his hopes:

> To can each argumentative, backsliding representative
> For bouncing contradictory opponents of full victory.
> The senators hysterical and anti-hemispherical
> For chasing them, erasing them and hastily replacing them.
> With men of perspicacity and infinite veracity
> Who'll seize each opportunity to build a world community
> To make the peace assurable, Dumbartonish and durable
> For clarity, prosperity and global solidarity.[68]

For students at the School for Political Action Techniques and subsequent audiences at Henry Wallace rallies, SFA and the Progressive Party wanted Joseph McGinnical's goals—equality, civil liberties, full employment, a balanced budget, and world peace—to be the nation's goals as well. Progressive Party members were inspired by the possibility of a racially integrated United States, where the majority of people, women and men alike, could be fully employed and live in a world free from imperialism and the threat of atomic weapons. Moreover, Progressives were striving for a society where cultural, economic, and political differences did not outweigh the peaceful perspective that everyone was an inhabitant of One World.

Miss Farmer speaking to the audience in a scene from Les Pine and Anita Short's *Joseph McGinnical, Cynical Pinnacle, Opus II.* *Courtesy of the Tamiment Library and Robert F. Wagner Labor Archives, New York University.*

Mr. Taft Can Dig It, Mr. Hartley Can Haul It

A political tourbillion occurred between the initial Stage for Action performances of *That They May Win* in December 1943 and Henry Wallace's failed bid for the presidency in 1948. By the end of 1947, Wallace and the labor unions were on icy terms following Truman's veto of the controversial Taft-Hartley Act and its subsequent ratification.[69] The frigid relationship between Progressives and labor is reflected in *That They May Win*'s script changes between 1944 and 1948. In 1944, "the unions got to get delegations together and go to the Mayor," but by 1948, "[the union] ain't interested. My brother-in-law also has this problem. He went down to the union. He tells them his problem. He talks to them. They listen very carefully. They got a solution . . . what is it? His family are still eating meat once a week."[70] However it was not that unions were disinterested in the plight of Danny and other outspoken union members (though the play does mirror a growing public impatience with labor's supposed abuse of power and "arrogant attitude" regarding its position of political superiority following the war).[71] Rather, what these lines demonstrate is the desperation of the Progressive Party campaign following Truman's momentous decision to veto the Taft-Hartley Act on June 20, 1947. In spite of the long-term, felicitous relationship between Wallace and the labor movement, and regardless of congressional Democrats' failure to sustain the president's veto, the majority of AFL and CIO labor unions viewed Truman's veto as an act of solidarity and therefore saw little advantage in risking support of a third party. Miller's 1948 version of *That They May Win* attempted to appease liberal union members who remained disillusioned by how labor was treated in the United States. These same union members believed Truman would be unable to reverse Taft-Hartley if reelected. However, this group did not represent the labor union majority, and as the union vote was crucial in the 1948 election, Truman's veto of the Taft-Hartley Act ultimately sealed Wallace's fate.

Between the end of the war and June 1947, the labor movement was highly critical of Truman's policies on housing and inflation, the government's seizure of the coal mines, and Truman's request of authority by Congress to draft striking workers.[72] The president's special counsel, led by Clark Clifford, understood that repairing the relationship between Truman and labor was essential for a Democratic victory in 1948. Late in the fall of 1947, Clifford presented Truman with "a forty-three page confidential memorandum . . . a blueprint for Democratic strategy in 1948."[73] One of the key propositions outlined in the "Clifford Memorandum" was to invite labor leaders to the White House and ask for their advice on general political policies. "No human being," Clifford's memorandum stated, "can resist the glamour, the self important feeling of 'advising' a President on anything."[74] Truman accepted and followed Clifford's procedural blueprint, but despite slowly rebuilding his relationship with major union leaders, he could not overcome the contentiously antilabor and conservative Eightieth Congress.

Meeting for the first time in January 1947, the Republican congressional cadre was gifted with new brooms by George Bender of Ohio. The cards attached to the brooms read, "Here's yours. Let's do the job, to sweep away the cobwebs which have cluttered up our thinking."[75] The cobwebs to which Bender was referring were New Deal and wartime policies still in existence following the war. The New Deal legislation that Republicans found most troublesome was the National Labor Relations Act (often referred to as the Wagner Act) of 1935, which facilitated unionization and collective bargaining and allowed union members to designate their own representatives for wage and conditions negotiations. Republicans also resented the wage stabilization policy announced by President Roosevelt on April 27, 1942, and confirmed by Congress six months later.[76] In order to counteract the incredible strength (and therefore unified voting power) of labor unions prior to the 1948 presidential elections, the Eightieth Congress overwhelmingly approved an omnibus bill coauthored by Republican politicians Senator Robert A. Taft from Ohio and Representative Fred A. Hartley Jr. from New Jersey. Historian R. Alton Lee's careful research has revealed that this particular piece of legislation was brought into being through the efforts of Republican congressmen and Dixiecrats but was also assuredly "the brainchild of the National Association of Manufacturers and big business," as is clear by the number of lawyers and lobbyists representing these agencies who were paid to assist the House and Senate committees.[77] Be that as it may, the Taft-Hartley Act was also responding to what has been called the "most lively domestic drama of the day . . . at a time when the nation was fully aroused against organized labor."[78] Taft and Hartley argued they were only collaborating on legislation that met the approval and needs of their constituents, and in the wake of an exceptionally turbulent postwar labor environment, their argument carried weight.

Ultimately, the Taft-Hartley Act implemented the following changes that had a direct impact on the power of labor unions in the United States:

- It established an eighty-day cooling-off period for what the president or attorney general deemed national emergency strikes.
- It forbade unions to make expenditures or contributions in any national primary or general election.
- It barred federal employees from striking.
- It permitted states to enact "right to work" laws prohibiting compulsory membership in a union shop.
- It prohibited Communist Party membership in unions by requiring union officials to sign a noncommunist affidavit annually or risk forfeiting the union's rights.[79]

It was this final prohibition—section 9-H of the act—that was especially devastating to Wallace's electability. Henry Wallace was not a Communist, nor did he directly invite Communist Party of the United States of America members into the Progressive Party, but he never shunned them, and they were some of his staunchest supporters. Perhaps Wallace's most blatant anticommunist statement occurred in June 1948 when addressing a small audience in Center Sandwich, New Hampshire. Wallace stated, "I'm never going to say anything in the nature of red-baiting. But I must say this: if the Communists would run a ticket of their own this year, we might lose 100,000 votes but we would gain three million. I know if the Communists really wanted to help us, they would run their own ticket this year and let us get those extra votes."[80] There were, of course, members of labor unions who also supported Communism, but once Truman vetoed Taft-Hartley and regained the support of labor, he worked quickly to prohibit simultaneous membership in a union and the CPUSA. Despite two minutes of chanting "We want Wallace!" by a capacity crowd at a CIO-sponsored anti-Taft-Hartley rally in Madison Square Garden in June 1947, few of those supporters pulled the lever for Wallace in November 1948. In fact, much of labor's supporters turned against Wallace in order to protect themselves in the red-baiting atmosphere of 1947 and 1948. In order to understand labor's Brutus-like response, it is worth noting Richard J. Walton's assessment of labor's reaction to section 9-H of the Taft-Hartley Act:

> At first all wings of the labor movement refused to [sign a noncommunist affidavit] as a matter of principle, but then the ranks began to break. This put Communists on the spot. If they did not sign, they were not eligible to hold office. If they did, they were guilty of perjury. … One or both factors forced Communist officeholders in the labor movement to choose between their unions or the Communist Party. Over a period of months most of these "influentials," as they were called in Communist circles, chose their unions.[81]

The majority of political historians focusing on the 1948 presidential election recognize that the most strategically advantageous political decision Harry Truman made was vetoing the Taft-Hartley Act, and it mattered not that his veto was overturned and that the Labor-Management Relations Act of 1947 went into effect. Truman won the 1948 national election because labor opted not to support the formation of a third party and instead remained politically faithful to its traditionally Democratic roots. Truman himself stated in a 1961 interview that "labor was responsible for his election and [he] is convinced that he won by using the Taft-Hartley Act as an issue."[82] Despite Truman's strategy, he recognized that Wallace would still pose a threat to the Democratic Party in 1948. He never had to dirty his hands again in order to thoroughly devastate the Progressive Party's campaign, however; instead, the majority of the remaining attacks on Wallace came from Republicans, Dixiecrats, and fellow liberals involved with Americans for Democratic Action.[83] Wallace's open criticism of the Marshall Plan and other international policies, his stance on nuclear weapons, and his pro–civil rights platform made him an easy target to link directly to a Communist agenda.

Although instrumental in shifting the political climate of the post–World War II United States, the passage of the Taft-Hartley Act did not cause the initial fracturing of SFA's delicate skeleton. That event occurred a year earlier and was directly related to SFA's shift toward national expansion and open support of the emerging Progressive Party agenda. On August 15, 1946, Peggy Clark—one of the four founding members of SFA—broke off her relationship with the group, stating, "Since I do not feel that your new perspective for Stage for Action is a realistic one and as a result can make no contribution to the new expanded dreams; I hereby tender my resignation from the Play Board, the Production Department, the Executive Committee, and the Board of Directors of Stage for Action."[84] Clark's resignation occurred within days of Perry Miller's stepping down from the group, and neither of them would participate in any future SFA activities. Following Miller's and Clark's exits in 1946, only two of the original founders, Berilla Kerr and Donna Keath, remained as members of the board or sponsors of the group. On the heels of Wallace's infamous "The Way to Peace" speech at a NC-PAC rally in New York City on September 12, 1946, and his subsequent dismissal from Truman's cabinet as a direct result of this speech, SFA was named a Communist front.[85] Peggy Clark escaped the group just in time, and Perry Miller was "named" in only one congressional hearing, though many other members were not so lucky. A significant number of SFA artists involved after the 1946 shift toward supporting the NC-PAC and the Progressive Party suffered immeasurably for their involvement with the group.

Perhaps it is not surprising that the plays produced after the summer of 1946 are more politically provocative than those penned during the first two and a half years of SFA's existence. August 1946 through November 1948 saw SFA producing work that substantiated its position as the premier social activist theatre group of the late 1940s—the sole national theatre group dedicated to promoting a specific political party—and, as chapter 3 addresses, foundational in the production of pro–civil rights performance. Despite the eventual downfall of the group due to a combination of red-baiting and the massive electoral defeat of Henry Wallace in the 1948 election, its backing of a defeated political movement resulted in a repertory of plays highlighting social issues significant to Progressives. SFA's performances during the immediate postwar period and the cadre of artists involved anticipated the radical agendas adopted by social activist theatre practitioners in the latter half of the twentieth century.

3. YOU'VE STILL GOT A VOICE

STAGE FOR ACTION PERFORMANCES covered a wide range of topics, from advocating for childcare to promoting antinuclear war policies.
Each performance directly challenged a societal injustice, and although
many of the plays were originally inspired by specific regional grievances,
scripts written in New York after 1946 often made their way to other SFA
branches, thus becoming more national in tone and scope. The societal
issue that SFA concerned itself with most consistently during its five-year
existence, and one the Progressive Party campaigned on, was the struggle
for civil rights. As newspaper columnist and SFA supporter Louis Untermeyer wrote in 1948, "I will vote for Wallace because I believe with him
. . . that our country can't be considered a true Democracy until all men,
regardless of color, creed, or race, can live and work together without
intimidation or discrimination."[1] SFA, in accordance with Progressives,
responded directly to post–World War II race conflicts in order to bolster
civil rights activism. The insufferable treatment of black citizens was by
no means a new topic in the theatre when the members of SFA adopted
it as a cause in the mid-1940s. During the 1930s, for example, groups like
the Workers' Laboratory Theatre (with its productions of *Scottsboro* and
Newsboy) and the Theatre Union (with *Stevedore*) addressed the treatment
of black citizens in the U.S. judicial system. What separates SFA's plays
about the mistreatment of black Americans from these earlier works is
that they do not merely highlight the problem of racial prejudice; instead,
they demand new laws addressing issues of inequity, thereby highlighting
the group's name: Stage for *Action*. Additionally, through plays such as
Skin Deep and *Talk in Darkness*, SFA countered much of the social and
scientific thought of the period, suggesting that—aside from differences in
the levels of melanin and carotene found in pigmentation—fundamental
biological differences between races do not exist.

Last, and perhaps most significant, what set SFA apart from most of the earlier social activist theatre groups in the arena of civil rights was not merely the content of its plays or its casting of a large percentage of black actors but rather the inclusion of an unprecedented number of black sponsors and board members. SFA supported integration at every level of its organization during a period in American politics when such support automatically earned one the label of "liberal" (and often "Communist" as well). As one military intelligence officer involved in the Truman administration's loyalty program argued in 1947, "A liberal is only a hop, skip, and a jump from a Communist. A Communist starts as a liberal."[2] The paranoid post–World War II powers pounced at the opportunity to attack any group seeming to undermine "Americanism." Various documents written by prominent civil rights leaders and activists operating during the Cold War era illustrate that integration supporters were constantly attacked as being un-American. Paul Robeson, a great supporter of equality and a board and advisory member of SFA, was consistently harangued for his integration advocacy. In a July 13, 1949, letter to members of the Council on African Affairs, Dr. W. A. Hunton, secretary of the council, challenged the House Un-American Activities Committee's "notorious" mistreatment of black Americans, making explicit reference to a recent Robeson speech. Hunton stated that when the HUAC, "and its constant smearing of those who do not subscribe to its own brand of Americanism, turns its attention to the opinions of Paul Robeson regarding the Negro peoples' attitude toward war against the Soviet Union, it's obvious that the Committee is not concerned with and does not dare place in the record the full context of what Robeson actually said on this subject."[3] Addressing the HUAC's apathetic response to a surge in postwar violence against black Americans, Hunton continued, "This same committee which has pursued a persistent and deliberate do-nothing policy with respect to the protection of Negroes against outrageous mob violence and other un-American practices, and has even called the fight against these evils 'Communist inspired,' now sets itself up as the judge of the 'loyalty' of Negro Americans."[4]

In contrast to the HUAC's actions during the 1940s, SFA was committed to civil rights during this period when support of "equal rights for all" was suspect, given this "all" might very well include people the government considered an enemy. The group's policy of integration raised the suspicion of HUAC watchdogs and assisted in earning SFA the label "Communist front." Communism and civil rights may at first seem like strange bedfellows, but the partnership between prominent Communists and black civil rights leaders in the United States began during the 1920s, when the Communist Party of the United States of America championed the formation of labor unions. Although Communist control of many labor unions in the United States would not occur until the 1930s, as early as 1928 the Comintern of Moscow was pressuring the United States (through its "black belt" initiative) to push for equality of the races and racial integration of labor unions. SFA was sponsored by many CIO-affiliated labor unions. The CIO, which formed from a dissident group of AFL (American Federation of Labor) members under the leadership of John L. Lewis in 1935, was the more forward thinking of the two major umbrella labor bodies. CIO leaders acknowledged that black workers toiled in some of the most underappreciated jobs in production; they were highly likely to labor under the dirtiest, most back breaking, and dangerous conditions (and for the lowest pay) in most of their affiliated unions. Understandably, black workers would often break strikes in order to improve their working conditions. It therefore made strategic sense for the CIO to seek out and organize black workers, particularly given that CIO organizers tended to be "less provincial, less wedded to traditional racial attitudes" than their AFL counterparts.[5] Even at the height of the Red Scare, many of the Communist-run unions retained racially underrepresented members. Explained a black miner, "I've never known a Communist in the labor movement to mob a man outside city hall, lynch him, castrate him, and everything else, even shoot him on sight. . . . It's the good white man who does that, you see. So, why am I going to go out and fight somebody who doesn't do the things that the good white folks have done."[6] Clearly not all black union members were Communists, but equality, particularly in a time when few political groups or organizations were offering it, inspired significant loyalty.

The message of racial equality garnered focus at every level of Communist Party life, demanding racial integration of each union, school, and social event it supported or controlled. The CPUSA sponsored multicultural events, promoted black culture in its curriculum, and advanced black Americans to leadership positions within many party branches. It was the first political party in the United States to field a black citizen for national office: in 1932 James Ford ran for vice president on the Communist Party ticket. In 1943 Benjamin Davis Jr. was elected to the New York City Council under the Communist Party; two years later the Democratic Party endorsed Davis for reelection as well. In a period when Jim Crow racism was affecting the livelihood of many black Americans and destroying the lives of some, the CPUSA offered what appeared to be genuine opportunity for social, political, and economic advancement.

That the CPUSA promoted racial equality during the 1940s is illustrated by responses to the passage of the Ives-Quinn Bill in New York. The Ives-Quinn Anti-bias Bill, which was signed into law by Governor Thomas E. Dewey on March 12, 1945, established a permanent antidiscrimination commission in the state for the purpose of "the elimination of discrimination on racial or religious grounds in the hiring, promotion or the discharge of employees; with enforcing provisions barring labor unions from discriminating in the admission or expulsion of members on racial or religious grounds; and with preventing similar discrimination by employment agencies."[7] In reaction to the passage of the bill by a vote of 109–32 and after the failure of three proposed amendments, Assemblyman William M. Stuart stated, "This bill cannot work. . . . It is a definite part of the communist program and part of a communist pattern to disrupt social and economic relations in the United States."[8] This is only one of the many indicators of just how closely some government officials associated Communism and civil rights during the 1940s.

However, it was not only Republican assemblymen from upstate New York districts with "few members of racial or religious minorities" who attempted to railroad legislation promoting equality.[9] The U.S. House of Representatives challenged any notion that Communism could assist in ending educational, racial, or religious disparity in America through its 1949 publication *100 Things You Should Know about Communism*. The work offers a dialectical discourse on the truths and fallacies of Communism and its role in society. Question 26, for example, asks, "But don't the Communists promise an end to racial and religious intolerance?" The government responds, "Yes, but in practice they have murdered millions for being religious and for belonging to a particular class. Your race would be no help to you under Communism. Your beliefs could get you killed."[10] In a period when the Progressive Party was the most assertive champion of civil rights and Progressives were simultaneously called out as under the control of a murderous, totalitarian philosophy, standing up for equality during the late 1940s was arguably a subversive act.

The potential dangers of the political climate did not stop members of SFA from advocating for the Ives-Quinn and Austin-Mahoney Bills in New York, as well as for the federal Fair Employment Practices Act and a federal civil rights amendment. It is not clear what primarily drove SFA's interest in tackling civil rights in its plays, though there are several possibilities, including the Progressive Party's political platform, labor union interests, and the CPUSA. Certainly SFA's pro-integration performances were directly at odds with many government-sponsored performances of the World War II period, such as the USO *Minstrel Shows* that in Albert Wertheim's appraisal offered "racist humor . . . while enacting the kind of comedy based on the presumed naïveté and inferior intelligence of dark-skinned subalterns."[11] The personal beliefs of SFA members were also critical in determining the group's focus on civil rights. For example, Bunny Kacher of the Chicago SFA branch stated that the group was under the leadership of Paul Robeson and focused on "civil rights, housing, and labor organizing" and on "getting the message around that was important"; the group supported "a lot of good causes."[12] Robeson, perhaps the most openly defiant of the "unfriendly" HUAC witnesses, was a dynamic and multitalented performer, a tireless advocate of civil rights, and Henry Wallace's stump speech and song associate on the 1948 Progressive Party campaign trail. Robeson's leadership of SFA's Chicago unit, as well as his sponsorship of the national organization, reveals a direct link between SFA and the Progressive Party and provides additional explanation for the group's focus on racial equality in its postwar performances.

Several SFA plays debate issues significant to civil rights during the 1940s; these include Edward Chodorov's *Decision* (1944); Charles Polacheck's *Skin Deep* and Paul Peters's *And No Wheels Roll* (1945); *All Aboard* by Ben Bengal and *Dream Job* by Arnold Perl (1946); and *Dress Rehearsal* by Jerome Bayer and *Talk in Darkness* by Malvin Wald (1948). Although all of these plays are significant to SFA's discussion of civil rights, it is the scripts' specific indication of racially integrated casts—as in *Skin Deep, All Aboard, Dream Job,* and *Talk in Darkness*—that did the most to advance civil rights as well as to spur government interest in the group.

Skin Deep

The career of *Skin Deep* author Charles Polacheck illustrates the versatile accomplishments common to many members of SFA. He also, as a little-studied participant in mid-twentieth-century American theatre and television, is representative of artists from this period who have been overlooked by academic scholarship. Prior to writing for SFA, two of his songs—"Italian Infantry" and "Help Yourself"—were produced by the social activist predecessor to SFA in Illinois, the Chicago Repertory Group. In addition, he was an actor and performed in the Playwrights' Company production of Elmer Rice's *Two on an Island* at the Broadhurst Theatre in 1940, as well as in the original production of Marc Blitzstein's *No for an Answer* with Carol Channing and fellow SFA performer Lloyd Gough in 1941. A singer as well as a music arranger, Polacheck was a member of the touring branch of the Almanac Singers with Pete Seeger and Woody Guthrie and a member of People's Songs, working as a stage manager for one of its famous hootenannies. He arranged the songs for fellow SFA member Arnold Perl's play *Dream Job* in 1946 and performed these songs with future legendary blues star Brownie McGhee at Carnegie Hall on March 31, 1946.

After his brief career with SFA, Polacheck became a television producer and director from the late 1940s through 1960, working on programs such as *Charade Quiz, Captain Video and His Video Rangers, Colonel Stoopnagle's Stoop, Voice of Firestone, The Edge of Night, The Far Horizon, Recital Hall*, and *Wide World TV*. He translated and directed the final act of a televised production of Puccini's *La Bohème* in 1949, which ultimately led to his position as director for the first season of the *NBC Television Opera Series*, for which he directed Kurt Weill's *Down in the Valley*, Johann Strauss's *The Bat*, and Bizet's *Carmen*. He produced and directed Tchaikovsky's *Pique Dame*, with an English translation by fellow SFA writer Jean Karsavina in 1952. During the second season of the program, Polacheck also served as associate producer. He concluded his work with the televised opera program by translating Strauss's *Salome* in 1954.

In 1953 Polacheck was honored with a Christopher Award for his work on the Easter edition of the *Voice of Firestone* program. The Christopher Awards were established in 1945 by a Roman Catholic group and were dedicated to honoring creative works that "restore the truths of Christ to the market place, thereby changing the world for the better."[13] It is surprising that in the same year that many SFA members were blacklisted for their Communist ties—ties that many in powerful religious and government positions saw as embracing anti-Christian values—Polacheck escaped government scrutiny and was publicly honored by a religious institution.

Polacheck never turned his back on confrontational performances during the height of the Red Scare. While his television career blossomed, Polacheck continued his relationship with the theatre, directing in August 1949 Bertolt Brecht's play *The Private Life of the Master Race*, translated by Eric Bentley for People's Drama Inc. (a founding member of the Off-Broadway Theatre League and splinter group of SFA; see chapter 5). But he balanced this production with safer (or at least more centrist) work, such as translating Puccini's *Gianni Schicchi* with Herbert Grossman for television in 1951; later the same year, they lent the translation to the Metropolitan Opera for a benefit performance supporting the Free Milk Fund for Babies. In April 1959 Polacheck, known at that point primarily for his television work, produced an evening of Noh plays for an off-Broadway theatre. Polacheck completed his professional theatre career in 1964 by writing a musical version of Oscar Wilde's *Salome*.[14]

The scant biographical information available on Charles Polacheck provides a potential explanation for why he is not even listed as the playwright on the extant typescript of *Skin Deep*. His authorship is clear, however, since *Skin Deep* was so significant to its immediate time period that each newspaper article reporting on a performance of the piece and the racial tensions it addressed named Polacheck as the playwright.[15] I surmise that the extant copy of *Skin Deep* housed at the Schomburg Library Rare Books Reading Room was donated by Oakley C. Johnson. Johnson was a guest professor of English and placed in charge of the Little Theatre at Talladega College in Alabama during the 1946–47 school year. Searching for productions to direct at Talladega, Johnson contacted Abram Hill, a board member of both the American Negro Theatre and SFA, for script recommendations. *Skin Deep* was suggested, and Johnson states it was Talladega's "most popular production, staged seven times in a single year."[16] The piece was so popular the students took it on tour, performing before both white and black audiences in Talladega, Montgomery, and Birmingham. In his reflection of the performances, Johnson writes, "Excitement, thrills, laughter—that's the recipe for entertainment. And *Skin-Deep* gives them all, plus *social content*. . . . I have often in my heart thanked the unknown authors of *Skin-Deep* for a very skillful, effective, and socially valuable dramatic vehicle."[17]

The Talladega students performed for audiences ranging in size from fifty to one thousand people, and in feedback questionnaires collected after the performances, audiences repeatedly commented that *Skin Deep* "would help break down barriers between white and black."[18] The play was performed by an all-black, primarily female cast portraying all the characters, black and white, female and male. Although Talladega College's performances of *Skin Deep* are not the first on record, they are significant because they suggest social activist performance occurring in the segregated South twenty years prior to the arrival of the Free Southern Theater, which is generally understood to be the first touring company of black artists performing for predominantly southern black audiences about civil rights issues.

SFA began rehearsals for *Skin Deep* on March 25, 1945.[19] In October 1945 *Skin Deep* was performed at a youth conference under the auspices of the Greater New York Federation of Churches at the Marble Collegiate Reformed Church. Less than a month later, on November 9, the integrated cast performed at Benjamin Franklin High School after a breakout of racial violence in and around the school. In 1945 Benjamin Franklin High School, an all-boys school located in East Harlem, had a student population of 50 percent white (primarily of Italian ancestry), 30 percent black, and the rest undisclosed.[20] The school was founded by Dr. Leonard Covello in May 1941 to "play a central role in the social reconstruction of East Harlem . . . serv[ing] as a catalytic hub for creating and strengthening social networks and fostering community norms of civility, trust, and reciprocity."[21] This "civility" faced a serious setback on September 27 and 28, 1945, when a student demonstration over increased pay for athletic coaches turned violent: "Street fighting broke out in which knives flashed, [and] stones and bottles were flung from roof-tops" as five hundred students and their guardians engaged in rioting.[22] The riot swelled on the second day to nearly two thousand white and black students battling each other as well as against plain-clothed and uniformed police officers. Five black students were detained at the scene and arraigned for carrying "dangerous weapons" including "knives, an ice-pick, a baling-hook, and a razor." None of the white students, "throw[ing] stones and bottles and assailing [black students] with sticks, bats, and clubs," were arrested.[23]

The Mayor's Committee on Racial Unity argued that "the incident was not a race controversy but a dispute growing out of a fight. . . . There was nothing of any startling nature that happened Sept. 27 or 28, but the possibilities of serious happenings in the community are not only present but growing greater month by month," concluding that "the need for city-wide attention cannot be ignored."[24] Newspaper reports suggest the riot was the culmination of a series of events including "a dispute over a basketball game between a Negro and a white team on Thursday, in friction over dominance of the school's activities between the student bodies of each race, and in reports which had a Negro teacher striking a white student."[25] Leaders of the East Harlem community and Benjamin Franklin High School made it clear that although the initial incident may have appeared on the surface to be nothing more than a disagreement between riled-up adolescent boys, there were indeed deeper sociological causes.

These events at Benjamin Franklin High School were not isolated incidents. Racial tensions were steadily escalating in the early 1940s all over the

United States, and especially in major urban areas such as Detroit, Chicago, and New York City. Despite warnings from prominent religious and political leaders, these tensions exploded into violence after the war. In late June 1943, Reverend Adam Clayton Powell Jr.—a city councilman and eventual sponsor and advisory council member of SFA—warned that the 1942 Detroit race riots would soon be replicated in New York City if immediate proactive attention was not paid to the mistreatment of the black community in New York. Challenging the mayor and police commissioner to take responsibility for the rising racial tensions in the city, Powell declared, "If any riots break out here in New York, the blood of innocent people, white and Negro, will rest upon the hands of Mayor Fiorello La Guardia and Police Commissioner Lewis Valentine, who have refused to see representative citizens to discuss means of combating outbreaks in New York."[26] Powell's warnings that La Guardia and Valentine were not preparing properly for a rising tide of racial unrest inspired the formation of a subcommittee "to handle aspects of a campaign to counter-act propaganda designed to foment racial conflicts."[27] Despite these actions, the Harlem riots—which resulted in five deaths, four hundred injuries, and property damage estimated at $5 million—began on August 1, 1943, less than two months after Powell's speech. Although Mayor La Guardia and many others denied these were actually race riots, the events were bred out of general dissatisfaction with the discrepancies in job opportunities, criminal punishment, housing, and recreational facilities between black and white communities.

One year later, in June 1944, another prominent leader, Malcolm Ross, chairman of the Fair Employment Practices Committee, again attempted to draw attention to the racially discriminatory hiring practices of employers and the problems they would cause when an estimated one and a half million black veterans returned from war looking for work and expecting equality in return for serving their country. Ross attempted to push through the original Ives-Quinn Bill, which had been in process for over a year. However, Governor Dewey, presumably fearing the bill's passage would threaten his campaign for president in 1944, stalled the bill's movement, and no legislation providing for fair employment practices (and therefore the possible easing of racial tensions) was enacted until the spring of 1945. As Ross predicted, many returning veterans could not find work in New York City and other large urban centers, and racial tensions escalated yet again after the war. The Benjamin Franklin riot, as well as confrontations between white and black students that subsequently took place in other parts of New York City, clearly demonstrates that racial tension was threatening to unravel the city's fragile postwar fabric. Benjamin Franklin High School officials looked to Stage for Action and its production of *Skin Deep* to mend the problems facing their community, which speaks to the agency the group had at this moment in its existence.

Skin Deep was adapted from the pamphlet *Races of Mankind*, written in 1943 by Columbia University anthropologists Ruth Benedict and Gene Weltfish. *Races of Mankind* was intended to combat the blatant racism of U.S. segregationists such as Mississippi senator Theodore Bilbo. During debate of the Wagner–Van Nuys Bill to make lynching a federal offense, Bilbo declared that "one drop of Negro blood placed in the veins of the purest Caucasian destroys the inventive genius of his mind and strikes palsied his creative faculty."[28] Up for reelection in 1945, Bilbo ranted that an integrated society would result in a "motley melee of miscegenated mongrels" filled with "mestizos, mulattoes, zambos, terceroones, quadroons, cholos, musties, fustics, and dusties."[29] Bilbo was only one of the many outspoken racist politicians in office during SFA's tenure, a group that included Strom Thurmond, George Wallace, and John E. Rankin. Although *Skin Deep* does not make direct reference to any specific politician, it is clear that select government officials' messages of racism were an impetus for the creation of the play and that their rhetoric was embodied in the character of Hitler.

Not only does *Skin Deep* offer a revealing, dramatic historicization of racial politics during the immediate post–World War II period, but the epilogue of *Skin Deep* allows for a closer examination of both the mise-en-scène of SFA performances and their purpose:

> Stage for Action, which composed and published the play, SKIN-DEEP, is an organization of professional people of stage and radio with headquarters in New York City. Stage for Action composes plays on important subjects for the purpose of combining entertainment with information that will help build a better America. . . . Since we bring these plays to you and don't ask you to come to a regular theatre to see us, we must ask you to imagine all the glamour and expensive scenery of a Broadway play. For instance, the opening scene of the play on the bus. We can't put a real bus on the stage, so we have put these chairs here to represent the bus.[30]

The play does indeed begin with a confrontation on a southbound bus between a black veteran and the white driver, with other bus riders becoming involved. A college professor on board acts as both mediator and narrator for the play. He leads the riders of the bus (and therefore the audience) to various significant landmarks, including a medical tent in the South Pacific during World War II, a blood specialist center and a psychologist's office in New York City, and the Tuskegee Institute. These sojourns introduce the riders to an injured white soldier (receiving the blood of a black medic) and the spirits of both George Washington Carver and Adolf Hitler. The trips were designed to address racial stereotypes while also educating audiences about cultural history. At each stop, common prejudices of the 1940s regarding racial differences in blood type, brain size, intelligence, and contributions to civilization are debunked, and the riders on the bus ultimately realize that their racism supports Hitler's overarching message of "hate." At the climax of the play the spirit of Hitler shouts gleefully,

> My idea is: HATE! Hate the Jews; hate the Russians; hate the foreigners; hate the Catholics and hate the dirty, stinking, black niggers! And you do it. You fall for it. Look what happens in your Tennessee in the town of Columbia. Look what happens in your great state of New York in Freeport, Long Island! That's right. Hate them, jim-crow them, starve them, terrorize them, shoot them, kill them. Be like me. Be supermen. Be NAZIS![31]

Blood transfusion scene in Charles Polacheck's *Skin Deep. Courtesy of the Tamiment Library and Robert F. Wagner Labor Archives, New York University.*

The original version of *Skin Deep* was penned sometime between the initial publication of *Races of Mankind* and the outbreak of violence at Benjamin Franklin High School. A close reading of the extant script indicates that the play was likely adapted in 1946 in order to address an upsurge in violence toward returning black veterans, especially the 1946 Columbia, Tennessee, race riot. This riot erupted on February 26 following an altercation in a store between two veterans, one black and one white, concerning repairs of a radio owned by the black veteran's mother. Though the historical record is full of discrepancies, it seems that James Stephenson (the black veteran) threw the clerk of the store (the white veteran) through the window for threatening his mother. The Stephensons were arrested for disturbing the peace but released after paying a fifty-dollar fine. Later that day James Stephenson was again arrested, this time on the charge of assault with the attempt to commit murder. This charge was brought by the father of the store clerk. Word of the arrest and subsequent release of Stephenson quickly spread through town. By nightfall a white mob had gathered around Mink Slide, an area of Columbia populated primarily by black residents. The population of Mink Slide threatened retaliation if the mob attacked. When four white policemen entered the neighborhood that night, the residents of Mink Slide opened fire on the officers, critically injuring one of them. More than one hundred black residents were arrested following the attack. While under police custody on February 28, two of the black prisoners were shot and killed by their interrogators. Further rioting ensued, and Governor Jim Nance McCord called out the National Guard.

The riot garnered national attention for the severity of violence perpetrated by both civilians and police officers. The riot had broader significance for postwar race relations because the defense lawyers in the case, led by Antigua-born Zephaniah Alexander Looby, successfully won acquittals for twenty-three of the twenty-five black defendants, despite facing an all-white jury. The case catapulted Looby to fame and earned him the title "Mr. Civil Rights."[32] He continued fighting for racial equality into the 1960s, becoming one of the most respected attorneys in Tennessee.

Of course, *Skin Deep* was not revised in 1946 to highlight the rising career of Looby. Rather, the revisions were intended to alert audiences to increases in racial violence toward black veterans and cultural minorities of all backgrounds following the end of the war. At the very beginning of *Skin Deep*, Sergeant McGinnis, a black veteran, stops at the front of the bus to speak with the soldier to whom he gave his blood at the Iwo Jima company aid station. The white bus driver, seeing that McGinnis has not moved toward the back of the bus, responds to this inciting incident:

DRIVER. Get back in the rear of the bus, black boy.

WHITE VET. Why you lousy civilian . . .

NEGRO VET. Take it easy, soldier.

WHITE VET. What right has he got to talk to you that way?

DRIVER. I'll do more than talk. Go on, boy, don't make me tell you twice.

WHITE VET. Take your hands off him.

DRIVER. Listen, you damn Yankee . . .

WHITE VET. I said take your hands off. (*He throws the Driver back into his seat.*)

DRIVER. You asked for trouble, and, by God, you're going to get it. (*He picks up a club. Vet disarms him and sits down.*)

WHITE VET. Take it easy, Jackson. You'll live longer.

DRIVER. Let go of me. I'll show that uppity, black ape . . .

WHITE VET. Leave that man alone. He's a friend of mine.

DRIVER. A friend of yours?

WHITE VET. Sure. We both belong to the same lodge. The ancient and honorable Order of the Ruptured Duck.[33] He's an ex-service man, and so am I. And you're not going to push him around. Not while I'm here.[34]

The professor intercedes not long after this exchange, stopping the argument before it escalates into actual violence. Encapsulated in this brief and incendiary scene is not only the violence of Columbia but also the discrimination taking place throughout the United States immediately following the war. Gordon Allport, a psychologist and social ethics professor who founded the Harvard University Department of Social Relations in the 1940s, reported that racial and religious bigotry actually increase during and after periods of war:

War and its aftermath multiply and augment our frustrations. . . . There are the minor irritations of gas shortages, red tape of rationing, mounting taxes and higher prices. Both wage-earner and white collar workers are fearful for the future. Our worries give us the pinioned feeling which makes us want to attack something—something visible, near-lying and outlandish. Minority groups, being visible, near at hand, and a bit outlandish provide the outlet we need. We don't care particularly what we attack them for. If one excuse (The Jews all keep to themselves) is proved invalid, we seize another (They pry into Christian groups).[35]

Toward the end of *Skin Deep*, views similar to Allport's—as well as to those of *Races of Mankind*'s authors—are performed for the audience, illustrating how war exacerbates the anxieties that lead to bigotry and prejudice:

PSYCHOLOGIST. These prejudices are based on fear.

GEORGIA B. How do you mean?

PSYCHOLOGIST. Most people are afraid of something.

DRIVER. I'm afraid of losing my job.

NEGRO GIRL. I'm afraid of a penniless old age.

GEORGIA B. I'm afraid of sickness with no doctor.

WHITE VET. (*Enters*) I'm afraid of losing my money and all I have. But why? Why am I afraid? Whose fault is it?

ALL. It's your fault! It's your fault! It's your fault! (*Pointing at each other and overlapping*)

DRIVER. It's the Negroes' fault! (*Others echo him*)

NEGRO GIRL. It's the Jews' fault! (*Others echo her*)

GEORGIA B. It's the Catholics' fault! (*Others echo her*)

WHITE VET. It's the foreigners' fault! (*Others echo him*)[36]

Ultimately it is Sergeant McGinnis who stops this argument, and by the end of the play it is decided that "our differences are only skin deep. Under the skin, we're all brothers."

The overarching message of the play resonated with the lived experiences of many returning veterans. Sociologist Henry A. Singer, who spent four years researching soldiers in interracial platoons during World War II, convincingly argued that their attitudes regarding racial equality showed significant improvement following the war. Singer's findings validate SFA's intentions that "through creative and educational mediums it is possible to compete successfully with [those] insidious influences," a reference to such postwar American Fascist groups as the St. Sebastian Brigade of Charles Coughlin, the "gentile-only" American Order of Patriots, and the anti-Semitic Christian Veterans of America.[37] Singer continued, "By each of us participating in the social action force in our communities and by making democracy work in the classrooms, the offices, the shops, the subways, the recreation halls, the taverns, the cafeterias, the clubs, and anywhere when the opportunity for good human relationships presents itself, further advances will be possible."[38]

Skin Deep closes with the riders realizing that their prejudices have been fostered by socially constructed fears and that the last thing they want to do is fall prey to a message espoused by Hitler. Prior to the denouement, one of the most alluring moments of the piece occurs, one certain southern members of Congress and the HUAC would no doubt have viewed with great interest. The white veteran on the bus questions Jim Crow laws, observing that "some states make their own laws on how and where Negroes can love, marry, go to school, vote, ride on trains, and stuff like that. And if the people don't change the laws, they stay that way, no matter how they may conflict with the other laws in the Constitution."[39] The piece ultimately suggests, in barely masked propaganda, that Americans need to question at a personal level how beliefs are started, probe why certain laws are enacted, and challenge those laws that they find "Fascist" and reminiscent of Hitler's rhetoric of hate.

All Aboard

In 1946 Ben Bengal was well established in leftist theatrical circles. He was the playwright of *Plant in the Sun*, a piece written in 1936 about young sit-in strikers in New York. Originally produced by the Theatre of Action, it was subsequently staged by the New Theatre League, which awarded *Plant in the Sun* a prize for being the "best play dealing with the problems of youth in America."[40] It became the go-to strike play during the late 1930s and, according to novelist and historian Jay Williams, a "welcome alternative to *Waiting for Lefty*, which had been performed beyond endurance."[41] Bengal also co-authored the play *With Honor* under the auspices of the New Theatre League in 1941. *All Aboard* was first published in the September 1944 issue of *Theatre Arts*, the editor's note stating that it was written for the War Writers' Board and dedicated to Paul Robeson.[42] By the time SFA produced a significantly revised version of Bengal's play, he had moved into film writing, which may explain why

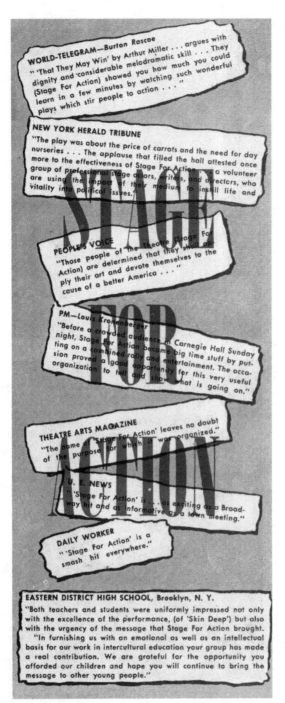

SFA brochure cover, circa 1946, with a review of *Skin Deep* at the bottom. *Courtesy of the Tamiment Library and Robert F. Wagner Labor Archives, New York University.*

this short piece was his lone collaboration with the group. He spent the next three years fully immersed in the film industry and, perhaps in an attempt to dodge the blacklist, wrote the screenplay for *Illegal Entry* in 1949, which supported cracking down on illegal immigration and had financial backing from the government. This, however, did not prevent Bengal from Hollywood blacklisting, as Leo Townsend named both Bengal and fellow SFA playwright Ben Barzman as Communists in a 1951 HUAC hearing. Bengal was subpoenaed and appeared before the committee on March 12, 1953.

All Aboard is set in a passenger coach on a train headed south after World War II. Three white GIs are enjoying their travels until the arrival of Lenny, a black GI. At this point one of the white soldiers, Shreveport, refuses to stay in the same car. The action escalates when the "Old Man" sitting in the same train car demands that Lenny move to the front of the train. When Bakokus, a Jewish GI from New York City, defends Lenny, the Old Man demands that all foreigners be removed. Shreveport stands up for both Lenny and Bakokus when the Old Man calls the latter a "goddam Jew bastard," and eventually it is the Old Man who is removed from the train, all the while threatening to report the blatant violation of Jim Crow laws to the local government.[43] Another character on the train, "Middle Aged Man," responds to the incident by declaring, "To hell with the Mason-Dixon line! If he was good enough to die for us, he's good enough to ride with us, Goddamit!" His wife, too, expresses her distaste for the display: "My God, if this isn't the most disgusting thing that I ever witnessed in my whole life." The play concludes with Bakokus asking, "Anybody else want to get off the train?"[44]

The writing in *All Aboard* is blunt and predictable and the characters hyperbolic, in accordance with many of the agitprop plays popularized by various workers' theatres of the 1930s from which Bengal drew direct inspiration. Nine years prior to the Alabama bus boycotts, Bengal and SFA used *All Aboard* to argue that it is those who do not believe in civil rights for all who are on the wrong track. Bengal arguably wrote the play in response to Irene Morgan's highly publicized 1944 revolt against Virginia bus segregation laws, actions that resulted in a Supreme Court hearing and the civil rights anthem "You Don't Have to Ride Jim Crow." This song was initially produced in 1947, the year that *All Aboard* became one of the most popular pieces in SFA's repertoire. Additionally, this was the year of the "Journey of Reconciliation"—when sixteen black and white freedom riders traveled two weeks by bus through Virginia, North Carolina,

Tennessee, and Kentucky to test the limits of the Supreme Court's recent decision to strike down the segregation of passengers on interstate buses. But 1947 was also the year yet another national incident involving mass transit took political center stage.

In May 1946, "over sixty organizations including the American Federation of Labor, the American Veterans of World War II, the National Urban League, and the NAACP sent representatives to a White House conference for the purpose of organizing the American Heritage Program and inaugurating the Freedom Train."[45] The Freedom Train, a traveling shrine dedicated to displaying historic artifacts symbolizing the "dignity and freedom of the individual," was scheduled to visit 315 cities in all forty-eight states.[46] The artifacts included "George Washington's copy of the Constitution, Thomas Jefferson's Bill of Religious Freedom, Francis Scott Key's manuscript of *The Star Spangled Banner*, the Emancipation Proclamation, and the German treaty of unconditional surrender that ended World War II in Europe."[47] Every city planned special events around the arrival of the Freedom Train, including "Community Rededication Weeks" with pageants where community members recited the "Freedom Pledge" and "The Nine Promises of a Good Citizen."[48] Number 6 of the nine promises stated, "In thought, expression and action; at home, at school and in all my contacts, I will avoid any group prejudice based on class, race or religion."[49] The *Good Citizen* pamphlet accompanying the Freedom Train tour emphasized that intolerance and prejudice were a "manifestation of insecurity and ignorance" and a form of bullying used by "rabble-rousers and demagogues."[50]

In what might seem a surprising move, the Alabama NAACP blocked the Freedom Train from stopping in its city. Its December 24, 1947, announcement explained that the NAACP did not believe that Birmingham, a city renowned for its atrocities against blacks, should have the privilege of hosting an event of such national significance. The city's past actions exhibited a blatant disregard for the ideals of racial equality and religious freedom that the *Good Citizen* pamphlet prescribed and the artifacts on the Freedom Train embodied. Although blocking the Freedom Train from making its patriotic stop in Birmingham did not change Jim Crow laws in Alabama, it did represent a moral victory for black citizens across the South, making the final line of *All Aboard*—"Anybody else want to get off the train?"—all the more prescient.[51] Due in part to its resonance with important flashpoints in the fight for racial equality, Bengal's play quickly became a touchstone performance.

The NAACP included a performance of *All Aboard* at a New York City mass membership rally in April 1947.[52] As was often the case with SFA performances, *All Aboard* was not a stand-alone feature of the event. The plays of SFA regularly served as the opening act or afterpieces for lectures regarding prominent social issues or were sandwiched between speeches by politicians, labor leaders, and public intellectuals. At the NAACP rally for example, SFA was on the same bill as Congressman Adam Clayton Powell Jr., Senator Kenneth Sherbell, and NAACP lawyer Franklin Williams. One month earlier, in March 1947, following a weekend run of *All Aboard* at the Theatre Des Artistes in New York City, Philadelphia audiences experienced a performance of Bengal's play featuring New York actors James Edwards (recently of the Broadway production *Deep Are the Roots*), Bob Howard, and Estelle Evans.[53] *All Aboard* was preceded at this Philadelphia event by a lecture titled "The Klan Rides in Pennsylvania" by James H. Sheldon, administrative chairman of the Non-sectarian Anti-Nazi League. The Philadelphia Council of the American Jewish Congress sponsored the program, which was free to the public.[54] What is significant about these events is how a variety of organizations used *All Aboard*, and other SFA productions, in order to replicate onstage the national debates surrounding social issues and in doing so created a discursive model immediately accessible to audiences.

Dream Job and *Talk in Darkness*

Dream Job by Arnold Perl was influenced by state and federal debates surrounding equal rights in employment occurring in the immediate postwar era. Malvin Wald's *Talk in Darkness* targets the same ideas as presented in *Skin Deep* but does so in a much more realistic style. Neither play shared the same robust production history as *Skin Deep* or *All Aboard*, but they remain significant to this study because they illustrate how dedicated Stage for Action was to producing works about racial equality. It is also through acknowledgment of their respective writers that the interconnectedness of SFA artists with the fields of radio and film, and therefore with the cultural moment as a whole, is reinforced.

Dream Job was first performed as part of an evening titled *Theatre Parade* at Carnegie Hall in the spring of 1946. Dubbed "thoughtful and dramatic" in a review in the *Worker*, the journalist continues, "The cast did a magnificent job and acted every move and word as if they were literally living the situation at the given moment." The reviewer also highlights that the piece was originally intended for the radio; however, "with the war's end, the brass hats in control of the radio program apparently decided there had been enough of that radical stuff about racial equality and specifically the shameful treatment of returning Negro servicemen, so they banned it."[55] Perl's *Dream Job* sets out in simple language the story of a young black army mechanic and pilot named Ted. Returning from the war with a Purple Heart, Ted finds a segregated homeland where he is denied service in a bar and unable to find a job because of his race. This leads him to mourning the time he spent in the military because it allowed him to experience freedoms he would never know as a civilian in the United States. Speaking to his sister Cora after another job rejection, Ted bitterly explains:

> They teach us how to fix things, how to be experts. They even teach us how to fly a plane. . . . So you can go back and think about how to fly a plane while you're running an elevator. So you can think about Diesel engines while you're scrubbing floors. Took me up to the heights . . . showed me what a man can do. What they want to raise me up for? So they can smash me down twice as hard. (*Long Pause*) I wish they never did it.[56]

Ted is eventually reunited with his army buddy Sam, who finds him a position as a mechanic at the plant where he works. Initially, Ted is reluctant to accept the position because he fears the boss will fire him at a moment's notice because of his race (last to be hired, first to be fired), but Sam convinces him otherwise. It is through their conversation that the main argument of the play is forwarded:

> SAM. Then listen to this. (*Pause*) Our plant is a union plant, Ted. And we signed a contract that forbids discrimination against any man because of his color, nationality or creed.
>
> TED. You . . . . you got that in the contract?
>
> SAM. We have. And more and more unions are making the same contracts every day.
>
> TED. I . . . . . . I didn't think there was such a thing?
>
> SAM. There is, Ted. Now, are you going to take that job?
>
> TED. Boy . . . . am I!!!
>
> SAM. And we'll all keep on building the union as strong as we can. That's the surest guarantee that you, as well as ourselves, will never lose that feeling of being men. (*They shake on it.*)[57]

Dream Job, with its clearly gendered discourse, may seem somewhat romanticized to contemporary readers. But it invites further exploration as it addresses a number of civil rights issues, doing so in politically volatile rhetoric (for the 1940s) and offering another glimpse into a post–World War II radical writer's repertory.

Arnold Perl was named in *Counterattack*'s 1950 *Red Channels* pamphlet, a list of 151 U.S. radicals and the supposedly subversive organizations they joined, for writing *Dream Job* and other works challenging the suspect treatment of marginalized individuals by the United States and other international governments. For example, Perl, like Arthur Miller in *That They May Win* (see chapter 2), broached the challenges of raising children during the war as well as the difficulties of providing adequate daycare and education for the millions of "war babies" orphaned by the conflict. He also grappled dramaturgically with the plight of Palestinian immigrants. I argue that Perl was not labeled a Communist for any one of these topics, however, but rather for his opposition to media censorship. In 1946 Perl blew the whistle on the army for banning his radio drama *Assignment Home*, which offered many of the same arguments that *Dream Job* does.[58] In 1948 Perl blew the whistle again when he publicly stated the Mutual Broadcasting System (MBS) changed its original intentions of dramatizing the report of the President's Committee on Civil Rights due to "protests from persons and interests in the South."[59] The shifting of the "original intention of employing the dramatic form . . . in favor of straight readings" for the radio report on civil rights is critical to understanding the effect of social activist theatre, particularly that of SFA, on audiences.[60] The head of MBS's educational department stated that a dramatized version would "distort the actual" and would not "permit coverage of the entire report."[61] But if we consider this statement in connection with southern protests and the many revisions Perl was encouraged to make in his script, it becomes clear that possible obfuscation of the report was not the primary issue. Instead, the station's leadership was concerned that a dramatization would be more agitational, more of a call to action, than a less presentational approach.

Perl suffered approximately nine years of television and film blacklisting because of being named to the *Red Channels* list, and several of the actors and directors he worked with in radio and SFA—including Ralph Bell, Howard Da Silva, Lloyd Gough, Mitchell Grayson, and Martha Scott—followed similar or worse fates. As the Red Scare subsided, however, Perl slowly regained his foothold in the arts, becoming a prolific television

writer during the 1960s. Today he is best known for writing and directing the original 1972 film *Malcolm X* and is credited as screenwriter with Spike Lee for the 1992 version. Additionally, as the copyright owner of Sholem Aleichem's stories, Perl had input into and gained residuals from both the original and subsequent productions of *Fiddler on the Roof.*

The SFA performance of *Dream Job* at Carnegie Hall, produced as part of its *Theatre Parade* program on March 31, 1946, probably earned Perl little money (and no residuals), certainly when compared with *Fiddler on the Roof,* but it does emphasize the shift in the overall purpose of SFA that occurred in 1946. Press releases and advertisements for the variety show performance touted performers such as Mildred Bailey, Imogene Coca, Eddie Condon, and Billie Holiday with Fred Keating as master of ceremonies and sponsorship provided by Margaret Webster, Moss Hart, William Morris Jr., Frank Kingdon, Martha Scott, Louis Kronenberger, José Ferrer, Barbara Bel Geddes, Oscar Serlin, and many others.[62] The group announced a transformation in its mission at the *Theatre Parade* performance from using drama to sustain public support of the war effort to engaging audiences with dramatic public instruction on vital issues of the day. Seemingly overnight, SFA moved from a company of volunteer theatre professionals operating within acceptable theatrical and political boundaries (because of its nationalist, pro-war orientation) to a group of militant outlaws who in less than a year would be named as a subversive group before Congress. The plays produced after 1946, which included *All Aboard* and *Talk in Darkness*, would be used by the government as evidence of support for radical causes and therefore grounds for, at best, congressional subpoena and, at worst, blacklisting.

Despite Joseph Lieberman stating that Malvin Wald's play *Talk in Darkness* was one of the "most popular plays in Stage for Action's repertory" in 1948, newspaper records indicate it was not as well received as *All Aboard* or *Skin Deep.*[63] The play did, however, have an afterlife following the dissolution of SFA. The interracial Harlem Unity Theatre produced Wald's *Talk in Darkness* and Ben Bengal's *Plant in the Sun* as a part of its evening titled *Contrasts* in September 1949.[64] Part of the selling point for Wald's play was his recent success as a screenwriter. He cowrote the Academy Award–winning film *The Naked City* in 1948 with Albert Maltz and would have a prolific career as a film and television writer. Dubbed a "groundbreaking, gritty drama," *The Naked City*, suggests film historian Leonard Maltin, paved the way for popular crime dramas of today because it deglamorized police work and followed the "day-to-day, mundane activities of the police."[65] The seething realism exacted in Wald's screenwriting is exactly what makes *Talk in Darkness* one of the more contemporary-sounding scripts in SFA's repertory. Set in a recreation room of a U.S. Army hospital in September 1946, the piece revolves around two soldiers, one black and one white. Both were blinded during the war, and they soon learn they are from the same block in Brooklyn. The two soldiers are chatting amicably and sharing memories of their youth when they discover they are not of the same race. It is soon revealed that Mike Vecchio (the white soldier) and his gang used to beat up black citizens on the block simply for stepping onto their corner. Russ Peters was one of the people often roughed up by the gang. At the climax of the play, Russ questions if Mike will attempt to change the old neighborhood's perspectives on race relations when they are discharged from the hospital:

> MIKE. I said I was sorry. I didn't know the score.
>
> RUSS. Why didn't you? Did you have to believe every lie you ever heard? Didn't you ever question your friends or your neighbors—or your father and mother? They taught you to hate us—in school, on street corners, on the baseball field. (*Bitingly*) "Eeny, meeny, miney, moe, catch a nigger by the toe." They gave it to you along with your teething ring. One world for the whites—another for the black. That's how it was in school. And that's how it was in the Army! The only thing they didn't provide was Jim Crow bullets . . . What did we fight for? What did the guys in my outfit die for? What did I lose my eyes for? Ask yourself why? You've still got a voice.[66]

Typical of the propaganda formula, Mike promises he will return to the old neighborhood and fight for racial equality. Yet the transparent language and denouement of the play should not be dismissed, particularly when coupled with its production in an election year fraught with immense consequences for black citizens. SFA's post–World War II plays focusing on civil rights were an extension of Henry Wallace's and like-minded liberals' thinking about, as well as advocacy for, the Progressive Party platform through theatrical activism.

The presidential race of 1948, which pitted Democratic incumbent Harry S. Truman against Republican candidate Thomas Dewey, proved especially intense because it was the year that the Democratic Party split three ways. As discussed in chapter 2, Henry Wallace ran on the Progressive Party ticket, promoting antiwar sentiments, calling for the elimination of the

HUAC, and fighting discrimination against black citizens and women. The Communist Party rallied behind Wallace, despite his subtle attempts at separating from its endorsement. Although Wallace initially found strong support "among voters who had no ties to the pro-Soviet left," as the campaign continued and Wallace's anti–Marshall Plan stance garnered increasingly negative media attention, American Communists became an "obvious and intrusive part in the third party."[67] Following the Progressive Party's convention in July 1948, pro-Republican outfits, such as American Business Consultants (publishers of *Counterattack*), started referring to Wallace's supporters as members of the "Commugressive Party."[68] Neither the Communists nor SFA wavered in support of the Progressive Party during the 1948 campaign season, and the unflappable backing of assumed subversives unfortunately lost Wallace a tremendous number of votes by Democrats leaning a little closer to the center.

The second group that split off from the Democratic Party during the 1948 election was the States' Rights Party, better known as the Dixiecrats, led by Strom Thurmond. Its platform supported Jim Crow laws and continued racial segregation in the South. One final candidate also ran for president: Norman Thomas, an ordained Presbyterian minister and pacifist who ran on the Socialist Party ticket. The election eventually came down to Truman versus Dewey, though Wallace and Thurmond each won approximately 2.4 percent of the popular vote, or more than a million votes each. In the end, Truman carried twenty-eight states (303 electoral votes) to Dewey's sixteen (189 electoral votes), enjoying a margin of more than two million popular votes over his opponent.

Although Truman vehemently denied that Wallace's pro–civil rights stance affected any of the Democratic Party's platform in the 1948 presidential election, he was strongly advised to adopt some of Wallace's rhetoric on equality in order to appeal to minority voters. While Truman maintained some of the Progressive Party's views regarding civil rights, he was no match for its actions. No other presidential candidate before Wallace did as much to bring national attention to issues of equality and civil rights during his campaign. The Progressive Party platform demanded the desegregation of public schools, the eradication of Jim Crow laws, equal rights for women, public daycare, and immigration reform. The Progressive Party also revolutionized political campaigns by inviting a black man named Charles P. Howard to give the first keynote speech at a political convention. Howard was an Iowa lawyer, a civil rights activist, and a World War I veteran when he broke down the color barricade for speaking at a national political event.[69] The Progressive Party convention had nearly three times the number of black delegates as the Republican and Democratic conventions combined, and "the interracial character of the gathering went well beyond mere tokenism."[70] One of the black delegates participating in the Progressive Party convention in Philadelphia stated it was "the first time his people had walked into a public place where it didn't occur to them to look for their own people or feel self-conscious."[71] Acknowledging that timing is everything in a political campaign, President Truman strategically issued Executive Order 9981 on July 26, 1948, while the Progressive Party convention was in session. The order declared "that there shall be equality of treatment and opportunity for all persons in the armed services without regard to race, color, religion or national origin."[72] This historically and politically significant move on Truman's part could not, however, undercut Wallace's unprecedented campaign tour of the southern states. Wallace refused to "speak before segregated audiences, to sleep in segregated hotels, to eat in segregated restaurants. Wallace's open defiance of Jim Crow focused on a national shame" and in doing so forced Truman and the Democratic Party to take a firmer stance on promoting civil rights.[73]

Even before his 1948 electoral victory, Truman governed a country that was in a constant state of anxiety. The United States was responsible for introducing atomic weaponry into modern warfare, the extent of the Holocaust's atrocities were clearer than they had been during the war, the Cold War was a perceived constant threat, and Americans were paranoid and scared. Truman hesitantly supported civil rights, but he also authorized an unparalleled attack on civil liberties through his federal loyalty pledge, the unbridled espionage antics of Herbert Hoover and the Federal Bureau of Investigation, and the HUAC inquiries. Although black Americans experienced small social advances under the Truman administration, on the whole his time in office was marked by repression, containment, and overwhelming fear. This fear was debilitating to many social agendas because the threat was undefined and the enemy boundary-less. Neighbors, coworkers, or relatives could operate as informants, and a person's actions—no matter how innocently undertaken—might warrant investigation. It is not wholly surprising that in this climate, many (though far from all) social activist performance groups dissolved.

The first wave of internal conflict and resulting exodus from SFA followed its participation in the School for Political Action Techniques in June 1946 (see chapter 2). Several founding members of SFA resigned as the group morphed into a national organization supporting a progressive agenda, but no archival evidence indicates that SFA's focus on civil rights was a factor for people leaving the group. Peggy Clark, for example, was a longtime supporter of civil rights and continued teaching stagecraft for an additional two years at the American Negro Theatre after resigning from SFA.[74]

Wallace's political loss in November 1948 spelled the end of SFA; however, this did not protect its members and sponsors from red-baiting. Black SFA artists and sponsors who openly advocated for civil rights were especially targeted by the government as being subversive or un-American. In 1948 Ferdinand C. Smith became one of the first SFA members to face prosecution due to Communist affiliations. In March 1948 SFA sponsored a benefit performance of Sidney Alexander's *Salem Story* for the interracial Sydenham Hospital in Harlem (see chapter 4). Smith—a black Jamaican-born board member of both SFA and Sydenham, a staunch supporter of civil rights, and one of the highest-ranking black union leaders in the United States—missed the performance because he was awaiting deportation on Ellis Island for his Communist-related activities.[75]

Smith was not the only black member of SFA who feared targeting by the U.S. government for supposedly subversive activities. Actor Gordon Heath (who had a leading role in *Dream Job* at Carnegie Hall) and his partner Lee Payant (who performed in SFA's *Open Secret* the same year) moved to Paris in 1948 to start a cabaret called L'Abbaye, which became one of the most popular venues for expatriates in France until Payant's death in 1976. As an interracial homosexual couple participating in a supposed Communist front theatre, Heath and Payant could not avoid HUAC attention and considered 1940s France more hospitable to both blacks and homosexuals.

Some black members of SFA stayed in the United States, continuing their outspoken activism while facing government investigation. At a well-publicized conference of the Committee for the Negro in the Arts in July 1949, Canada Lee and Paul Robeson, as well as fellow SFA sponsor Howard Fast, spoke out about the "indecent treatment" of black citizens in the United States. Robeson "predicted the death of American democracy if Negroes and 'progressive' artists in this country did not unite with the twelve indicted leaders of the Communist party to overthrow the 'guys who run this country for bucks and foster cold war hysteria.'"[76] During this summer, which witnessed the infamous Peekskill riots, a telegram sent to Robeson suggests that many other theatre artists supported Lee's, Robeson's, and Fast's continuing civil rights advocacy: "The rights and liberties of many Americans have already been taken from them while the rights of the rest of us are increasingly being threatened. The lifelong fight you have waged against reaction is a tribute to the spirit of man and an inspiration to all lovers of freedom. The members of the theatre join you and back you in your fight. Noble ideas cannot finally be suppressed."[77] His passport revoked in 1951, subpoenaed by the HUAC in 1956, Robeson was caught in a "conjunction of antitheatrical discourse, highly theatrical displays of power, and coerced performances of the accused [that were] marshaled to regulate and contain [his] activist performances."[78] Ultimately, Robeson's activism could not be suppressed, though Canada Lee's was. Despite consistent denials of Communist affiliations, Lee, a longtime sponsor and board member of SFA, was blacklisted and died penniless from uremia on May 9, 1952, unable to find work in the United States since his outspoken support of Progressives and civil rights in the summer of 1949.

SFA's very public shift in focus in 1946 to supporting the development of a third political party and attacking "native fascism"—or what Fredi Washington in the *People's Voice* labeled "domestic fascism"—elicited almost immediate government interest in the group.[79] This interest evidently frightened some members with promising or already successful careers and dissuaded them from continuing with the organization. Many conventional historical narratives emphasize that the fear of government backlash (and therefore loss of personal and professional stability) significantly hindered the civil rights movement, slowing progress to a crawl. Theatre historian Cheryl Black explains that while "U.S. participation in World War II provided an optimum moment to combat domestic fascism, the moment was lost to postwar anxiety over the perceived threat of Communism."[80] But recently uncovered archival evidence contradicts the narrative that civil rights activism in theatre abruptly ended during the Cold War and emerged in whole out of the New Left movement during the late 1950s. For example, spin-off theatre companies were born out of the defunct SFA units across the nation, and People's Drama Inc. in New York City, which focused entirely on racial disparities, was the direct descendant of the original SFA branch. Although the gloomy and cautionary tale of the dangers of social activism pre-détente are accurate, there simultaneously exists a need to recuperate the people and groups continuing the fight for civil rights during the early Cold War. Many of these artists marched on, rallying for equality, global solidarity, and peace through theatrical means well into the 1950s and beyond.

4. THE PEOPLE'S VOICE MUST SOUND LOUDER

STAGE FOR ACTION ENTERED 1948 by channeling all of its dramaturgical force into an unrelenting wave of plays intent on exposing the flagrant civil liberties violations practiced by the House Un-American Activities Committee. However, government intimidation in the wake of Henry Wallace's election loss and the continuing efforts by the HUAC against members of SFA hushed the group's antifascist thunder, which ultimately faded away in 1948. The militant leftist consciousness that had permeated the political ether since the 1930s slowly dissipated over the course of the year, washed away by a rising conservatism. But despite this conservative backlash, the radical Progressives of the immediate postwar era continued their struggle into the fifties and beyond, providing the structure for the mystical militants of the 1960s New Left.

George Santayana expounds, in admittedly one of the more belabored quotes of the twentieth century, "Those who cannot remember the past are condemned to repeat it." Cliché or not, invoking Santayana is appropriate when analyzing the repetitive actions of the U.S. government concerning civil liberties violations. Following the attacks on the Pentagon and the World Trade Center on September 11, 2001, the U.S. government responded by passing the "Uniting and Strengthening America by Providing Appropriate Tools Required to Intercept and Obstruct Terrorism Act of 2001" (better known as the "USA PATRIOT Act") as well as the subsequent Homeland Security Act in 2002. The USA PATRIOT Act—intended "to deter and punish terrorist acts in the United States and around the world"—includes among its provisions an enhancement of domestic security and surveillance, improved border protection, immigration reform, and "removing obstacles to investigating terrorism."[1] The Homeland Security Act allowed for the creation of the Department of

Homeland Security, which President George W. Bush stated would allow for "the most significant transformation of the U.S. government in over a half-century" in order to realign the "current confusing patchwork of government activities into a single department whose primary mission is to protect our homeland."[2] Many provisions of the USA PATRIOT and Homeland Security Acts build upon previously passed federal laws of the 1940s, such as the Alien Registration or Smith Act (1940), which made it illegal to advocate the violent overthrow of the government or to belong to any group devoted to such an advocacy, and the National Security Act (1947), which allowed for a restructuring of the military and intelligence agencies in order to streamline the chain of command regarding national security. It was in fact the National Security Act that President Bush was referencing regarding his "most significant transformation of the U.S. government," as this was the law resulting in the creation of the Department of Defense and the Central Intelligence Agency.

The Smith Act and the National Security Act of the 1940s were opposed by members of Stage for Action because of their ability to overreach their stated intentions of protecting the country from domestic and international terrorism. Members of SFA agreed with the opinion of retired U.S. Marine Corp major general Merritt Edson that following the passing of the National Security Act, "a Brass Curtain . . . is spreading over the nation. Behind it, continuing efforts are being exerted to fashion an American replica of the Prussian general staff system which destroyed all vestiges of democracy in the German nation, which plunged that country into four wars within three quarters of a century, and which has left Europe devastated, police-ridden and bankrupt."[3] Ultimately SFA members perceived that the U.S. government was becoming increasingly tolerant of civil liberties violations and that the "war had long-lasting repercussions for free expression."[4] One of the clearest examples of this, and perhaps the easiest to dramatize, was the instatement of the HUAC as a permanent standing committee in 1945 and the committee's subsequent actions. Through analysis of the plays *The Investigators* by Lewis Allan, *You're Next!* by Arthur Miller, and *Salem Story* by Sidney Alexander, this chapter elucidates the multiple points of collision between SFA and the HUAC and concludes with the repercussions—fatalities even—of the impact. The plays provide concrete evidence that SFA explicitly questioned the overreach of the U.S. government into the personal lives of citizens. In producing these plays, SFA directly challenged the legality of laws recently enacted that aimed at curtailing civil liberties while simultaneously protesting the actions of the House Un-American Activities Committee. Produced within a year of SFA being named a Communist front group before the HUAC by Walter S. Steele, these three plays illustrate the risks SFA artists were willing to take in order to protect the freedoms of their fellow U.S. citizens.

The Investigators

The first sense an audience member watching Lewis Allan's *The Investigators* engages is auditory as the opening stage directions read "Laugh in the dark, serio-comic, like the villain gloating over his innocent victim before committing his Dastardly Deed."[5] This is indeed an appropriate initial sound cue for a play amplifying the devious actions of the HUAC and its often less-than-reputable informants. The short musical piece involves a group of unnamed investigators attempting to prosecute a Mr. Smith for subversive actions because he publicly calls for "higher wages" and "no discrimination."[6] When Smith attempts to cross-examine the paid informant hired by the investigators and brings in a lawyer on his behalf, he is quickly removed from the stand. Offstage, the investigators' cronies attempt to brainwash Mr. Smith and turn him into a robot. Ultimately their plan fails, and the investigators are defeated.

Lewis Allan, the pseudonym of Abel Meeropol, was a prolific song-writer and poet with a penchant for theatre. His most well-known song is "Strange Fruit" (1938), based on his poem "Bitter Fruit" written in 1936 after he saw a particularly gruesome photograph of a lynching in the newspaper. The song was made famous by occasional SFA performer Billie Holiday on her album *Lady Sings the Blues*. "Strange Fruit" was not Allan's lone piece of activist music, however. He had a long history of writing political music and collaborated during the 1930s with members of the Communist Composers Collective. Other songs of his included the brazenly titled "I Kissed a Communist (Was My Face Red)" and "Is There a Red under Your Bed?," penned during a period much more congenial to those with Communist sympathies. He also enjoyed a thirty-year friendship and writing partnership with Communist composer and SFA supporter Earl Robinson. Allan and his wife, Anne (née Shaffer), were members of the Theatre Arts Committee (TAC), along with fellow SFA performer Will Geer. The TAC was a performing arts organization operating from 1938 to 1941 that produced topical cabarets in order to provide financial aid to Spanish Democracy and other Popular Front causes. Allan, who wrote for his college's humor magazine as an undergraduate, frequently contributed songs and sketches for TAC performances. When not composing for the TAC, both he and Anne were employed as teachers in the New York City public school system. According to Nancy Kovaleff Baker, Allan greatly appreciated the work of Bertolt Brecht, Kurt Weill, Clifford Odets, and Marc Blitzstein.[7] During the 1940s and 1950s Allan collaborated on songs with Weill and Lehman Engel, the conductor of Blitzstein's musical *The Cradle Will Rock*.

It is unclear exactly when Allan wrote *The Investigators*, but the most likely date of creation is between 1945 and 1948 (based on the standing status of the HUAC).[8] *The Investigators* is only one of many SFA productions challenging the activities of the HUAC. The House Un-American Activities Committee had existed on a temporary basis since 1938 but, as noted above, became a permanent committee in 1945. It was a standing committee for the next thirty years, with the heyday of its hearings occurring during the late 1940s through the 1950s, when its primary concern was investigating Communist infiltration at all levels of American society. Regardless of the precise date of its writing, *The Investigators* was not the first creation to pique government suspicions about Allan's political affiliations. In 1941 he was investigated by the Rapp-Codert Commission looking into Communist infiltration of the educational system. Although he was relatively unscathed by this early investigation, seven years later Allan and his wife were forced from their stable Hollywood life, where Allan had been writing songs for the movies, due to the blacklist. They began a decade of frequent moves in order to dodge HUAC subpoenas.

Allan was openly critical of the HUAC hearings (and later of Senator Joseph McCarthy), writing not only *The Investigators* but also such pointed songs as "Riding the Broom" and "Ballad of the Hollywood Ten." However, he and his wife's most outwardly political, and simultaneously selfless, act was adopting Julius and Ethel Rosenberg's two young sons following their parents' execution in 1953. During the 1950s and 1960s Allan composed several musicals and continued his political activism. He was outspoken in his distrust of Richard Nixon and the Vietnam War, and in 1973 the National Endowment for the Arts commissioned Allan to write the text and lyrics for a cantata titled *The Song of the Liberty Bell* emphasizing the "role of minorities in American democracy."[9] Allan died on October 29, 1986, of complications from Alzheimer's.

The Investigators, at only six pages in length and lacking any serious character or plot development, is reminiscent of a 1930s agitprop. Despite its length, the play focuses on a wide swath of concerns facing Progressive Party members: the tightening of government control over labor unions, the labeling of all Communists as "subversive," the corrupt investigative processes of the HUAC, race relations in the South, and the stifling of intellectual freedom in the United States. The characters include the Investigators, the Victim, the Rat, and the Lawyer. The final character, the Robot, is meant to symbolize the U.S. government's "synthetic creation[,] the perfect citizen of a perfect well-regulated nation" whose spirit has been "cut in proportion—a sort of intellectual abortion."[10]

All of the characters are broad stereotypes, and Allan suggests in his stage directions that "the sketch should be done in a highly stylized manner both in the reading of the lines and in movement, and it should have a nervous, staccato effect, especially from the Investigators. The Rat should be a broad burlesque of all stool pigeons. The other characters should be handled simply, underplayed for effect."[11] The absence of a required set or props and the flexible cast size make *The Investigators* an ideal piece for town hall meetings or political rallies. It is easy to understand why the play would be chosen for a Wallace campaign meeting and performed by SFA. The end of the piece was revised slightly by the Chicago Arts Committee for Wallace so that the Robot breaks out of its brainwashed routine and triumphantly shouts, "Wallace in '48!" as the Investigators run offstage screaming.

But *The Investigators* deals with more than targeting Communists. It brings to the fore growing problems in the conservative climate of the late 1940s, including the devaluation of intellectual freedom and the whitewashing of American society with regard to politics, ethnicity, religion, and culture. In using a robot to symbolize the perfect American citizen, *The Investigators* draws on popular novels and films of the 1940s that use robots, zombies, and outer-space body snatchers to illustrate (depending on the creator's political beliefs) the brainwashing of American citizens by the government or by Communists. Even government officials with justifiable fears of espionage, war, or revolution questioned what the homogenizing of American society through the forced suppression of difference would mean to our creative and intellectual output. Lewis Allan spent his life combating what he saw as racist, anti-Semitic, and antidemocratic activity by the government in his songs, poems, and plays. He argued that freedom of thought was foundational to the American way of life. *The Investigators* claims that the corrupt HUAC members valued only the citizen who abdicates his or her right of free speech:

Why if everybody had concealed thoughts it would be a terrible blow!
And if they thought out loud they might even gather a crowd
And then where would our profits go?
We have our own idea of the kind of citizen
Who fits into our conception of society.
Somebody very safe and sane.
With an arrested brain.[12]

In his excellent research on filmmaker Carl Marzani and the history of left-wing documentaries during the Cold War, Charles Musser discusses a film version of *The Investigators*, listed in the 1948 Union Films catalog as part of the "Films for Wallace" series. Musser describes the short film, which runs eleven minutes, as "fun and snappy, lampooning the unfunny House Un-American Activities Committee."[13] The film score was composed by Serge Hovey, who studied under Hann Eisler.[14] The actors cast in the film version of *The Investigators* all came from the ranks of the John Lenthier Troupe.[15] Musser stated that the film, and the play upon which it was based, echoed Wallace's opposition to the way Congress had "struck at civil liberties" and "smeared men of the highest integrity who are willing to accept public office."[16]

Two years after both SFA and Union Films championed Lewis Allan's *The Investigators* as propaganda for Wallace's presidential run, Supreme Court justice Robert H. Jackson, a longtime adversary of the HUAC, issued a revealing opinion. Jackson's ruling addressed the potential menace of Communism to American society as well as the even greater dangers facing a nation in which political and business leaders felt it was their right to prosecute people based solely on their "beliefs or opinions, even though they may never have matured into any act whatever or even been given utterance." Justice Jackson and Lewis Allan seem to have shared fears of where the United States was headed:

> Our forefathers found the evils of free thinking more to be endured than the evils of inquest or suppression. They gave the status of almost absolute individual rights to the outward means of expressing belief. . . . This is not only because individual thinking presents no danger to society, but because thoughtful, bold and independent minds are essential to wise and considered self-government. Progress generally begins in skepticism about accepted truths. Intellectual freedom means the right to re-examine much that has been long

taken for granted. A free man must be a reasoning man, and he must dare to doubt what a legislative or electoral majority may most passionately assert. The danger that citizens will think wrongly is serious, but less dangerous than atrophy from not thinking at all. . . . The priceless heritage of our society is the unrestricted constitutional right of each member to think as he will. Thought control is a copyright of totalitarianism, and we have no claim to it.[17]

The idea that freedom can be achieved only through reason and an individual's right to uncensored outward expression is also at the core of another SFA production, *You're Next!*, by Arthur Miller.

You're Next!

As discussed in chapter 2, Miller was committed to SFA for the entirety of its existence, a commitment that included writing plays for the group, hosting events, auctioning off scripts to raise funds for it, and directing his own script for a benefit performance. The goal of Miller's efforts was likely to educate and entertain a society able and willing to create necessary and positive change. He writes in his autobiography, *Timebends*, that his formation of political and dramatic sensibilities occurred simultaneously and "deepened the presumption that should [he] ever win an audience it would have to be made up of all the people, not merely the educated or sophisticated, since it was this mass that contained the oceanic power to smash everything . . . or to create much good."[18] *You're Next!*, following in the vein of Miller's earlier SFA offering, *That They May Win*, realizes Miller's dramaturgical aspirations by evoking a powerful optimism toward "the people's" ability to produce change when their voices can be heard.

The protagonist of *You're Next!* is Jerry Marble, a successful barber in "an industrial community" called Libertyville. In typical 1940s argot, Jerry is an "ace." He is admired and has a great sense of humor, and as the narrator of the play points out, "Even the big-shots who come into his shop, go big for Jerry."[19] But Jerry courts trouble because of his political affiliations and convictions. He believes that every U.S. citizen has the right to free speech and that it is the duty of Americans to support people in places like Yugoslavia, Greece, and even Russia: "The war made him realize, along with a lot of other folks, that there were fine people in the other countries, and now he finds it kinda hard to forget it."[20] Jerry even goes so far as to set out on his barbershop countertop, adjacent to his collection jars for cancer victims, collection jars for the antifascists in Spain and for Russian war relief. Additionally, when Fletcher, a local butcher, comes in for a haircut and asks Jerry to "put in a good word" for him with the local plant workers, Jerry politely declines because he believes Fletcher should have "helped them out during the strike" instead of charging them full price for meat when they couldn't afford it.[21] Fletcher threatens Jerry that there will be trouble if the plant workers don't start buying their meat from him again, but Jerry refuses to use his popularity with the workers for Fletcher's economic gain when he "let them starve for seven weeks" and then expects their forgiveness and patronage now that they have returned to work.[22]

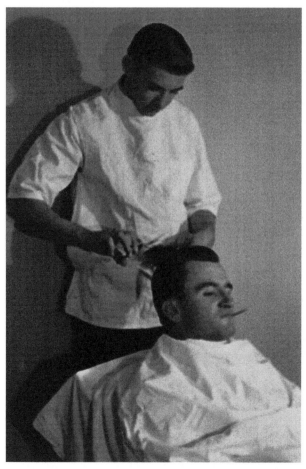

"I don't like the attitude around here." Scene from the Washington SFA production of Arthur Miller's *You're Next! Courtesy of Schlesinger Library, Radcliffe Institute, Harvard University.*

Many of Jerry's aforementioned free speech acts—openly supporting antifascist and pro-Soviet causes as well as criticizing neighbors who price-gouged striking workers—proved suspect in the late 1940s. However, Jerry's troubles increase significantly when an election for a judge takes place. The incumbent judge had handed down an anti-picketing injunction in a recent union strike, an action repudiated by the pro–free speech and pro-union Jerry. This affront leads him to hang a poster for the challenger—Progressive candidate Dan Kelly—who is also being supported by the labor unions and the CIO-PAC. Not long after, a lawyer friend of Jerry's named Matty enters the shop and encourages him to take down the poster and hide his collection cans under the counter. Matty warns Jerry that his confrontational political actions are going to put him in danger of being called up by the Rankin Committee (a pseudonym for the HUAC). As Matty explains,

> All right, Jerry, now listen to me. I spend a lot of time in the court-house. There's a certain judge who is trying to get reelected, and it looks bad for him because of what he did in the strike. He is getting set to pull a Red hunt. You know what that means? It means that one of these days you're going to pick up the paper and it's going to say that the people behind Kelly are all communists.[23]

Jerry responds to the warnings by removing the collection cans from the counter, but he keeps the poster of Kelly up because, as he says, "It's a free country, ain't it? What can they do to me? I got a right to tell Rankin to go to hell if I want to."[24]

One can only imagine the audience response to Jerry's hypothetical telling-off of John E. Rankin, longtime member of the HUAC and the man responsible on January 3, 1945, for raising a successful amendment to congressional rules making the Un-American Activities Committee a standing committee of the House.[25] In an audience of labor union members, Progressives, and potential fellow travelers, Jerry would appear the ultimate political rebel. His actions would most likely have elicited wild applause and cheering from the audience, though likely little response from the HUAC. However, when Republican J. Parnell Thomas became chairman of the HUAC in 1947, this change in leadership was reflected in subsequent versions of *You're Next!* That year began the tensest period of government investigation into supposedly subversive activities by members of the performing arts in the United States. The audience reaction in 1947 to Jerry's stoicism regarding his accusers may have been vastly different; the government's response most certainly was. In addition to the volatile content of the play, *where* it was performed also influenced the HUAC's interest in it, in its playwright, and in the group performing it. There exists from 1947 a rare reference directly linking Arthur Miller to the Communist Party, and it is in conjunction with *You're Next!* During the height of a New York City drive for members, the Brooklyn Communist Party sponsored an event in which Henry Winston (then secretary and future chairman of the national organization of the Communist Party of the United States of America) spoke about the party's position on Greece and Turkey, topics directly referenced in the play.[26] Two other political speakers, Gil Green and Peter V. Cacchione, voiced concerns about Communist recruiting challenges in Chicago and the Washington witch hunt, respectively. The entertainment for the evening was none other than "Arthur Miller's Smash Hit" *You're Next!*[27] It mattered not that Miller may not have authorized this performance or that SFA was not mentioned in the advertisement. In a moment in which life truly imitated art, the fact that Miller's play, which he donated to SFA, was advertised in direct connection with the Communist Party would have raised investigators' suspicions.

Adding fuel to the fire, beginning in early 1948 SFA ramped up its support of Henry Wallace while performing a number of plays clearly distrustful of, if not directly hostile to, the HUAC. SFA not only staged its political views in plays like *The Investigators* and *You're Next!* but also circulated them (and in large print). On October 20, 1948, Arthur Miller, as well as numerous other SFA members and supporters, were listed as being "For Wallace" in a large *New York Times* ad sponsored by the National Council of Arts, Sciences, and Professionals. SFA's social activist maneuvering in this most politically delicate of years illustrates not only its dedication to progressive causes but also its extreme naïveté regarding Cold Warriors' (politicians actively pursuing anti-Soviet policies and postures) power of censorship. Walter Goodman states that 1948 "stands as the most celebrated year of the Committee on Un-American Activities, a year of threat and counterthreat to which the Committee responded with enormous gusto, grasping and sometimes throttling its opportunities. . . . It showed itself at its best and at its vicious worst."[28] Between 1948 and 1956 many of the Progressive Party supporters listed in the October 1948 *New York Times* ad were subpoenaed by the HUAC for alleged Communist ties. Miller, for example, was called before the committee on July 25, 1956. His trip to Washington, D.C., earned him a contempt citation for responding to a request for Communist Party names thusly: "I could not use the name of another person and bring trouble on him. These were writers, poets, as far as I could see, and the life of the writer, despite what it sometimes seems, is pretty tough. I wouldn't make it any tougher for anybody."[29] Miller appealed the contempt citation for two years, during which time he could not travel abroad because the State Department continued to hold his passport. A court of appeals overturned the contempt ruling in September 1958, judging that Miller had not been "adequately apprised that he risked contempt if he refused to answer questions on grounds of conscience."[30] For SFA members and supporters, the actions of the HUAC proved a bitter rejoinder to a group of people who continuously performed and voted their conscience.

Salem Story

Seven months before Miller's name was plastered in the *New York Times* as being "For Wallace" and only two months before he signed on as a vice chairman for the "Brooklyn Wallace for President Committee," another play addressing civil liberties violations by the HUAC, Sidney Alexander's *Salem Story*, was performed by SFA.[31] Miller is connected to this SFA play as well, given it foreshadows the most renowned theatrical hailing of the New England witch trials: Miller's 1953 play *The Crucible*. It is arguable that Miller's play is a mythologized dramaturgical adaptation of historical events often supplanting the original craze. As evocative as his portrait is, however, Miller was not the first playwright to dramatize these infamous trials. Nor was he the first playwright to conceive of the HUAC as a modern-day witch hunt that correlated accused subversives of the twentieth century to the Proctors and Coreys of the seventeenth. William Carlos Williams, for example, penned a musical with composer Thomas Canning about the HUAC titled *Tituba's Children* in 1950, three years before Miller's play emerged. The Williams play is partially based on "Cotton Mather's Wonders of the Invisible World," a chapter he contributed to a 1933 book of essays titled *In the American Grain*. Additionally, thirteen years prior to *The Crucible*'s appearance, a verse radio play by Sidney Alexander, *Where Jonathan Came*, was broadcast over the airwaves. The piece subtly attacks the actions of the Dies Committee using the Salem witch trials as a backdrop. Alexander subsequently revised the radio play, and it was staged by SFA under the title of *Salem Story* in 1948.

In contrast to the ease of associating Miller with SFA (thanks to a lengthy archival trail), discerning similar connections between playwright Sidney

Alexander and his relatively obscure play *Salem Story* is a far more arduous task. SFA produced the piece, along with the third iteration of Miller's *That They May Win*, during its 1948 season. Alexander's theatrical experience seems limited to writing *Salem Story* and two other plays—*The Hawk and the Flesh* and *The Third Great Fool*. Born in New York City in 1912, Alexander graduated from Columbia University in 1934 and served in the army during World War II. He is best known today as a novelist, but during the 1940s Alexander was considered a "well known radio and short story writer," additionally composing several collections of poetry early in his career.[32] He published in the *New Masses* from 1935 to 1947, overlapping the period Miller was employed by the magazine (under the pseudonym Matt Wayne). It is intriguing to think that Alexander could be one of the two aspiring playwrights working at the *New Masses* in 1939 who had "written unproduced plays" that Miller thought "showed talent."[33] Alexander won the prestigious PEN award for his translation of a work on Italian history in 1970, the first award for translation offered by the PEN International.[34] From the 1950s through the 1980s, he spent long periods of time in Italy, returning to the United States between 1963 and 1967 to teach in the fine arts department of Syracuse University. While in Italy, Alexander worked for the *Reporter* magazine and as an independent scholar, often reviewing poetry or novels for the *New York Times* and other publications. He returned to the United States in 1983 and subsequently taught at Virginia Commonwealth University. His final work was a translation of Horace's *Odes and Satires* in 1999; he died soon after its publication.[35]

Although Alexander had very little connection to the professional theatre world, his poetry and novels are in complete alignment with the progressive perspectives espoused in many of SFA's plays and by members of the group. In *The Man on the Queue*, which was published in 1941 and contains the text of the radio play *Where Jonathan Came*, one finds the crux of Alexander's personal philosophy. Selden Rodman states in the introduction of this collection that Alexander is "fight[ing] his way out of the jungle of 'proletarian' clichés of over-simplicity and 'intellectual' clichés of over-complexity."[36] The collection is riddled with attempts at merging the intellectual, political, and artistic while simultaneously speaking to a multitude of reading audiences and classes. Miller commiserated with Alexander's yearning for a way to blend political philosophy with artistic merit, writing in 1947 that "art, at least good art, stands in contradiction to propaganda in the sense that a writer cannot make truth but only discover it. . . . All one could say was that a philosophy could help an artist if it challenged him to the sublime and turned him from trivializing his talent."[37] It is evident that although they were dedicated Marxists, both Alexander and Miller were even more passionate about creating work of artistic significance.

Alexander's work as a welfare investigator in Harlem, as well as his personal reactions to war and the Holocaust, inspired his second collection of poetry, *Tightrope in the Dark*, which was published in 1950. Maurice Irvine, reviewing the collection for the *New York Times*, stated that the poems—not unlike the works in his first collection—fall into two groups, "those which are rather intimate and sensitive," referencing the poems dedicated to Alexander's wife, Frances, "and those of social protest." Irvine continued, "To walk 'tightropes in the dark' is to be concerned about and to believe in hope of a better world."[38] Alexander—as a creative writer with an exhaustive expertise in the areas of art, history, religion, and politics— always found ways of including his opinions in even his most historically grounded works, and *Salem Story* does not stray far from this approach.

Originally produced as a radio play in 1940, *Where Jonathan Came* was arguably written in reaction to the formation of the HUAC under Martin Dies Jr. on May 26, 1938. In Rodman's appraisal of the radio play, he considers it as drawing on the "usable past" with the "dramatic intention to tell a story of such obvious immediacy that the reader is directly involved."[39] The phrase "usable past," often traced to a 1918 essay by Van Wyck Brooks, has been a guiding force in the fields of new historicism and cultural history and provides the key for interpreting both Alexander's and Miller's (as well as William Carlos Williams's) plays regarding the Salem witch trials. The concept of the usable past, of bringing the past into discourse with the present, "permits a two-way exchange to occur. In its use in the present, the past becomes subject to the interpretive fashions, and, potentially, the political demands of the present."[40] The usable past concept allows historians to conflate—though not distort—the historical and the present. This is what Alexander, Miller, and Williams aim at achieving: a dramatized, extended historical metaphor (of course, taking creative license with the historical material, which all three do, violates professional historians' understanding of the usable past concept).

Continuing the analysis that Alexander's play is embracing a usable past, Milton Allen Kaplan places special focus on *Where Jonathan Came* in his work *Radio and Poetry*. Kaplan identifies Alexander as one of the few poets during the 1940s taking advantage of the rich possibilities found in the "incidents and personalities" of history.[41] But it is Samuel Sillen who offers the most provocative review of *Where Jonathan Came*: "This play, which has distinct implications for our own witch hunt days, deserves to be much better known. The basic moods of Alexander's verse are present here: his warm sympathy for the underprivileged and oppressed, his indignation at those who provoke hatred and usurp power, his admiration for those who have the courage to fight for a progressive idea at what ever personal cost."⁴² This review, published in the *New Masses* in 1941, could as easily be a description of Miller's *The Crucible* as of the little-known Alexander play composed more than a decade before Miller's highly lauded work.

When considered with the rest of SFA's performances, *Salem Story* (as *Where Jonathan Came* was eventually titled) does not fit into the group's standard repertoire. The language of the play is melodic and well-crafted prose, and its multidimensional characters and loftier style are more similar to other mainstream plays of the time than to the agitprop or "proletarian grotesque" of many SFA productions. The production was an outlier for SFA because it was performed in benefit of the Sydenham Hospital.⁴³ Sydenham was New York City's only interracial hospital at the time, providing medical services to much of Harlem.⁴⁴ One of SFA's direct connections to Sydenham Hospital was a shared board member: Ferdinand C. Smith, the Jamaican-born vice president (other records state secretary) of the powerful National Maritime Union in 1948. In March 1948, he faced deportation proceedings under the Smith Act due to his participation in the CPUSA and subsequent labeling as an "undesirable alien."⁴⁵ Perhaps the more significant connection between the hospital and SFA, however, was their shared belief in equality. As discussed in chapter 3, SFA was dedicated to civil rights in its postwar rhetoric as well as in its performances. It seems appropriate that the group would fight to keep Sydenham open as it was the only hospital in the United States "where all racial barriers have been lowered, so that Negroes sit on the board of trustees, practice medicine and surgery, conduct research and nurse the ailing."⁴⁶ SFA, operating as one of the only interracial theatre groups in the United States during the 1940s, perhaps felt a kinship with Sydenham and therefore rushed to its aid.

The score of SFA's production of *Salem Story* was composed by Herbert Haufrecht with choreography by Valentina Litvinoff, scenic and lighting design by Ralph Alswang, and direction by Gene Frankel.⁴⁷ In 1948 Frankel was serving as executive director of SFA. An undated SFA press release for the event describes *Salem Story* as "a dynamic new play by Sidney Alexander, prize winning author, dealing with the witch hunt of an earlier day"; touting "a cast of thirty, featuring several prominent Broadway actors and a special score and dances composed for the play, it will tell the story of our ancestors' early fight against thought control."[48] Alternately, the *New York Herald Tribune* stated the performance was attempting to achieve "a fusion of drama, music, and dance . . . [and] fluidity of motion throughout the seven scenes without blackouts or lowering of the curtain."[49]

Interest in *Salem Story* would perhaps end here were it not for the play's similarity to Arthur Miller's 1953 production of *The Crucible*. Miller was entrenched in SFA, not only as its most prolific playwright but also as a meeting host and leader. It is highly probable that Alexander and Miller knew each other through the *New Masses* and SFA and as occasional writers for *The Cavalcade of America* radio program.[50] It is also intriguing that Alexander won the PEN award the year after Miller completed his four-year engagement as the president of this international group. However the two writers may have encountered each other, the similarities between *Salem Story* and *The Crucible* cannot be ignored.

The plays share the same basic plotline and major characters. Both Alexander's and Miller's plays open in the house of Reverend Parris, who expresses his anger with certain citizens of Salem for their backward or "yeoman" behavior, absence from the meetinghouse, and inappropriate provisions of firewood. In Alexander's play, Parris lashes out at the towns-people in a conversation with his wife, stating, "I tell you this village is filled with evil people: beggars without property, tavern-keepers, bawds, thieves, preachers of rebellion, Horned prophets erecting idols of pride and Gods of non-conformity . . . Those whose only law is the lumpy average will of all of them . . . That kind is dangerous here in Salem: A cancer that would eat away our property and home and righteousness . . ."[51] Parris, along with the Reverend Cotton Mather, are the clear antagonists in Alexander's play. By contrast, Miller's Parris appears as a bumbling fool and a cog in the machinery of Salem's political and religious insanity. Other major differences between the two pieces include their lengths: *Salem Story* lasts only six scenes and an epilogue, while *The Crucible* runs four acts. Additionally, *Salem Story* lists only ten named characters: Giles, Martha, and Abigail Corey; John Burroughs (betrothed to Abigail Corey); Samuel Parris and his wife and daughter; Hagar; Cotton Mather; and a Prophet.[52] The rest of the "cast of thirty" comprise mostly unnamed townspeople who are in the group scenes, whispering accusations against the Coreys during underscored and choreographed moments in the play. Completely absent from *Salem Story* is the adultery plot device.[53] The piece instead focuses wholly upon a corrupt religious system that allows the accusations of a few disgruntled citizens, a superstitious European servant, and a handful of young girls to destroy the lives of otherwise innocent people. But without doubt Alexander alludes to recent history. The HUAC, as well as the totalitarianism of the Nazi regime, resonates in lines such as "All Salem is accuser and accused, and conscience like a coward hides between," as well as "O you can't imagine the horror that burst the pod in Salem centuries

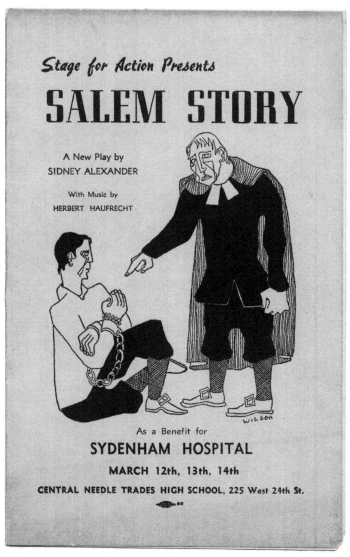

SFA program cover for 1948 production of Sidney Alexander's *Salem Story*. *Billy Rose Theatre Division, the New York Public Library for the Performing Arts, Astor, Lenox, and Tilden Foundations.*

ago: you would not dream such horror: not even today when fact outdoes the imagined dream—when the nightmarish goosestep walks in the sun."[54]

Miller's *The Crucible* is a historical fiction drama exploring the Salem witchcraft hysteria from the perspective of John Proctor, Elizabeth Proctor, Reverend Parris, and Abigail Williams. Miller stated in 1958 that he wrote the play

> not merely as a response to McCarthyism. . . . It is examining the questions I was absorbed with before—the conflict between a man's raw deeds and his conception of himself; the question of whether conscience is in fact an organic part of the human being, and what happens when it is handed over not merely to the state or the mores of the time but to one's friend or wife.[55]

One of the subplots in the play involves John Proctor's brief sexual affair with the teenage Abigail Williams, who subsequently accuses Elizabeth Proctor of witchcraft. Near the end of the play Elizabeth Proctor lies about her knowledge of the affair to protect her husband's honor and inadvertently sentences him to death. In the final scene of the play John Proctor refuses to sign his name to his witchcraft testimony and therefore hangs.

Similarities between *Salem Story* and *The Crucible* are plentiful. Although each playwright takes great liberties with the usable past, especially regarding the ages of Reverend Parris's daughter and Abigail Williams, there also exist significant lines drawn directly from historical testimony in both plays. For example, the questioning of Martha Corey features a line from the Salem trial records: "How can you know that you are not a witch and yet not know what a witch is?"[56] Additionally, each play includes a near-reversal, an *almost* peripeteia, in close proximity to the climax of the play when the judges question their own motives during the trials.

Perhaps the most significant comparison the two plays invite is revealed through the journey of their protagonists. Both playwrights present a man unwilling to commit perjury before a corrupt legal proceeding in order to save his own life. The protagonist in each play refuses public confession to witchcraft and in doing so spares Salem through his martyrdom. One major difference between the two characters is that John Proctor has a temporary moment of weakness near the end of *The Crucible*, allowing his confession to be written, while Giles Corey stands mute at his trial and is pressed to death. While this is Corey's fate in both plays, as well as in the historical record, in *The Crucible* Elizabeth Proctor suggests that Corey stands mute to protect his property and posterity. Miller writes of

Corey, "Old Giles must be spoken for, if only because his fate was to be so remarkable and so different from that of all the others. He was in his early eighties at this time, and was the most comical hero in the history."[57] Miller's character description of Corey suggests he read both the original court documents (which is intimated in his autobiography) and the mammoth WPA collection on the trials (which Miller scholar Brenda Murphy supports).[58] Regardless, Miller's work ultimately portrays Giles Corey as a feeble-minded, aged loon responsible for his wife's demise.

Sidney Alexander presents a vastly different Giles Corey characterization. In *Salem Story*, Corey is a stoic and perceptive protagonist, defending his wife until the very end of the play. Alexander's Giles Corey *is* Miller's John Proctor, their similarity magnified by casting choices of the protagonist in both plays. The production of *Salem Story* in March 1948 starred twenty-eight-year-old Walter Matthau, a World War II veteran and recent student at Erwin Piscator's Dramatic Workshop. Matthau was not an elderly man (albeit supernaturally strong, as Giles Corey supposedly was) past his mental prime but a quick-witted and powerful young actor just emerging in the New York theatre scene. In comparison, Arthur Kennedy was thirty-nine years old when he originated the role of John Proctor in *The Crucible*. Also in Alexander's play, Giles Corey is allowed a final courtroom speech of his own (rather than having his death described by another character):

> I will not plead. If I deny, I am convicted already in this court where ghosts appear and swear men's lives away. If I confess, then I confess a lie to buy a life that will be death in life: a shivering skin, a crouching in the dark . . . No, I will not plead. I will not bear false witness against anyone, not even against myself . . . whom I count least . . . If there is any grain of guilt in me, fear was that guilt: the long silence; the shameful turning of the back: the downcast eye at the murderous procession . . . but now I taste death bitter-sweet upon my lips . . . and soon the heavy weights shall crush my life . . . and yet if one word were to save me, and that word were not the truth . . . if it did swerve a hair's breadth from the truth . . . I would not say it.[59]

The major distinction between Miller's John Proctor and Alexander's Giles Corey is that the latter has no apparent flaws and is the victim of a corrupt system, while the former, a much more nuanced character, has sinned and takes responsibility for it. It is this single shift in protagonist characterization that marks the significant difference between *Salem Story* and *The Crucible*.

Although Arthur Miller never publicly discussed his multi-year involvement with Stage for Action, archival evidence overwhelmingly suggests that he would have known about Alexander's play and gone to see it, especially as it was being performed as a benefit event sponsored by the group and was an award-winning play, having won the annual Maxwell Anderson Award sponsored by Stanford University. Miller did however speak and write at length regarding his inspiration for *The Crucible*. He states that the work was partially inspired by the HUAC hearings and McCarthyism, by the fear for self-preservation espoused by "people who had had only the remotest connections with the Left who were quite as terrified as those who had been closer," and also by his fascination with guilt and social compliance.[60] He claimed that he started actively researching the Salem witch trials in the spring of 1952 after someone gave him a copy of Marion Starkey's *The Devil in Massachusetts*.[61] William Carlos Williams also cites Starkey's work, as well as a 1948 visit to the historical records in Salem and Charles Upham's *Salem Witchcraft*, as fodder for his *Tituba's Children*.[62] Starkey's book was first published in 1949 (a year after SFA performed *Salem Story* and Alexander received the Maxwell Anderson Award) and was drawn from primary sources on the witch trials, nineteenth-century historical treatments of the trials, and her background in psychology, "particularly of the Freudian school."[63] It is clear from reading Starkey's work that Miller was heavily influenced by it, and Brenda Murphy, in her chapter on *The Crucible* in *Congressional Theatre*, offers analysis of how Starkey (as well as novelist Merle Miller and writers for the *Nation* and *New Republic*) strengthened the public association of the Salem trials with the HUAC.

I have no doubt that Miller was influenced by all of these works, but I contend that another significant inspiration for Miller was the 1948 SFA performance of Alexander's *Salem Story*. Too many parallels exist between these two artists for the overlap in their plays to be mere coincidence. They were colleagues at the same publications, worked on the same radio programs, and participated in the New York City unit of SFA. One year after *Salem Story* was performed, Winifred Cushing—Mrs. Parris in the SFA production—performed in the premier production of *Death of a Salesman* as The Woman. The following year, in 1950, another *Salem Story* actor, Salem Ludwig, was cast in Miller's adaptation of *An Enemy of the People* along with fellow SFA performers and sponsors Fredric March, Florence Eldridge, Lou Gilbert, Art Smith, and Michael Strong.

The final piece of evidence I offer concerning the influence of Alexander's work on Miller is found in the very title of Miller's play. In an interview with Miller in 2000, he argues that the word "crucible" was largely absent from twentieth-century vocabulary. He states one of the reasons *The Crucible* initially failed on Broadway was because of the title: "Nobody knew what a crucible was."[64] It is quite possible that Miller's title, consciously or not, was inspired by the climax of Alexander's play, in which the character of the Prophet speaks to the townspeople, saying, "The after is shaped now: the fruit falls near the tree: Hate and you shall be hated: kill and be killed! . . . . The *crucible* is here; the mold foretells the form!"[65]

Miller admits in his autobiography that he often drew inspiration from the works of great playwrights. They were something to build from, and he wrote by "pretending that the works of Chekhov or Euripides or Ernst Toller were brand-new or not yet finished, still open to revision and improvement, trying out choices different from those their authors had made. I imagined them no longer marble masterworks but improvisations that their authors had simply given up trying to perfect."[66] Perhaps Miller viewed *Salem Story* as an improvisation Alexander gave up on and *The Crucible* as an attempt to perfect it. It is feasible Alexander gave Miller permission to use his metaphorical idea in order to "try out" different choices. Or, to accept the theory of John C. Thirlwall, editor of William Carlos Williams's plays, the "genial coincidences" between works "show . . . that alert minds and sensitive spirits are often drawn to similar subjects."[67] Alexander and Miller held similar political perspectives and operated in the same artistic and social bodies, SFA being their most obvious connective tissue. Regardless, Arthur Miller was not the first playwright to link the Salem witchcraft hysteria with the red-baiting of the HUAC. Miller, Alexander, and Williams had many compatriots on the road to Salem who appreciated the rich metaphorical potency that an especially abhorrent moment in history—this horrific usable past—held for U.S. audiences.

Unfortunately for Stage for Action, its ability to dramatize the overreach of the HUAC earned it as many enemies as it did friends. One of the group's most politically connected detractors was Walter S. Steele, longtime managing editor of the *National Republic*, who testified to the HUAC about SFA's supposed Communist affiliations and its methods of cultural persuasion in 1947. But it was more than just SFA's stage performances and training schools that endangered the group with conservatives. Founding SFA member Donna Keath was a national board member of the American Federation of Radio Artists (AFRA), and four other SFA members (Felix Knight, Paul Mann, Minerva Pious, and Ann Shepard) served as New York AFRA delegates. The connection between SFA and

AFRA is illustrative of SFA's simultaneous onstage and on-air presence. As early as 1944, Arthur Miller's *That They May Win* was performed over the air, and in 1947 congressional hearings, one of the most significant accusations against SFA was its endorsement of the application by the People's Radio Foundation (PRF, considered a Communist front) for an FM broadcasting license so that it could continue producing its plays over the airwaves. In late December 1946, SFA and the American Negro Theatre teamed up to perform several plays on-air in support of the PRF in a program titled *Adventure Radio* that was directed by Milton Robertson and included an interracial cast.

The PRF, spearheaded by attorney Joseph Brodsky and political activist Rockwell Kent, was created to produce "for the first time a radio station . . . owned and operated in the interest of the community, free from business pressures."[68] Its mission was to "offer honest labor news, promote international friendship, fight race hatred, educate the community, and offer opportunity to developing artists."[69] As these were all social issues SFA supported, it was strategically advantageous for the group, especially with a number of radio personnel already involved, to stand behind a venture with the potential to substantially broaden its audience.

The PRF collected a number of foes equal to, if not greater than, its supporters, however. In late 1946, the ultraconservative and vociferously anticommunist radio and television evangelist Reverend James Hargis spoke out against the PRF's application for an FM license specifically because it was receiving the support of SFA, which he charged was "steeped in red propaganda, taught to ridicule our religious concepts, morals, our institutions and Constitution," continuing, "It is easy to deduce the type of material which will be sent over the air waves to etherize the people into acceptance of these philosophies so that their task of destruction may be easier and more rapid."[70] Because politically questionable groups such as SFA supported the PRF, the Federal Communications Commission rejected the PRF's bid for one of the five remaining FM licenses available for labor union groups in the spring of 1947, and the PRF disbanded a year later due to attacks from both the Left and the Right.

It is plausible that Donna Keath was also responsible for bringing the early radio writer Norman Corwin into the SFA fold, as she performed in a March 7, 1944, Columbia Broadcast of Corwin's *Studio Primer* with fellow SFA performers Ralph Bell and Minerva Pious. Keath became chairman of SFA one month later and Corwin was subsequently listed as a sponsor for the SFA benefit performance in April at the Henry Hudson Hotel.

Corwin spoke at the benefit and allowed the first act of his play *Untitled* to be performed that evening. Hargis, in his 1946 report on SFA, called Corwin "a person who deserves further attention. During the recent hearings by the FCC . . . evidence was submitted to show that this same Norman Corwin (biggest individual money raiser for left front movements) would contribute to programs broadcast by the station if and when the PRF was granted a license."[71] For her work in solidifying the relationship between SFA and radio, Keath was rewarded by being named to the *Red Channels* list in 1950 and blacklisted.

In 1952 the U.S. Chamber of Commerce published a highly influential pamphlet calling for "an untrammeled investigation and prosecution of Communists, the complete exclusion of Reds and fellow travelers from all agencies and professions affecting public opinion . . . particularly those in the entertainment field."[72] The Red Scare and McCarthyism reached their apex in the early 1950s, but by then SFA was defunct. What the hearings of 1952 through 1956 achieved was to solidify SFA's stature in public discourse as a Communist front group and to assure its absence from legitimate theatre history records for over half a century. But as historian Jacqueline E. Jung asserts, "The meaning of art is necessarily determined belatedly and subject to revision as part of an ongoing historiographical process."[73] Dismissing a theatre company due to its contemporaneous political labeling is a misuse of historiographical method as well as a historical disservice. Although the availability of congressional testimony suggests that SFA did include Communist members, distance from the moment, in conjunction with a variety of archival sources, allows historians to reinterpret the group's position in the historical record.

Walter S. Steele testified that SFA, in cooperation with People's Songs and the New Theater, was "staging Communist plays in New York," citing *Waiting for Lefty*, *The Cradle Will Rock*, *The General and the Goats*, and *All Aboard* as the offending material.[74] Just to illustrate how quickly alliances turned during the Cold War, Elia Kazan, who was a guest speaker at a pro-SFA forum the year before Steele's testimony, named prominent SFA members in his HUAC hearing on April 10, 1952. Gene Frankel, executive director of SFA when the group disbanded, "never had a good thing to say about Elia because of that." Frankel left New York City for a period of time during the 1950s and headed to the Midwest "to avoid the whole blacklisting and continue directing plays."[75] Jerome Robbins, acclaimed choreographer and director best known for the original Broadway production and film of *West Side Story*, declared Edward Chodorov, the long-standing chairman of SFA's board and one of its most ardent supporters, a Communist on May 5, 1953. Robbins also called out SFA's *Satire Matinee* (a politically topical cabaret held Sunday afternoons at the Café Society and sponsored by the group) and Progressive Party supporter Jack Gilford as "red."[76] There were many more prominent theatre personnel who participated amicably with HUAC hearings. Their naming of names contributed directly to the Subversive Activities Control Board ruling that the Communist Party—as well as its members and affiliate organizations (and therefore SFA)—must register as a subversive organization. This ruling acted as a perfunctory gag order for all members and sponsors of SFA that has lasted into the twenty-first century.

But silence does not always protect. Philip Loeb—SFA performer and board member, as well as an original member of the Group Theatre—committed suicide on September 1, 1955, because of his inability to find work after being named in the *Red Channels* list and HUAC hearings. Canada Lee, a sponsor and board member named in the HUAC hearings, would die penniless and alone after being banned from forty television shows. Pert Kelton—a prominent radio and stage actress married to another SFA member, Ralph Bell—suffered her first heart attack after being named in *Red Channels*. Will Geer, also named in *Red Channels* and an original member of SFA, was called before the HUAC in 1951 and was unable to find work for over a decade. The actor Sterling Hayden named SFA sponsor Karen Morley at his hearing in 1951, though her acting career had already been demolished in 1947 for refusing to testify at her own HUAC hearing. One SFA artist after another faced blacklisting or worse. In contrast to many other SFA members, Arthur Miller rose in prominence after his HUAC hearing and his refusal to "name names," although this in no way diminishes the courage of his act.

Much has been written about the direct influence, both perceived and actual, of the Moscow-based Comintern in the day-to-day operations of CPUSA-affiliated mass organizations or front groups. Although the Comintern and high-ranking officials in the CPUSA had some influence over the daily mechanics of front group operations, the people involved with these groups rarely adhered absolutely to the party line, nor were they all dupes of a brainwashing umbrella group intent on secretly coercing people into the Communist Party or overthrowing the government. A significant number, though not all, of front group members knew that an organization was somehow connected to the CPUSA and "collaborated with the party, believing it to be the most effective ally they could find" in the political climate of the late 1930s and early 1940s.[77] Even Henry Wallace was guilty by association, but most non-CP-affiliated members of front groups, as well as rank-and-file CPUSA members, did not adhere to the unquestionably dictatorial tenets passed down from Moscow to the CPUSA. Instead, the vast majority of these people saw the progressive work many of these groups were doing and felt a compulsion to collaborate out of altruism. The intentions of many of the front groups were socially positive despite the official policies of the political party, being at their best misguided and at their worst heinous.

Of course this opinion was not shared by most people involved in prosecuting alleged Communists. In *The Techniques of Communism*, Louis Budenz, a former Communist turned FBI informant, wrote that it was not significant that the government could *prove* Communist Party membership; instead, a person's affiliation was justifiable evidence for prosecution. Budenz stated, "It is the *records* of pro-Communists in education, government, or other agencies which should be primarily considered, therefore, and not whether technically they can be proved to be Communists. If those records reveal a consistent aid to Soviet Russia, its fifth column here, and its fronts, then these individuals are enemies of the United States and should be recognized as such."[78] Budenz was suggesting that it did not matter if a person actually admitted to being a Communist; regardless of the fact that people might "plead the Fifth," their affiliations could still prove them to be one. Howard Fast, author and SFA sponsor imprisoned for contempt during his HUAC hearing, reacted strongly to Budenz and others who questioned the validity of pleading the Fifth Amendment. Fast retorts,

> The Communist who declares he is a Communist finds that his life has become both complex and dangerous. If the Communist Party member who is asked this question should invoke the Senator's [McCarthy] suggested attitude of pride and disdain, as every Communist witness in this position unfailingly has, he would not be allowed to do so under the guarantee of the Fifth Amendment; for his previous waiver of the privilege of the Fifth Amendment would destroy his subsequent use of the privilege. Therefore, his unwillingness to become a stoolpigeon, a police informer, would be rewarded with a year in prison for contempt of Congress, and fines which could be as high as $10,000.[79]

In many ways, Budenz's political stance that silence or invoking the Fifth Amendment did not absolve a Communist of his or her guilt matches the stance of many SFA members, who believed that actions—or what people do and the company they keep—speak much louder than words. As Jerry Marble in *You're Next!* protests, "The people's voice must sound louder."[80] Although SFA members were prevented, either by fears of government retaliation or by their own psychological blockades, from responding to Jerry Marble's call, there were many others during the 1950s who did. On buses and baseball fields, in schools, on streets and on stages, resounding voices sounded for free speech, equality, and change.

5. A PEOPLE'S THEATRE IN EVERY SENSE

MARXIST THEORIST GEORGI VALENTINOVICH Plekhanov argued that works of art reflect the psychology of the class or ideology the artist represents. Stage for Action reflected a post–World War II progressive ideology, inclusive of all its political and class contradictions, yet endeavored collectively for a world in which peace and equality were guiding spirits. But it was operating during the 1940s, which historian Chester Eisinger refers to as containing an inner reality of "fear, terror, uncertainty, and violence, mingled with sad satisfactions and a sense of relief at victory."[1] He concludes that "fear encouraged silence and acquiescence; it discouraged dissent. The strained inner face of the forties revealed a yearning for withdrawal from this unmanageable and hellish world."[2] SFA existed in conflict with Eisinger's appraisal of the 1940s through its open support of racial equality, position on the necessity for federally funded early childcare, demands for nationally mandated fair employment and voting practices, and call for the dissolution of the House Un-American Activities Committee. Although SFA did not witness these social changes during the 1940s, the majority of its artists and audiences experienced measurable improvement in these areas during their lives.

There remain, however, two social issues addressed in SFA performances that have yet to move any closer to resolution in U.S. culture: the destruction of all atomic weapons and the independence of Puerto Rico. The two final plays considered in this study, *Open Secret* by Robert Adler and George Bellak and *Who Are the Weavers* by Joseph Shore and Scott Graham Williamson, remain exceptions in the SFA repertory. *Open Secret* was written in response to the dropping of the bombs on Hiroshima and Nagasaki and to the reactions of atomic scientists following the war when control of atomic weapons landed in the hands of the military. It was the belief of Henry Wallace that "only the United Nations should have atomic bombs" and individual countries must be stopped from building "atomic bombs, guided missiles and military aircraft for bombing purposes."[3] Wallace made these pronouncements, along with statements critical of U.S. foreign policy, in his widely covered National Citizens Political Action Committee–sponsored speech at Madison Square Garden on September 12, 1946. This speech, considered "greatly embarrass[ing]" to the Truman administration, led directly to Wallace's dismissal from the cabinet.[4] It also resulted in a revised draft of Adler and Bellak's *Open Secret*, which had its premier performance at the Cherry Lane Theatre in December 1946.

In comparison, *Who Are the Weavers* was intended for SFA's 1949 season but ultimately was never performed by the group. The play addresses the role of the United States in eviscerating the Puerto Rican economy and advocates for the island's independence, which was a platform issue of Wallace's Progressive Party. Although this production never came to fruition because all of the SFA branches dissolved following the 1948 national election, the group continued influencing social activist performance even after its dissolution. Therefore I conclude this study by addressing SFA's legacy, including its involvement, vis-à-vis Gene Frankel and Lee Nemetz, in creating the Off-Broadway Theatre League in New York City and its role in inspiring future social activist theatre across the United States.

Open Secret

Open Secret by Robert Adler and George Bellak was based on Dr. Louis Nicot Ridenour's playlet *Pilot Lights of the Apocalypse*, originally published in *Fortune* magazine in January 1945. Interest in Ridenour's short play about the dangers of atomic warfare was plentiful during the mid-1940s. It was published in newspapers across the country, and many college and high school groups—both national and international—produced the play. Adler, in letters written to Ridenour, admitted that he and Bellak unconsciously modeled *Open Secret* after Ridenour's play and because of the similarities wished to include him as a third author on the piece. Ridenour agreed to the inclusion of his name on any publications or performances of *Open Secret* and requested one-third of any profits.

Driven by his combined knowledge of "physics, weapons and human behavior," Ridenour wrote *Pilot Lights of the Apocalypse* because he felt compelled to "do all that can decently be done to avoid an atomic-armaments race."[5] Adler and Bellak had no scientific impetus for creating *Open Secret*; however, they did share Ridenour's ethical stance regarding atomic warfare. Additionally, as members of the social activist performance group Stage for Action, which by this time was operating as the theatrical propaganda arm of the burgeoning Progressive Party, Adler and Bellak might have felt compelled to advocate the anti–atomic weapon views of their political affiliation.

Although Adler and Bellak's venture into nuclear physics may seem somewhat puzzling, Ridenour's foray into playwriting was, in many ways, a natural outgrowth of his understanding of the intersections between science, politics, and literature. For example, he reviewed George Orwell's *Animal Farm* for the *Saturday Review of Literature* in 1946, was a columnist on science- and nonscience-related items in the *Atlantic Monthly*, enjoyed a lifelong friendship with Thornton Wilder (who was his professor at the University of Chicago), and corresponded often with renowned essayist and novelist Philip Wylie. Ridenour surrounded himself with the leading scientific and literary minds of the day. His own writing of fiction—both short stories and plays—and the fact that he welcomed involvement with the publication of *Open Secret* create the characterization of a multifaceted man, passionate about learning and dedicated to educating as well as preserving humanity. Ridenour never backed away from the debate surrounding atomic weapons and publicly stated his moral stance on the relationship between science, war, and the responsibility of the scientist: "God told Moses, 'Thou shalt not kill'—not 'Thou shalt not kill with atomic energy, for that is so effective as to be sinful.'"[6]

Ridenour's public denunciation of war, inclusive of atomic weaponry, indicates the vital difference between the scientific perspective on atomic energy and the layman's stance. The vast majority of scientists involved with the discovery of nuclear fission in no way repudiated their inquiry or considered it in violation of any assumed human ethics codes. The etymology of the word "science" originates in the fourteenth-century root participle meaning "to know." The need for knowing is of course not the driving force behind all contemporary scientific discoveries, and the pursuit of knowledge is vastly different from its application. Some of the scientists who aided in the discovery of nuclear fission were practicing pure science. They never imagined its use as a global weapon. Alternatively, many of the physicists who applied their knowledge of atomic energy to developing the bomb also ascertained its potential for cancer radiation therapies. Science is arguably a-ethical. Scientists are not.

Open Secret is a play that challenges its audience to question the U.S. government's ethics, which means that even with a fictitious plot, the characters in the script required believability. In a 1946 response to Adler and Bellak's first draft (titled "Top Secret" at this point), Ridenour critiqued at length what he considered the significant flaws of the script, especially the protagonist Brigadier General Shulman, who is supposedly a celebrated atomic physicist. Ridenour wrote,

> If he [Shulman] was in fact unable to tell the difference between puzzling out a gimmick to establish projectiles in a satellite orbit and "an experiment in pure science," I would never put my dough on him to win a Nobel prize. Just at this moment, when everybody is confused about science and technology—when legislators are disposed to restrict the former because of the wartime accomplishments of the latter—it seems to me of the utmost importance to make perfectly clear the distinction between the two. Your B. G. Shulman, though he may have a degree in physics, is an engineer in the hire of the Army and nothing else. I have been that myself, and a scientist at another time, and I can assure you there is a difference. A very profound difference. For God's sake, don't mislead the public any more. They are confused enough already.[7]

Ridenour not only was concerned with Adler and Bellak's protagonist but also took great issue with their description of the atomic defense underground chamber setting and its employees. Ridenour argued their laboratory seemed "the slap-happy pinochle-playing repository of the entire atomic defense of the United States. Now it is well known that I don't have much respect for the military or for the political mind, but I can scarcely bring myself to believe that either soldiers or politicians would behave with the great ineptitude that you imply."[8] Dr. Ridenour's concerns about the inaccuracies of the original version of *Open Secret* were based on his prolific technical and academic knowledge. Ridenour was an expert on atomic weaponry, war weapons in general, and the academic fields of physics and chemistry. A letter from J. R. Oppenheimer in May 1943 stated that although Ridenour would be invaluable to the Los Alamos Project, he was irreplaceable as the assistant director of the radiation laboratory at MIT.[9] His group at MIT developed the XT-1, the automatic tracking radar that served as the developmental prototype for the SCR-584, which was a radar-guided antiaircraft system. During 1944 he served in Europe as chief radar adviser to General Carl Spaatz, who then commanded the U.S. Strategic Air Forces.

In a letter to Ridenour dated April 5, 1946, Adler described the similarities and differences between *Open Secret* and *Pilot Lights of the Apocalypse*. He concluded this letter by noting that he and Bellak were "not equipped, however, to bring to our script the authority and the technical-knowhow which so definitely glows through yours."[10] Upon receiving Ridenour's criticism of the original draft, Adler and Bellak revised the piece significantly. The new character of Shulman, they wrote to Ridenour, "although he is symbolic of the dialectic growth of science, is as a character, merely an engineer in the hire of the Army."[11] The changes made in the script were substantial enough to satisfy Ridenour. He agreed to his name being included in all future publications of the script, such as in Margaret Mayorga's *Best One-Act Plays, 1946–1947* and those published by Samuel French in 1948. Additionally, it was Ridenour's widow, Gretchen, who renewed the copyright license on the play in 1974.[12]

The setting of *Open Secret* is an underground chamber in the U.S. Atomic Control Center. The piece opens with a presentational prologue in which the protagonist sets up the scenario. The audience members therefore become students in General Shulman's nuclear physics course, and he explains during his direct address why this will be their final class together:

> I imagine that most of you know that I have been engaged on experiments dealing with latest devices employing fast chain reactions [*He smiles a bit.*] what our less scientific friends call atomic bombs. I presume also that since most of you are fairly intelligent, you have been following the controversy concerning international control of atomic energy. There is no need to tell you what my position has been on this matter ... Because I have maintained that our sole possession of a huge stock pile of atomic bombs constituted a threat to world peace, because I believed that powerful elements in this country were waving an atomic club over the rest of the world, because I wrote and published numerous articles arguing that a policy of atomic secrecy was impossible, and if pursued would lead inevitably toward this country's becoming the focal point of world hatred and suspicion, I have been called less polite names than traitor in the columns of the national press ... Still, I am a scientist, and an American citizen. This is the last class I will teach because I have just been appointed a Brigadier-General in the United States Army. As technical supervisor I will work with the atomic control team. .... So, I can think of nothing else to say except to wish you luck in your future work and

to caution you to remember that science is not only an exciting study, a fascinating chase; it is also a sacred trust that each true scientist holds for all humanity. . . . Good-by.[13]

And so it is in the very opening soliloquy of the play that Ridenour's stance regarding the ethical responsibility of scientists emerges. *Open Secret* highlights the fundamental shift in civilian scientists' roles and the usurpation of dominance by applied science during the atomic age. The civilian scientists involved with the Manhattan Project, the Metallurgical Laboratory at the University of Chicago, and the Los Alamos facility caught U.S. physicists in a new contextual net, which has yet to be undone: the direct association of science with military operations. It became evident during the developmental phase of the atomic bomb that scientists could no longer "leave the unpleasantness of war to the soldiers."[14] Scientists now had "a special responsibility in helping resolve the problems posed by the new weaponry. . . . Physics—and science more generally—which heretofore in their lives as practitioners had been an *end*, was being transformed into a *means* for the state."[15] So necessarily the question (controversy, as General Shulman calls it) of who held authority over nuclear energy was at the forefront of many minds—scientific and not—during the late 1940s. Percy Bridgman, Harvard physicist and Nobel Prize winner, in December 1946 observed flatly, "If society would only abolish war, 99 percent of the control of scientific discoveries would vanish."[16] When the United States became the first country to successfully develop a nuclear weapon, it sparked an international race to harness the power of nuclear energy and create more nuclear weapons. *Open Secret* dramatizes the possibilities of global nuclear war and plays on the fears of citizens living in a postatomic world, but it also spotlights the conflicting realities of ethical science and patent law.

Louis Ridenour's involvement with *Open Secret* grants the play an authoritative voice that other fictionalized literary works debating atomic weapons control could not boast of. Perhaps Ridenour's participation in the creation of *Open Secret* was inspired in part by the disappointing limitations set by the Atomic Energy Act of 1946. The act established the Atomic Energy Commission (AEC) as well as the eighteen-member Senate and House Joint Committee on Atomic Energy, which (to American physicists' alarm) gave the government direct control over all fissionable material. It also condoned the confiscation of the ores as well as the actual land of private citizens if the AEC found that the property in question might result in the production of fissionable material. Likewise, the act clearly states that any public lands found to contain materials "peculiarly essential to the production of fissionable material . . . are hereby reserved for the use of the United States."[17] The Atomic Energy Act of 1946 directly challenged Ridenour's ethical objections to nuclear weapons, authorizing the commission to "conduct experiments and do research and development work in the military application of atomic energy; and engage in the production of atomic bombs, atomic bomb parts, or other military weapons utilizing fissionable materials."[18] The act established the punishments of "death or imprisonment for life" for those found guilty of conspiring with another nation regarding atomic energy with the "intent to injure the United States" and lesser punishments of fines and jail time for sabotage or espionage without the intent to injure the United States. A person could not be hired to work with the AEC or fissionable materials until the FBI investigated his or her "character, associations, and loyalty."[19] Although the stated intention of the Atomic Energy Act of 1946 was the "development and control of atomic energy," development of atomic *weapons* was plainly the focus of the act. Passage of the act granted the U.S. government and military complete authority over any mandates or decisions regarding this power.[20]

These decisions were in total opposition to the declaration made only a year earlier by the Federation of Atomic Scientists, which was supported by Henry Wallace. The federation called for education of every citizen "to the realization that 1) there can be no secret; 2) there can be no defense; and 3) there must be world control."[21] The scientists' objectives were to edify "civilian ignorance, and to modify the attitude of military authorities" in particular, in order to loosen the closeness with which the army had held the power of decision over the atomic potential of the United States, not only during but since the end of hostilities.[22] In the *Bulletin of the Atomic Scientists of Chicago*, to which Ridenour was also a contributing writer, the scientists called for "an enlightened bill," one "looking forward to international cooperation and peaceful development of atomic energy."[23] Sensing that the declarations made by the Federation of Atomic Scientists were not being acknowledged, Ridenour contributed a chapter (along with Albert Einstein, J. R. Oppenheimer, Leo Szilard, and many other prominent physicists) to a work titled *One World or None* commissioned by the federation and published in March 1946. In the end the federation's fears were justified as the Atomic Energy Act, signed into law by President Truman on August 1, 1946, reconstituted the power of the government in controlling atomic energy, keeping its dangers secret from the American public, focusing research on the production of atomic weaponry, and obliterating any possibility of international cooperation in its development (thereby exacerbating the tense relationship between the United States and the Soviet Union). Ridenour and his *One World or None* colleagues were not quelled by the congressional argument that a respected scientist would be assigned to the AEC. Regarding this decision, scientists remarked, "To the military mind, one scientist may be as good as another; if one leaves he can be replaced by another one. This is the spirit in which Hitler let the best German scientists leave the country. He thought that he could find adequate replacement among servile nonentities with party membership cards."[24]

The Federation of Atomic Scientists feared that rising tension with the Soviet Union would taint congressional views on atomic energy. In what became a prophetic questioning of U.S. governance, the scientists demanded, "Will the Congress, in despair over the momentary—and perhaps passing—international troubles, enact legislation which will create, in the tissue of our public life, a malignant tumor of irresponsible military rule; which will stifle science in the name of a futile 'security,' create a 'Maginot line' of a stock of atomic bombs, and start the whole world on the road to disaster?"[25] Although the federation achieved one of its goals, which was removing the power of atomic energy development directly from the hands of the military, the remainder of its concerns continued. In light of these controversies, Ridenour's involvement with *Open Secret* was in concert with his mission to educate the public about the dangers of atomic weapons in as many ways as possible.

Open Secret debuted under the auspices of Stage for Action on December 8, 1946, at the Cherry Lane Theatre in New York City. The cast included Nick Persoff, Richard Robbins, Salem Ludwig, Antoinette Kray, Lee Payant, Sy Travers, and Lee Nemetz with direction by John O'Shaughnessy.[26] The play reads as one of the more technically demanding performances by SFA, requiring significant light cues and a large rotating wall complete with "switches for launching and controlling atomic projectiles . . . three built-in radar screens and photographic devices. The remainder of the rear wall . . . is one huge light panel. The indicators on the panel are grouped in series of threes, labeled with the names of the major cities of the world, and subdivided into columns by nationality."[27] The set designer for the original production was Aaron Ehrlich. Ehrlich did not have a long career in theatre, leaving the stage to become a respected graphic artist and photographer before entering into nightly news production and then advertising. He eventually began working with the highly esteemed advertising agency DDB in New York City and produced the infamous

"Daisy" commercial for the 1964 Lyndon Johnson presidential campaign. It is perhaps ironic that Ehrlich, once employed as the designer of a play addressing the horrors of atomic weapons, would eventually oversee production of an iconic commercial ending in an atomic mushroom cloud.

In *Open Secret*, the United States' atomic warheads are all in orbit and controlled by one military commander in a centralized top-secret location. The commander, Major General Harris, has power over 2,700 orbiting missiles with one lone political scientist, Professor Cornel Lowery, as his adviser. Brigadier General Shulman informs the secretary of war that "the bombs will act as planets as long as our equipment controls them. There is no time limit. When desired, we can create an increase in gravitational pull on any individual bomb. That is, we can draw it from its orbit and direct its plunge to a specific point on the surface of the earth or any of the bodies of water."[28] Shulman bemoans throughout the play that what he has created for the military is "a terrible weapon" and a "perfect engine of destruction" with "no room for mistakes."[29] He offers the lone voice of reason in the command station but is outranked by both Major General Harris and the secretary of war. The play quickly reaches its climax when satellite images show that instead of 2,700 missiles orbiting the earth, there are 4,841, meaning that the United States is no longer alone in its top-secret mission.

Open Secret comes to its nihilistic close when one of the lights on the control board shows that San Francisco has been attacked. In a knee-jerk reaction, Major General Harris launches a missile at and destroys Moscow. Moscow quickly retaliates and destroys Madrid, which in turn hits Paris, which in a matter of seconds wipes out Buenos Aires. A few moments later the characters learn that it was a massive earthquake and not an atomic warhead that destroyed San Francisco. As the members of the underground control chamber attempt to rectify the situation by having the president announce in an international wire, "There is no war," U.S. cities come under attack one by one. Philadelphia, New York, Boston, New Orleans, Newark, St. Paul, Minneapolis, Shreveport, Seattle, Pittsburgh, and Washington, D.C., are all flattened before Major General Harris wires the order that "the United States will destroy all atom bombs and stock piles immediately." But it is too late. In the control bunker the lights go out, sirens scream, and the control equipment crashes down. Harris screams in futility, "But it was a mistake. Tell them it was a mistake. THERE IS NO WAR!" The final stage directions read, "In the darkness, only the red light can be seen going on and off. As the terrible sound of destruction rises, that, too, is extinguished. And now, as the sound fades to an eternity of silence . . ."[30]

The closing moments of *Open Secret* may read as hyperbolized, but when compared to the reports of physicists who visited Japan immediately following the bomb, the projected sense of desperation is chillingly accurate. Philip Morrison, involved with the Manhattan Project and Los Alamos, was one of the scientists reporting back about the impact of the atomic bomb in Hiroshima. In his chapter titled "If the Bomb Gets Out of Hand," Morrison describes Hiroshima's aftermath and the terror facing Japanese civilians. Then in a method not unlike in *Open Secret*, Morrison creatively projects the impact of an atomic bomb were it dropped on Manhattan, describing the destruction.[31] The majority of Morrison's narrative is dedicated to painstakingly detailing the human pain and devastation faced by New Yorkers. Morrison writes,

> From the river west to Seventh Avenue, and from south of Union Square to the middle thirties, the streets were filled with the dead and dying. The old men sitting on the park benches in the square never knew what had happened. They were chiefly charred black on the side toward the bomb. . . .
>
> The most tragic of all the stories of the disaster is that of the radiation casualties. . . . The people around them had never gotten away, but they had crawled, injured but alive, from the wreckage of homes or shops, from the elevated platforms, or from cellar stairways. . . . They were all lucky, as they said. . . . But they all died. . . . They died of unstoppable internal hemorrhages, of wildfire infections, of slow oozing of the blood into the flesh. Nothing seemed to help them much, and the end was neither slow nor very fast, but sure.[32]

Morrison's narrative is a casuist one, to be sure, in order to elicit an empathetic response from his readers. *Open Secret* is also intentionally exaggerated, yet based on the realities of Hiroshima and Nagasaki, the frenzied sensibilities of the postwar United States, and the overarching question of who or what entity had the ability to control atomic energy, it is easy to recognize why this heightened style was employed. There existed a necessity for an apocalyptic ending to the play because it was impossible for scientists to overstate the global ramifications of atomic weapons.

SFA's performance of *Open Secret* did not lead to the eradication of atomic weapons in the United States; however, two years after its premiere, and in the wake of the Truman Loyalty Oath of 1947, whereupon all civilian government employees underwent an extensive investigation by the government and those found "disloyal" were dismissed, eight scientists sent a telegram to the president protesting the loyalty oath and the procedures of the HUAC, suggesting they were depleting the atomic energy laboratories of "highly capable scientists and engineers."[33] The telegram was eventually reprinted in the *Bulletin of the Atomic Scientists* and points directly to the unexpected negative impact of government and military control over scientific experimentation, namely that the HUAC "is creating an atmosphere that makes men shun government work, thereby threatening us all."[34] *Open Secret* might have been a play about the dangers of atomic weapons and what happens when these weapons are placed under the complete control of people who do not understand their potentially devastating global impact, but it was also a part of a much larger conversation regarding the consequences in scientific and social development of demanding unquestionable loyalty to the U.S. government. This "loyalty" was subterfuge for a government-prescribed conformity resulting in the "uncritical and unquestioning acceptance of America as it is—the political institutions, the social relationships, the economic practices."[35] This unquestioning acceptance of life "as it is," of the United States "as a finished product, perfect and complete," was exactly what the artists of SFA spent five years pushing back against with their performances—and what many social activist theatre artists attempt through their work today.[36]

Who Are the Weavers

The expectation of conformity and acquiescence to political and economic conditions prescribed by the government extended to the U.S. citizens living in noncontinental geographies as well. In the unpublished collection of Stage for Action plays housed in the New York Performing Arts Library, editor Joseph Lieberman introduces *Who Are the Weavers* by Joseph Shore and Scott Graham Williamson as a play depicting "Americans who do not realize how cruelly poverty steps on our fellow-Americans of Puerto Rico."[37] Unlike the majority of SFA's performances, *Who Are the Weavers* enjoyed both a professional production and publication prior to the organization's inclusion of it in the repertory. *Who Are the Weavers* was first produced at Erwin Piscator's Dramatic Workshop, which originated as an educational unit of the New School for Social Research operating from 1940 to 1950. SFA shared a variety of connections with the Dramatic Workshop, including performers, playwrights, and directors, but perhaps the most significant tether between the two groups and *Who Are the Weavers* was that Joseph Shore produced his first play, *The Soldier Who Became a Great Dane*, with SFA.

Those versed in Piscator's work in Europe or the United States recognize how a play dealing with colonialism or imperialism easily found a place in the Dramatic Workshop's season. But SFA produced work only with actionable political outcomes, which means understanding its intentions for the play demands a more nuanced analysis of the cultural moment. Fully engaging the implications of *Who Are the Weavers* warrants an investigation into the social issues facing Puerto Ricans both on the island and on the continent due directly to U.S. congressional legislation. SFA intended to produce the play in order to underscore—just as its very first production, Arthur Miller's *That They May Win*, did—that change could happen only through democratic participation and voting.

Who Are the Weavers is set in a Puerto Rican shack that "has been made up of scrap lumber boards of various sizes."[38] It is the one-room home of José Ramirez and his family, consisting of his wife; twelve-year-old daughter, Mercedes; and ten-year-old son, Pepito. During the action of the play the audience learns that three additional children were born to the family, all dying in their youth from starvation-based illnesses. José is a jibaro, a word referring to the indigenous peoples of the interior mountain regions of Puerto Rico who primarily earn their living as sugar farmers. In the 1940s, more than 300,000 of the island's 1,000,000 arable acres were dedicated to sugar harvesting, which provided only a few months of employment annually.[39] José's income for an entire season of sugar cane harvesting is $75. In comparison, the average U.S. family's income during this same period was $4,237 with a median income of $3,216.[40] Surrounding the Ramirez's tiny hovel is an abundance of flamboyant trees with their scarlet blossoms and large fern-like leaves. The lush vegetation encircling the destitute family provides a potent visual metaphor for the duality of the country, rich in natural resources yet economically impoverished due in no small part to decisions made by U.S. legislation regarding prescribed overspecialization of crops, sugar quotas, rationing, and shipping embargoes enforced during the late 1930s and through the war years.

Señora Ramirez, in Spanish, speaks the first lines of the play, encouraging Pepito to eat the few pieces of steaming meat she has pulled out of a pot on their small charcoal stove. When her daughter, Mercedes, is also offered a plate of food, the girl begins wailing and refuses to eat. This outburst confuses her brother and enrages her father, but the arrival of two U.S. soldiers at the door cuts the argument short as the family frantically attempts to hide the meat and cover up its scent. Meat was highly rationed on the continent during the war and remained quite expensive—an occasional luxury—for the average U.S. citizen in the immediate postwar period. In Puerto Rico, meat was unattainable for most jibaro families during and after the war. The soldiers, or Los Americanos as the family refers to them, are Major Bierman (an army physician) and Technical Sergeant Whitey Martin (Bierman's assistant). They are making rounds in the village to check on the health of the children. Bierman, who has spent significant time in Puerto Rico, is clearly liked by the children and respected by their parents, while Whitey is a newcomer and is initially characterized as culturally ignorant and, by the end of the play, xenophobic.

Bierman concludes his medical examination of Pepito, who is suffering from stomach pains, stating: "Everything seems to be in order. Stomach a bit distended, and definite vitamin deficiency. Nothing that an adequate diet couldn't fix. [. . .] The boy is perfectly healthy. He just needs milk, fresh vegetables . . ."[41] The major's voice trails off, knowing that his prescription is impossible for the family to attain. He finishes his diagnosis sighing and speaking softly the lines, "He needs food. Just more to eat—that's all." José Ramirez responds with the proverbial Puerto Rican catchall, "*Ay bendito,* that's all . . ."[42] *Bendito* translates in English to "blessed," but this is a facile translation lacking the expansiveness of the phrase. *Ay bendito* is so potently complex that is has the simultaneous ability to conceal as much as it reveals. The phrase relies on mood and context for its meaning, which can range from compassion to anger to abject despair. The entire politics of *Who Are the Weavers* is located in José's utterance of this line, and whether it reveals sympathy, defeatism, fury, or even vindictiveness encapsulates the relationship between U.S. citizens born and living in Puerto Rico and those residing on the continent.

In Margaret Mayorga's publication of the play, it states that Robert Eley directed Frank Argento as José Ramirez in the Dramatic Workshop production; however, Dramatic Workshop archival records suggest that Castro A. Noste of 491 Sixth Avenue in New York City originated the role.[43] The casting discrepancies between the two scripts and contact addresses indicated in Piscator's records are significant, suggesting that Noste may have been a recent immigrant to the country (probably of Cuban heritage). I suggest Noste's recent immigrant status because while the remainder of the Dramatic Workshop actors lived in apartments across the city and listed contact phone numbers, Noste shared the same address as the New School for Social Research and had no available telephone number. Perhaps Noste, as an original member of the Dramatic Workshop cast, was able to share details regarding the lives of native Cubans as well as a half century of intense North American political and economic influence on the country. Although the historical relationship between the United States and Cuba differs from that between the United States and Puerto Rico, one need only reflect on the early twentieth-century quote "Behold the fair Isle of Cuba lying at the feet of the continent, awaiting only the magic touch of capital and enterprise to develop into its true and rightful position as the sugarbowl of the western hemisphere" to ascertain our colonial impulse regarding this island neighbor as well.[44] By the 1930s, U.S. economic influence over the sugar industry of Cuba was so severe that an analyst for the Brookings Institute noted it had "reduced rural Cuba to a condition bordering on serfdom."[45] Cuba—especially eastern Cuba, where Santiago and Guantánamo are located—faced a de facto occupation comparable to Puerto Rico's due to U.S. economic control of the sugar and coffee industries (the two most abundant Cuban crops in the 1940s). The majority of North American capitalists considered the two islands analogous from both economic and cultural perspectives, relying on them for cheap natural resources and strategic military positions resulting in less-than-equitable relationships unquestionably benefiting U.S. interests.

In a conflated era still complicit in racist casting processes but simultaneously haltingly opening the door to notions of color-blind casting, perhaps the innovative Piscator felt that Castro Noste was able to bring some agency or legitimacy to the production. Regardless, he is one of only two cast members with recognizably Latino surnames in either the Mayorga or Piscator casts (Aña Rios played Mercedes, according to the Mayorga publication), which is wholly unfortunate in a production set in an indigenous area of Puerto Rico and necessitating an acting ensemble of at least six inhabitants of this geographical area.

The politics of casting aside, Puerto Rican culture and identity was of growing concern to New York City residents. Although the majority of the cast and crew most likely had very little firsthand understanding of the lives of jibaros, what they assumedly did have intimate knowledge of was a small area of East Harlem recognized by outsiders as Spanish Harlem and known to the residents of the neighborhood, primarily Puerto Rican émigrés, as El Barrio. Historian Gerald Meyer describes some of the responses to El Barrio by nonresidents: "The xenophobic reaction was intense. Puerto Ricans became objects of extreme vilification in the press and they experienced general discrimination. This xenophobia reinforced many Puerto Rican's [sic] view that their stay in New York City was temporary and discouraged their acculturation."[46] The "Puerto Rican problem," as many anti-immigrationists termed the influx of U.S. citizens from the island to the continent following the war, quickly became a rallying point for Progressives in New York City who asked, "In these days, when brotherhood is being recommended and discrimination condemned, why are some people attacking the Puerto Ricans as interlopers and regarding them as less good citizens of the United States?"[47]

The U.S. government's political, economic, and social policies regarding Puerto Rico during its fifty years of colonial rule form the roots of the debate surrounding treatment of Puerto Ricans in New York City. Writing in 2007, Cesar Ayala and Rafael Bernabe astutely argue that neither participation in several growth periods of world capitalist economy nor its unique relationship with the United States "allowed Puerto Rico to escape a condition of extreme dependence on foreign direct involvements or its status as a relatively impoverished region under U.S. rule. . . . Puerto Rico's continued precarious economic and worsening social and ecological situation, secularly high unemployment rates, and lack of organic linkage between industry and agriculture are the result of this long colonial experiment in 'free trade' as a recipe for development."[48] During the 1940s, the economic issues facing Puerto Ricans on the island were championed by progressive New York City political leader Vito Marcantonio. What encouraged the Dramatic Workshop ensemble to produce *Who Are the Weavers* were the social debates surrounding the influx of Puerto Rican residents to New York City and its dramaturgical updating of Gerhart Hauptmann's *The Weavers*, including a trenchant criticism of capitalism and colonialism. However, what indisputably drew SFA to the play was the immediate potential impact the piece had on Puerto Rican rights in El Barrio and how this could turn into votes for the pro–Puerto Rican independence congressional candidate, Marcantonio.

Vito Marcantonio was the radical seven-term congressman of the Eighteenth District in New York City, which included "enormous economic and social contrasts to be found within its confines," from the tenement housing of East Harlem to the upper-class apartments on the East River.[49] His final congressional term occurred with the now-infamous Eightieth Congress, which came to power on January 4, 1947. Marcantonio was the sole American Labor Party member in a Republican- and southern Democrat–controlled Congress that set to work with all deliberate speed in "roll[ing] back or contain[ing] the progressive accomplishments of the New Deal era."[50] Marcantonio found himself in a constant—and quite often solitary—uphill battle to strengthen workers' rights and achieve some level of equality for minorities in the conservative climate of the early Cold War. Called by journalist Sidney Shalett "a screaming, snapping, effective tireless fighter for the man of the streets of East Harlem," Marcantonio battled relentlessly for the rights of Puerto Ricans in El Barrio and on the island, stating it was his "desire as a progressive to defend the most exploited victims of a most devastating imperialism."[51]

Vito Marcantonio was a sponsor of SFA during its five-year existence, and they shared a passion for achieving equality for all U.S. citizens, regardless of geographical status. He advocated anti–poll tax legislation, desegregation of the federal government, antilynch laws, the use of federal power to assure all people constitutional rights, and independence for Puerto Rico.[52] Prior to 1948, the only one of these social issues SFA had not addressed in its productions was the status and relationship of Puerto Rico to the continental United States. What encouraged SFA to finally produce a play about Puerto Rico was Marcantonio's relationship with Henry Wallace and the Progressive Party. Marcantonio campaigned for Wallace's presidential bid and was vocal at meetings in which the Progressive Party platform was debated and drafted. In the summer of 1948, at the national convention in Philadelphia, the right of independence for Puerto Rico and self-determination for all colonial areas of the United States found its way onto the Progressive Party's platform.

Ultimately, of course, independence for Puerto Rico did not occur. Post-1948 Puerto Rico "abandoned the vision of a planned, increasingly independent economy as counterpart to the New Deal in the United States and embraced the notion of industrialization driven by U.S. direct investments."[53] The final moments of *Who Are the Weavers* highlight the increase in Puerto Rican dependency on the United States as well as simultaneously animate the unbridled xenophobia on the continent. As the major and Whitey leave the Ramirez house, Mercedes runs after them and asks Major Bierman if it would be possible for him to provide them with another dog. The major is stunned as he realizes the meat he smelled cooking in the Ramirez household was that of their family pet. Whitey is disgusted and responds, "Eating dog meat? Why, them dirty greasers! Eating their own pooch! That's the lowest thing I ever heard! I said, every time you treat them like equals, they'll turn right around and show the stuff they're really made of. What're you going to do, Doc?" To which Major Bierman responds, "I'll try to get them another dog."[54]

This exchange between Major Bierman and Whitey epitomizes the dialectical debate surrounding Puerto Rico in the United States with Bierman sounding much like Henry Wallace and Vito Marcantonio. Wallace was soundly defeated in the 1948 election, and he, as well as other radical outspoken leftists during the immediate postwar period such as Marcantonio, quickly became a political pariah. SFA was collateral damage in the Cold War, and *Who Are the Weavers* has since faded into theatrical obscurity. But this brief episode in theatre history illustrates the interconnectedness of social activist performance and human rights. Puerto Rico's struggle for socially progressive independence was not fought solely on the island, nor is *Who Are the Weavers* relevant to Puerto Rico alone. Instead it is this play, as well as the majority of SFA productions, that emphasizes the interdependent aspects of radical acts engaging anticapitalist social and political transformation. In the words of historian Henry Farnum May, "It is the radicals who insist, from time to time, on asking the necessary but awkward questions and dragging the skeletons from the darkest closets. . . . Radicals alone can be counted on to stand by their own clear, if partial insights, to keep unpopular causes alive."[55] *Who Are the Weavers* did not achieve independence for Puerto Rico, but it did raise vital questions about U.S. involvement in Puerto Rican economics and threw the closet door wide open on larger concerns such as defending the victims of unchecked capitalism and colonialism in contemporary society. Like Vito Marcantonio, the play voted its conscience, and it was a conscience of radicalism in the face of great adversity.

Informers and Victims

It remains perplexing that SFA continued for as long as it did given Walter S. Steele's damning testimony before the HUAC on July 21, 1947, regarding its suspected Communist activities. Despite protests by prominent politicians, scientists, and performing artists, the HUAC hearings lasted until 1957, and during the decade of 1946 to 1956 informants "named" 40 percent of Stage for Action membership as Communists or subversives. Many SFA members were also called to testify before the congressional hearings, including Gertrude Berg, Canada Lee, Philip Loeb, Arthur Miller, Jean Muir, Jerome Robbins, and Paul Robeson. Some confirmed membership in SFA while others did not. Some of the members implicated in the hearings reestablished their careers, but many more did not.

Arthur Miller, writing in 1969 about Soviet writers who thrived during Stalin's regime (and perhaps about U.S. Communist and Communist-sympathizing writers as well), argued that a person trying to defend his or her past actions is "like a man trying to explain how he fell in love with a perfect woman who turned out to be murderous, vain, even insane, and cared nothing for him, a woman to whom he had dedicated his works, his life, and his highest idealistic feelings. How can you explain that, when the truth is now so obvious to your listener?"[56] Miller, like many writers attempting to explain, or apologize for, their support of the Soviets under Stalin, understood that hindsight is unforgiving when the devastation wrought is so immeasurable.

Another example of an artist attempting to defend his activist past is found in the person of Burl Ives. Ives, who performed in SFA's *Headline Cabaret*, is best known for his turn as Big Daddy in Tennessee Williams's *Cat on a Hot Tin Roof* (both on Broadway and in film). He voluntarily testified before the Senate Internal Security Subcommittee on May 20, 1952, denied having any connection to Stage for Action, and willingly named names in the hearing. Prior to his hearing, Ives stated that his participation in organizations later deemed subversive usually were for the benefit of "feed[ing], cloth[ing], or help[ing] someone."[57] Ives's statement aligns with the vast majority of artists who dedicated themselves to causes they felt were socially relevant regardless of their political affiliations. Historian Richard H. Pells suggests that members of the entertainment, state department, and scientific communities accused of Communist ties from 1947 to 1955 were often devastatingly lonely because they lacked any support or encouragement from the various institutions or guilds to which they belonged. Faced with economic, professional, and familial destruction, each defendant

> had to make that choice alone. . . . Given these lonely circumstances, the "friendly" witness should not be too facilely judged or condemned. . . . No one knows in advance how he will act when his work, his family, his future are at stake. Until we ourselves have passed the test more nobly than our predecessors, we ought to have compassion for both the informers and the victims.[58]

Historian Richard Hofstadter suggested in 1964, with many others supporting his argument since, that it is the government and not the informers or victims that should be admonished for the mistreatment of Communists and fellow travelers during the 1940s and 1950s. Hofstadter refers to the McCarthy period (and many other moments in U.S. history) as representative of the "Paranoid Style" in American politics. The psychological fear (what Hofstadter refers to as paranoia)—bordering on hysteria—permeating the nation during the late 1940s into the 1950s was played upon by politicians and encouraged a national policy of containment.[59] In many cases, this McCarthy-period paranoia stayed with people their entire lives. Personal interviews with Stage for Action artists exemplify the full range of reactions to the 1940s and reveal how SFA was involved in the political paranoia of the moment: Marvin Silbersher stated "political affiliation did not appeal to him" and that he was "somewhat annoyed by the political overtones" of the group. Bunny Kacher of the Chicago branch was open about her three-year involvement with SFA and plainly stated that the reason the group disbanded was "because of the red labeling."[60] Charles Polacheck reveled in sharing stories about directing opera on television but grew hesitant when speaking about his involvement as a playwright and performer with SFA, stating his concern for family and reputation. Perry Miller Adato, a glorious storyteller with the energy of a teenager, offered many details about the inspiration for founding Stage for Action as well as about the joys and stresses that came with running the group during its first two years; however, she failed to make any mention of the fact that she was named in a congressional hearing for her participation with SFA and the School for Political Action Techniques. Finally Marcia Haufrecht, daughter of Herbert Haufrecht, who composed the music for SFA's production of Sidney Alexander's *Salem Story*, stated that her father was "very political, very politically active" and "busy saving the world." Due directly to this political activism, "the FBI was coming to the door to talk to us."[61] Polacheck and Miller Adato were perhaps right to selectively edit their pasts in order to protect their families, because as Marcia Haufrecht admitted, being the child of an openly political artist during the Cold War meant always feeling "like an outsider."[62]

The collapse of any organization naturally calls its mission into question. The dramatic events of the HUAC hearings and the aftermath of the blacklisting have reframed the theatrical history of the 1940s around the stories of individual artists penalized for their beliefs. While it is easy to draw a correlation between the destruction of a single career and events such as the HUAC hearings, it is less simple to understand why an entire organization failed. Some of the reasons are obvious. The political climate of the 1950s discouraged individuals from claiming membership in SFA. The 1956 revelations concerning Stalin's genocides and crimes against humanity tainted the philosophies so many SFA members had embraced only one decade earlier. A lack of clear infrastructure within SFA meant that, despite its successes and rapid expansion from 1946 to 1948, it could not meet these rising external threats with a unified response.

While the original SFA form did not outlast the HUAC, a considerable number of its members found a way to translate the ideas and ideology of the group into their future work. Some studies submit that political and social activist performance focused on domestic issues was no longer fashionable or even possible in the Cold War climate, while others imply it never escaped the 1930s. Colette Hyman in her history of labor union theatre during the 1930s, *Staging Strikes: Workers' Theatre and the American Labor Movement*, suggests that "World War II shifted union leaders' attention away from domestic and internal union politics toward events abroad. . . . Eventually theatre would disappear from the agenda of union cultural and educational directors altogether."[63] In his conclusion of *Drama Was a Weapon: The Left-Wing Theatre in New York, 1929–1941*, Morgan Himelstein argues, "After [John Howard] Lawson's *Marching Song* in 1937, the story of the left-wing stage was anticlimactic. The new theatre movement was dying. Although plays of social significance were still written and produced, the playwrights' urge to protest and the spectator's desire to listen grew weaker as the nation grew stronger."[64] These statements represent a select few of more than forty years of scholarship establishing and reifying an absence of social activist theatre in the United States during the 1940s as well as the collapse of radicalism during the Cold War. Often dated as beginning with Winston Churchill's "Iron Curtain" speech on March 5, 1946, in Fulton, Missouri, the Cold War permeates Christopher Bigsby's analysis of Arthur Miller in *Modern American Drama, 1945–2000*. Bigsby identifies the "sense of alienation" invading U.S. culture and states that "the wider context for the political mood of the fifties was the collapse of a particular form of radical-liberal faith."[65] Bigsby continues by quoting Miller, who felt in 1953 "more and more frighteningly isolated, in life as in the theatre," suggesting that even playwrights directly involved with SFA felt that the Cold War period was bereft of the communal spirit experienced in previous decades.[66]

But we should be cautious when asserting that the isolation felt by many in the 1950s extends far back into the 1940s, as these assertions are at odds with the quantity of plays written and produced by SFA artists regarding domestic social problems and contradict the hundreds of thousands of audience members whom Marvin Silbersher recalls as "enthusiastic;" forming a "cross section" of humanity and "coming in from everywhere."[67] The social activist theatre of the 1930s, reinvented for 1940s audiences by SFA artists, was far from over when Miller began his commercial theatrical ascent and certainly not deceased when *The Crucible* premiered on Broadway in 1953. Many connections linked SFA writers, performers, and directors and the social activist plays featured off-Broadway during the early 1950s. The government also shut some of these early theatre outfits down, but often a company targeted by the HUAC would simply incorporate under a different name and relocate with the core people involved and the mission of the company essentially the same. This was especially true for theatre companies and artists interested in producing work about race relations. There exists a long list of companies from the late 1940s and early 1950s who shared similar casts and directors producing works about race and racism in the United States. By tinkering with the dominant narrative of the 1950s off-Broadway theatre movement, we may begin to understand the vast web of people excluded from, or overshadowed by others, in this history. Three of these many names are Robert Steck, Gene Frankel, and Lee Nemetz. Their theatre work during the 1950s is intimately linked to the birth of off-Broadway and the lasting legacy of Stage for Action.

People's Drama Inc.

Gene Frankel became acting executive director of SFA on February 18, 1947, and remained executive director until the New York group's disbanding. In the spring of 1948 he directed a benefit performance by SFA of Sidney Alexander's *Salem Story* in support of Sydenham Hospital, which was New York City's only interracial hospital at the time, providing medical services to much of Harlem (see chapter 4). By the spring of 1949, with the New York branch of SFA having dissolved, many of its members were involved with a group called People's Drama Inc., an off-Broadway theatre company described in newspapers as both an "interracial theatrical group" and "an experimental-theatre group."[68] Lee Nemetz, a performer with Stage for Action (along with his wife, Shirley Norris), was the second artistic director of People's Drama Inc., and Gene Frankel directed several of that group's productions: a revival of John Wexley's *They Shall Not Die* premiering in June 1949 (and performed for the next six months in the New York metropolitan region), Theodore Ward's *John Brown* (which ran during the summer of 1950), and Paul Peters's *Nat Turner* (running from November 1950 through May 1951).[69]

People's Drama Inc., though in existence only three years, is significant to U.S. theatre history for a number of reasons: under the leadership of Lee Nemetz it became one of five theatre companies in 1950 to establish the Off-Broadway Theatre League in a first attempt at solidifying labor details for off-Broadway productions; People's Drama Inc. specialized in the then quite new (at least to New York City audiences) arena-style staging under the tutelage of Gene Frankel; the company was interracial both in casting and the playwrights' work performed; and People's Drama Inc. continued the progressive social activist work begun by SFA.

Its inaugural production, Clifford Odets's *Waiting for Lefty*, was produced by SFA at the Knickerbocker Theatre in April 1947. People's Drama Inc. was called the New Theater (and alternately New Drama) at this time, and the play was produced as part of "An Afternoon of Social Theatre" and publicized as a "Special FDR Anniversary Program." While Frankel directed the two SFA performances on the afternoon's bill, Alfred Saxe directed *Waiting for Lefty* with a cast including SFA regulars Robert Adler (cowriter of *Open Secret*), Al Smith, Shirley Norris, Antoinette Kray, Lee Nemetz, and Marvin Silbersher. Silbersher is especially significant because he was involved with many of the social activist and experimental groups of the late 1940s and early 1950s, illustrating how intimately connected progressive artists and companies were during this period. He performed in SFA productions of *Open Secret*, *All Aboard*, and *The General and the Goats*; he also played the aging alcoholic but politically astute character of Don Quixote in the Dramatic Workshop performance of *Who Are the Weavers*.

The New Theater formed in early 1947 to provide an additional outlet (beyond SFA) for professional performers "who have found dissatisfaction in the banality of their Broadway roles, and wished to express themselves more completely on the progressive labor stage."[70] One of the New Theater's goals was establishing "progressive neighborhood theatre in different areas of New York City," which would eventually serve as a model for the rest of the country. Although initially raising funds by staging revivals of popular progressive plays such as *Waiting for Lefty*, it simultaneously launched "a plan to encourage young progressive playwrights" to join or write for the group.[71]

Following the success of its roof-raising, sold-out run of *Waiting for Lefty*, produced under the auspices of SFA, the New Theater in December 1947 joined forces with producer Michael Myerberg to stage a limited-engagement Broadway revival of Marc Blitzstein's *The Cradle Will Rock*. This production was directed by Howard Da Silva and conducted by Leonard Bernstein and included original SFA performer Will Geer. In the spring of 1948, the New Theater's productions included another performance of *Waiting for Lefty* as well as Irwin Shaw's *The Priest*. The group was advertised in the *New York Times* as a "cooperative," perhaps as politically dangerous a term in the late 1940s as "collective" was in the 1960s.[72] But the "cooperative" term was entirely appropriate in the case of the New Theater.

The organization's director during its first two years of existence was Robert Steck, no stranger to Communist-affiliated and cooperative-run organizations. He was the son of a Freethinking Society member who fell in love with theatre while attending St. Ambrose College in Iowa. Moving to New York City during the early 1930s, he joined the Workers' Laboratory Theatre's mobile troupe, Theatre of Action (see chapter 1), and wrote for *New Theatre Magazine*. An Abraham Lincoln Brigade member during the Spanish Civil War and captured after more than a year of fighting, Steck spent the next sixteen months under horrifying conditions and was not freed until after the war concluded. Serving as the activities director of the interracial Camp Unity in Wingdale, New York (when he was not fighting in Spain or serving in World War II), from the mid-1930s through 1952, he co-organized his own cooperative children's camp in 1957. Camp Unity is where Robert Adler and Elmer Bernstein's musical satire *Keynotes of Unity* was initially written and workshopped before SFA produced it in New York City during the fall of 1946. In an article addressing summer stock, camp, and barn venues, theatre critic Leo Shull elucidated the significance of these provincial performances, stating, "Many *Pins and Needles* sketches began life in these laboratories, and everyone is familiar with the contributions of the 'borscht circuit'—especially Camp Unity—to progressive theater."[73] Upon leaving the cooperative camp network, Steck taught history and social studies in the New York, New Jersey, and Connecticut public school systems from 1967 until 1978. Following his retirement from teaching, he spent "every Saturday standing in a Vigil for Peace on the Salisbury Green in Connecticut."[74] All evidence suggests that the New Theater was in very able hands when it was under the tutelage of the multifaceted Robert Steck; however, as with many theatre organizations during this period, turnover was constant and the reasons behind it were rarely openly identified.

By the summer of 1949 the New Theater had changed its name to People's Drama Inc., and Lee Nemetz had taken over for Robert Steck as the organization's director. Nemetz performed in *Open Secret* as well as in *The General and the Goats* with SFA and continued performing in People's Drama Inc. productions. The first production under Nemetz's leadership, *They Shall Not Die*, was originally written by John Wexley (an SFA sponsor) to protest the Scottsboro case during the 1930s. People's Drama Inc.'s production of the play was directed by Gene Frankel and performed in order to gain support for the Trenton Six trial. This trial, being heard by the New Jersey Supreme Court, involved the murder of a white used-goods store owner, William Horner, in Trenton during the winter of 1948. Six black men were convicted for the murder and eventually sentenced to death by electric chair, but the lower court was accused of mistrial and the verdict overturned several times. The case dragged on for more than four years in the New Jersey court system. Eventually only one of the six accused men was held accountable for the crime. Within days of the opening of People's Drama Inc.'s production of *They Shall Not Die*, leftist papers were calling

People's Drama Inc. poster for its 1949 production of John Wexley's *They Shall Not Die*. *Billy Rose Theatre Division, the New York Public Library for the Performing Arts, Astor, Lenox, and Tilden Foundations.*

it "one of the most important socio-cultural events in our town for some time" and hailing People's Drama Inc. for building "a permanent repertory of progressive plays, at low prices, done with fervent know-how."[75]

The white actors in *They Shall Not Die*, who were by then well known to progressive theatre audiences, were reviewed favorably in the papers. The cast included Salem Ludwig, Antoinette Kray, Lee Nemetz, Shirley Norris, and Bill Weaver. However, one reviewer also highlighted the performances of the black members of the acting company:

> I've mentioned the general high quality of much of the acting; but what stood out was the excellent ensemble performing of the Negro actors who played the defendants. Each gave evidence of being skilled actors individually but they also displayed a quality rare among even the best-equipped actors on the American stage: the ability to perform as a member of a group within the cast, described in the script as closely knit.[76]

One of these "skilled" actors was Earl Jones, the father of James Earl Jones, who faced attacks in the street and racial slurs for performing in the show. Additionally, while touring *They Shall Not Die*, People's Drama Inc. was banned from performing at the Labor Lyceum in Trenton by the police commissioner. This action led to the immediate involvement of the American Civil Liberties Union on behalf of the theatre company. General counsel for the ACLU, Arthur Garfield Hays referred to the banning as "a shocking and complete disregard for the right of free speech and assembly."[77] The physical attacks on the cast and the Trenton banning garnered People's Drama Inc. national attention and aided in its securing a physical theatre space the following spring: a garage at 212 Eldridge Street on the East Side. Not long after acquiring the theatre, a benefit performance was held to furnish the space. Performers at the benefit included not only People's Drama Inc. artists but also Gypsy Rose Lee, folk music group the Weavers, and Judy Holliday, among many others.[78]

Reviews of its second production, Theodore Ward's *John Brown*, ranged from laudatory to laughable, but it is telling of the group's significance at this moment that an off-Broadway production received a full review in the *New York Times*. Brooks Atkinson said the performance "is more like nervous tension than acting. . . . They eye each other warily like uncongenial animals locked inside a cage." He ultimately dubbed the performance "wholly inadequate."[79] Perhaps New York critics were not quite ready for Gene Frankel's directing style in 1950. As Atkinson admitted, "In the east, which is naturally more cautious, arena staging is still a novelty."[80] Eleven years later, with the experimental theatre movement and off-Broadway in full bloom, Frankel directed the now-acclaimed production of Jean Genet's *The Blacks*, which would consequently star James Earl Jones and a former People's Drama Inc. performer, Louis Gossett Jr. *The Blacks* performance was considered by Richard Watts of the *New York Post* "a kind of snarling ritual," and Walter Kerr used the phrases "animal ferocity" and "grotesque ceremony" to describe the "murky, hypnotic, sardonic and abrasive revel."[81] There is a tonal residue reminiscent of Atkinson's earlier wording in Watts's and Kerr's reviews, but a more experimental performance style had by this point become acceptable (even if not altogether appreciated) by the critics instead of tacitly admonished.

The theatrical and social boundary pushing by Frankel with People's Drama Inc. set the pace for the style of performance prevalent in off-Broadway performances for the next several decades. Additionally, akin to what its predecessor SFA had done, members of People's Drama Inc. merged with the artistic staff at Camp Unity and produced another progressive theatre offspring: Freedom Theatre. Beginning in the spring of 1950, Frank Silvera—who had performed in the original cast of *Anna Lucasta* on Broadway and *They Shall Not Die* for People's Drama Inc.—started the group with former New Theatre administrator Robert Steck. Although short lived, staging only three productions in the spring of 1950 (*Futurama*, *It Ain't Shanel*, and *Longitude 49*), the group was cofounded by a black performer and each of the casts was interracial, which is indicative of an increased interest in racial equality—or at least in nonmainstream performance—during the early Cold War.

As with many other successful off-Broadway and experimental companies of this period, some of People's Drama Inc. and Freedom Theatre's directors and performers moved on to Broadway and Hollywood, while others stayed content with the burgeoning off-Broadway market and social activist venues. Similar to their SFA predecessor, both People's Drama Inc. and Freedom Theatre were named on July 21, 1953, to the Department of Justice's subversive list. But by that point the two groups had already dissolved. In the years following the closure of People's Drama Inc., Lee Nemetz's "go-to" director, Gene Frankel, helmed several significant on- and off-Broadway productions, including the aforementioned *The Blacks*, *Indians*, *Volpone*, *Machinal*, *A Cry of Players*, *Enemy of the People*, *Brecht on Brecht*, and *To Be Young, Gifted and Black*. Nemetz cofounded the Drama Lab with Nola Chilton in 1953, a group deriving from Erwin

Piscator's by-then defunct Dramatic Workshop. Two years later he was a founding partner of Cuadro Productions with Chilton, John Howell, and Yale Wexler. They produced a revue penned by Mel Brooks and starring SFA artists Zero Mostel, Sono Osato, and Jack Gilford called *Once Over Lightly*.[82] In 1960 Nemetz founded yet another producing outfit in order to bring a musical about the Sacco and Vanzetti story, *The Shoemaker and the Peddler*, to off-Broadway.[83]

Regardless of its short existence, People's Drama Inc. remains crucial to theatre history chronology for a number of reasons: being a child of Stage for Action; advocating interracial theatre and promoting black actors and playwrights; and utilizing a raw, emotional, and ritualistic style of performance, which would become the mainstay of experimental performance during the 1960s and 1970s. Finally, and perhaps most important, in a period of increased conservatism and prescribed conformity, Steck, Nemetz, and Frankel were part of a group originating the Off-Broadway Theatre League, which fanned the flames of the off- and off-off-Broadway theatre movements. These movements and many of their artists have been instrumental in keeping alive progressive performance and social activist theatre in the United States.

SFA has connections to other social activist theatre groups as well, operating as a bridge between the 1930s and 1960s because it built upon the methods of the Workers' Theatre groups and the Federal Theatre Project of the 1930s. However, the groups of the New Left differed from their predecessors in the 1930s and Stage for Action in the 1940s by shrinking or limiting their ensemble sizes, focusing their agendas to one or two social causes, and increasing (in many, but not all cases) the commercialization of their groups. I am not suggesting these changes were conscious decisions on the part of 1960s social activist theatre collectives, but these trends possibly contributed to their longer existence. Perhaps the most significant change between SFA and the social activist groups of the 1960s, however, was the change in the political climate. The burgeoning of the New Left movement on college campuses, John F. Kennedy's presidential win, a massive economic expansion beginning in 1961, and youthful or "counterculture" responses to a long period of conservatism ushered in an unquestionably tumultuous political climate but ultimately one much more sympathetic to radical views on racial equality, women's rights, and other social reforms. The social activist theatre groups of the 1960s, such as the Free Southern Theater, El Teatro Campesino, Bread and Puppet, and the San Francisco Mime Troupe succeeded and flourished where SFA floundered. Certainly members of most of these groups also faced legal proceedings and even death threats, but somehow the slightly more lenient political atmosphere of the 1960s allowed these groups and their leaders to persevere, an option unavailable to Stage for Action.

John Gassner stated in March 1948 that "the social theatre of the 1930's is dead . . . because the alternative of revolution has lost its simplicity, as well as whatever attractiveness it once possessed."[84] Gassner continued in the same article to assert that once militant artists such as Blitzstein, Odets, and Shaw were made aware of the political climate change, their writing would morph with it "even if their sympathies are still ranged on the side of the common man."[85] The fact that half a year before the 1948 presidential election Gassner pronounced the death knell of social activist theatre in the United States speaks volumes about the uphill battle faced by progressive artists during the election season and into the Cold War. Furthermore, the guilt and disillusionment faced by many members of SFA in the wake of the HUAC hearings and the 1956 revelations about Stalin's atrocities must have been overwhelming. These troubled associations, combined with the brutal lesson of the blacklist, may help to explain why SFA has been wrapped in a shroud of silence for nearly sixty years. But to lose the legacy of Stage for Action means denying a significant part of theatre history and suggests that there were no positive attributes of the group or even of this time period.

There is still much to be learned by studying the methods, performances, and people of Stage for Action. Like its Federal Theatre Project predecessor, SFA understood that a national theatre dedicated to free or inexpensive performances was an ideal tool for educating and entertaining the masses. Referred to as "pioneers" in 1944, Stage for Action was heralded for "selling democracy" to audiences in its efforts of making "lasting peace a reality."[86] The plays produced by SFA and the people involved highlight the social needs and political climate specific to the 1940s because they were so intimately connected to the intricate issues of this moment. Harry Taylor in 1945 called the group "a child of this particular period: of a time of growing community consciousness, of powerful trade union organization, of widespread and increasing desire among people for more light and guidance on the social, economic and political facets of the day. . . . SFA is today's theater of the people."[87] It is instrumental to our understanding the intersection and history of twentieth-century U.S. activism and theatre. It offers an intriguing connection between civil rights plays like *Skin Deep* and *Who Are the Weavers* and the work of the Free Southern Theater and El Teatro Campesino.

Finally, artists of every political moment have a responsibility to their audiences in offering alternative viewpoints or methods of thinking. The existence of SFA, People's Drama Inc., Freedom Theatre, and a host of other like-minded groups suggests an alternative to the often-repeated belief that U.S. theatre during the early Cold War was apathetic to social activism. These post–World War II theatres, operating as a vital part of nonmainstream social activist performance during the 1940s and early 1950s, offered a multitude of Americans the opportunity to see, hear, and participate in a radically different theatrical event.

Stage for Action brought urgent social messages to its audiences through emotional as well as intellectual methods of performance in a moment when the gaps between different classes, races, genders, and ages were rapidly widening into chasms. Its means were simple. It brought theatre to the people in every imaginable venue for little to no cost to audiences and with very few sets or costumes. Its mission, however, was great: "Stage for Action is an idea—an idea that talent should be at the service of the community . . . that entertainment should have purpose . . . and that purpose must be exerted to prevent war, stamp out race hatreds, combat poverty."[88] The members and sponsors of SFA responded to the militant call that "Art is a weapon!" by turning it into a progressive instrument for peace, reform, education, and even entertainment. For those interested in the intersection between activism and theatre, Stage for Action's history serves as a powerful model, demonstrating the potential that social activist theatre possesses for fostering change.

NOTES

BIBLIOGRAPHY

INDEX

Notes

Introduction

1. Wolf, "Art Is a Weapon!," 230.

2. Gilbert, *Second World War*, 732.

3. *Headline Cabaret* and *Satire Matinee* were cabaret performances produced by Stage for Action in 1946 and 1947 in order to raise funds for its touring social activist theatre plays; "Brooklynite Produces 'Headline Cabaret,'" *Brooklyn Daily Eagle*, April 27, 1947, 29.

4. "Stage for Action Café Society Release," November 7, 1946, John Randolph Papers, Tamiment Library and Robert F. Wagner Labor Archives, New York University.

5. The Golden Gate Quartet, comprising singers William Langford, Henry Owens, Willie Johnson, and Orlandus Wilson, signed with Columbia Records in 1941. They recorded Zaret and Singer's "Atom and Evil" in 1947 for the label.

6. "Gadget" was the name used for the atomic bomb by many scientists working at Los Alamos during the war. See Schweber, *In the Shadow of the Bomb*.

7. Adato is Miller's married name.

8. Himelstein, *Drama Was a Weapon*, 4.

9. Friedman, "Contemporary Theatre for Working-Class Audiences," 197.

10. Wald, *Exiles from a Future Time*, xiii.

11. Ibid., 6.

12. Gassner, *Best American Plays*, xxi. To be fair, Gassner is writing of *commercial* theatre's output, and it would be inappropriate—in this or any historical moment—to consider Broadway the yardstick by which all U.S. theatre should be measured.

13. Sugrue, *Origins of the Urban Crisis*, 14.

14. This is Linda's line in act 1 of Arthur Miller's *Death of a Salesman.* Miller, *Collected Plays 1944–1961*, 195.

15. Du Bois, "Criteria of Negro Art," 168.

16. Kushner et al., "How Do You Make Social Change?," 62.

17. McDermott, "Workers' Laboratory Theatre," 121.

18. Ibid., 121–22.

19. Landy and Montgomery, *Theatre for Change*, xx.

20. Kleinman, *World of Hope*, 276.

21. Harry Taylor, "Stage for Action," *New Masses*, January 2, 1945, 29.

1. Theatre as a Weapon

1. Harry Taylor, "Stage for Action," *New Masses*, January 2, 1945, 30.

2. Samuel Sillen, "Stage for Action Moves Forward," *Daily Worker*, August 27, 1946, 11.

3. It is challenging to tabulate the exact number of artists participating in the different branches of Stage for Action over its five-year existence. "Thousands" is a safe estimate as already by early February 1946 Mildred Linsley, executive director of the group, had the names of eight hundred actors willing to participate with the group on file. See Beth McHenry, "The Lady with the 800 Actors," *Daily Worker*, February 6, 1946, 6.

4. Marvin Silbersher, phone interview with author, June 3, 2015.

5. Ibid.

6. Taylor, "Stage for Action," 29.

7. Eugene Gordon, "'Stage for Action' Takes Plays Directly to Its Audiences," *Worker*, April 8, 1945.

8. The Second International, also referred to as the Socialist International, was organized in Paris on July 14, 1889, as a federation of the world's Socialist—and overwhelmingly Marxist—parties. Interested in reforming capitalism in order to promote workers' rights, some of their original shared beliefs included the eight-hour workday, opposition to war and colonialism, and interest in reforming capitalism in order to promote workers' rights. Although the Second International was responsible for establishing May 1 as International Workers' Day, differing national opinions on entry into World War I led to the dissolution of the federation in 1916.

9. Marx, "Production and Consumption."

10. Saal, *New Deal Theater*, 54.

11. Samuel, MacColl, and Cosgrove, *Theatres of the Left*, xvii.

12. Rolland, "People's Theatre," 62.

13. Samuel, MacColl, and Cosgrove, *Theatres of the Left*, xx.

14. Philip Huston, *Equity Magazine*, quoted in "1940's: Hurry Up and Close That Big Show," *Equity Timeline 100 Years*, Actors Equity Association, http://www.actorsequity.org/AboutEquity/timeline/timeline_1940.html, accessed September 13, 2014.

15. "Roosevelt Lauds Show Business," *Billboard*, June 1943, 3.

16. Chicago Stage for Action promotional pamphlet, Stage for Action Collection, series XCIX, folder 1, Charles Deering McCormick Library of Special Collections, Northwestern University Library; promotional materials for Philadelphia Stage for Action from 1946 include the following additional national sponsors: Peter Frye, William Gailmor, John Gassner, Elinor Gimbel, Michael Gordon, Stanley M. Isaacs, Phillip Loeb, John T. McManus, Mrs. Arthur Mayer (Lillie), William Morris, Jean Muir, Minerva Pious, Rev. Adam Clayton Powell, Dr. Lawrence Reddick, Jerome Robbins, Channing Tobias, Toni Ward, and Frank Wilson. Edward Chodorov is absent from the Philadelphia list, Philadelphia Stage for Action promotional pamphlet, National Republic Records, box 104, folder 3, Hoover Institution Archives, Stanford University.

17. Chicago Stage for Action promotional pamphlet, Stage for Action Collection, series XCIX, folder 1.

18. Stage for Action informational pamphlet, J. B. Matthews Papers, David M. Rubenstein Rare Book and Manuscript Library, Duke University.

19. Cy Wagner, "Television Reviews: Balaban and Katz," *Billboard*, December 1944, 10.

20. "Television Reviews: 'Walk With Me,'" *Billboard*, February 2, 1946, 10.

21. Himelstein, *Drama Was a Weapon*, 14.

22. Ibid.

23. Burton Lindheim, "A Stage for Action: From the Bronx to Canarsie with the Players of Topical Problems," *New York Times*, May 14, 1944.

24. Chicago Stage for Action pamphlet, 1945–46, Stage for Action Collection, series XCIX, folder 1.

25. Himelstein, *Drama Was a Weapon*, 17.

26. Muray-Irizarry, *Rafael Ríos-Rey*, 46; George Barry, "'Keynote [sic] of Unity' a Militant Musical," *Daily Worker*, September 16, 1946, 7.

27. Quoted in Barry, "'Keynote of Unity,'" 7. Elmer Bernstein, whose filmography spans the 1950s through the 2002 film *Far from Heaven*, won an Academy Award for the score of *Thoroughly Modern Millie* in 1967. He also received two Golden Globe Awards, an additional thirteen Academy Award nominations, and two Tony Award nominations for *How Now Dow Jones* (1968) and *Merlin* (1982).

28. I.B., "'Keynotes of Unity'—Posies and Wafted Kisses," *Daily Worker*, October 3, 1946, 11.

29. Ibid.

30. Taylor, "Stage for Action," 29.

31. Although talk of forming a third party was taking place in liberal and Communist circles in the spring of 1946, it was not until the beginning of 1947 that Henry Wallace intimated he was interested in leading such an organization. See Yarnell, *Democrats and Progressives*, 15.

32. Gassner, "One-Act Play in the Revolutionary Theatre," 275.

33. Ibid., 257.

34. Mally, "Inside a Communist Front," 87.

35. Ibid., 85.

36. Membership ad, *Theatre Workshop* 1 (April–July 1937): 96.

37. Washington Stage for Action, "Report of the First Year, 1946–1947," box K, folder 393, Hilda Worthington Smith Papers, Radcliffe Institute for Advanced Study, Harvard University.

38. Records of the other declared branches of SFA—San Francisco, Los Angeles, and Cleveland—have yet to be discovered.

39. Stage for Action, "Membership Brochure 1946," John Randolph Papers, Tamiment Library and Robert F. Wagner Labor Archives, New York University.

40. Mally, "Inside a Communist Front," 84.

41. Ibid., 95.

42. Silbersher interview.

43. Some of SFA's contributing playwrights and members who were also active members of the LAW include Sidney Alexander, Lewis Allan, Samuel Barlow, Ben Bengal, Edward Chodorov, Harold Clurman, Norman Corwin, Ken Crossen, Arnaud d'Usseau, Howard Fast, John Gassner, Mike Gold, James Gow, Harry Granick, E. Y. Harburg, Elizabeth Hawes, Langston Hughes, Jean Karsavina, Louis Kronenberger, Millard Lampell, Peter Martin, Myron McCormick, Jean Muir, Dorothy Parker, Paul Peters, Burton Rascoe, Paul Robeson, Earl Robinson, Harold Rome, Norman Rosten, Johannes Steel, James Thurber, and John Wexley.

44. John Gassner quoted in Himelstein, *Drama Was a Weapon*, ix.

45. The CPUSA issued a public statement about the Nazi invasion only hours after the attack. Six days later a meeting was held by the national committee of the CPUSA, attended by 145 party delegates and led by Foster and Robert Minor, who both made speeches. Minor was standing in for General Secretary Earl Browder, who was serving a prison sentence in the Atlanta Federal Penitentiary. According to Bernard K. Johnpoll, the purpose of the national committee meeting on June 28, 1941, was

"to enunciate the new line and to calm the near hysteria that permeated the party ranks." See Johnpoll, *Documentary History of the Communist Party of the United States*, 37; and Foster, "New World Situation and Our Tasks," 11.

46. Quoted in Lieberman, *"My Song Is My Weapon,"* 81.

47. Ibid., 83.

48. Quoted in Satterfield, *"The World's Best Books,"* 152.

49. This debate has apparently ended as in the twenty-first century a large grouping of literary scholars included two of Ezra Pound's poems in the eleven "they felt were the most important in the American canon." See Malcom Gladwell, "Late Bloomers," *New Yorker*, October 20, 2008.

50. Max Lerner, "Artists and Fascists," *PM*, January 17, 1946, 2.

51. Marion Summers, "Social Art Must Breathe the Air of the Common Man," *Worker*, April 7, 1946, 14.

52. *Hearings before the Committee on Un-American Activities*, 80th Cong., 1st sess., 100 (July 21, 1947) (statement of Walter S. Steele, chairman of the national security committee of the American Coalition of Patriotic, Civic, and Fraternal Societies).

53. "Hollywood Writers Send Messages to Art Forum," *Daily Worker*, April 19, 1946, 12.

54. Ibid.

55. Wald, *American Night*, 61.

56. Arnaud d'Usseau, "The Theater as a Weapon," *New Masses*, June 25, 1946, 17.

57. Arnaud d'Usseau and James Gow, "Another Definition for Commercialism," *New York Times*, September 22, 1946, X1.

58. Quoted in Hill, *Lenin and the Russian Revolution*, 229. See also Samuel Sillen, "Lenin's Dream of a Culture Truly Belonging to the People," *Daily Worker*, January 13, 1946, 9.

59. Arvon, *Marxist Esthetics*, 39.

60. Quoted in Miller, "Concerning the Boom," 85.

61. Ibid.

62. Ibid., 86.

63. Ibid., 87–88.

64. Arthur Miller, "Are You Now or Were You Ever (II)?" *Guardian*, http://www.theguardian.com/books/2000/jun/16/history.society, accessed February 13, 2010.

65. Weigand, *Red Feminism*, 5.

66. Lindheim, "A Stage for Action."

67. Elena Mannes, "About," PerryMillerAdato.com, http://perrymilleradato .com/about/#_edn17, accessed January 25, 2016.

68. Ibid.

69. Bohn, *Historical and Descriptive Analysis of the "Why We Fight" Series*, 100.

70. "Perry Miller Adato," New York State Writer's Institute, http://www. albany.edu/writers-inst/webpages4/archives/pmadato.html, accessed September 14, 2014.

71. *Hearings before the Committee on Un-American Activities* (statement of Walter S. Steele) 52. *Red Channels: The Report of Communist Influence in Radio and Television* (1950) was a pamphlet publication of *Counterattack*, a right-wing journal that distributed materials aimed at combating Communism in the United States. Many of the artists named in the *Red Channels* list were eventually blacklisted.

72. The Congress of American Women was officially founded in New York City on International Women's Day, March 8, 1946. The group's national leadership included Gene Weltfish, Muriel Draper, Mary Van Kleeck, Susan Anthony II, and Elizabeth Gurley Flynn (among others), See Weigand, *Red Feminism*, 48–49.

73. Elizabeth Gurley Flynn's complete list of demands is quoted in Weigand, *Red Feminism*, 73–74.

74. *Hearings before the Committee on Un-American Activities*, 81st Cong., 2nd sess., 3520 (August 29–30, 1950) (statement of Alex Leith, freelance writer).

75. *Hearings before the Committee on Un-American Activities* (statement of Walter S. Steele), 115.

76. *Hearings before the Committee on Un-American Activities*, 82nd Cong., 1st sess., 1071 (June 19–July 13, 1951) (statement of Louis Ginsberg, treasurer of the Bookshop Association).

77. Mildred Linsley, "Frameup in Alabama," *New Masses*, January 31, 1939, 20; "Representatives Will Participate," *Daily Mail*, February 20, 1940, 1.

78. McHenry, "Lady with the 800 Actors," 6.

79. Ibid.

80. David Walsh, "American Folksinger Pete Seeger Dead at 94," *International Committee of the Fourth International*, January 30, 2014, http://www. wsws.org/en/articles/2014/01/30/seeg-j30.html, accessed March 25, 2014.

81. Stage for Action, membership pamphlet, Printed Ephemera Collection, box 97, Tamiment Library and Robert F. Wagner Labor Archives, New York University; ellipses in original pamphlet.

82. Elizabeth Lips, "Appeal Made for Hospital Volunteers," *Brooklyn Daily Eagle*, October 22, 1951, 11.

83. Schrecker, *Many Are the Crimes*, 8. Brackets appear in the original.

84. D'Usseau, "Theater as a Weapon," 16.

2. Progressive Insurgency

1. See Kleinman's *World of Hope*.

2. Eleanor Roosevelt, "My Day," *Times Recorder*, April 22, 1944, 4.

3. Martha Gellhorn was a field investigator for the Federal Emergency Relief Administration, an outstanding war correspondent and journalist, and a personal friend of Eleanor Roosevelt. She wrote the introduction to the edited collection of Mrs. Roosevelt's "My Day" columns; see Chadakoff, *Eleanor Roosevelt's My Day*, x.

4. Roosevelt, "My Day," 4.

5. Ibid. Living newspapers, which Russian theatre scholar Lynn Mally defines in the Russian tradition as an eclectic theatrical mix—"part broadsheet, part music hall, and part political rally"—first became popular in the United States during the late 1920s and reached their zenith under the Federal Theatre Project. See Mally, "Americanization of the Soviet Living Newspaper," 4.

6. Mally, "Americanization of the Soviet Living Newspaper," 21; see also Flanagan's introduction to *Federal Theatre Plays*.

7. Barnard Rubin, "Broadway Beat," *Daily Worker*, April 10, 1947, 12.

8. The largely unknown *Hiccupping Mr. Higgins* may have ended up on the American Federation of Labor four-part radio series titled *Story from the Stars*, for which Miller was one of the writers. His contribution was an eight-minute sketch titled *The Hiccups of Alfred Higgins*, in which the protagonist begs the audience for support in fighting the Taft-Hartley Bill. See Sam Chase, "Story from the Stars," *Billboard*, May 17, 1947, 11, 18.

9. Wald, *Trinity of Passion*, 210–35.

10. [Stage for Action], "Press Release—18 February 1947," J. B. Matthews Papers, David M. Rubenstein Rare Book and Manuscript Library, Duke University.

11. Ibid.

12. "Historical/Biographical Note," *Guide to the National Council of American-Soviet Friendship Records*, Tamiment Library and Robert F. Wagner Labor Archives, last modified June 2014, http://dlib.nyu.edu /findingaids/html/tamwag/tam_134/bioghist.html, accessed July 27, 2015.

13. Wallace, *Price of Vision*, 499.

14. "Historical/Biographical Note."

15. Perry Miller, "Stage Door to Action Letter: December 1943," Peggy Clark Collection, Music Division, Library of Congress.

16. Mayorga, *Best One-Act Plays of 1944*, 46.

17. Gaer, *First Round*, 414.

18. Ibid., 411, 415.

19. "War Work 'Orphan' to Get Day Care," *New York Times*, January 27, 1942, 18.

20. Gaer, *First Round*, 416.

21. "War Work 'Orphan' to Get Day Care."

22. Stage for Action benefit program, Peggy Clark Collection.

23. Miller, *That They May Win*, 53–54.

24. Gallaway and Vedder, *Out of Work*, 154. The Taft-Hartley Act amended the Wagner Act and other pro-union policies implemented during the New Deal.

25. Miller, *That They May Win*, 55–56.

26. Ibid., 58–59.

27. Arthur Miller, *That They May Win* [1944?], Stage for Action Collection, series XCIX, folder 7, 9, Charles Deering McCormick Library of Special Collections, Northwestern University Library. Based on the benefit performance cast list of *That They May Win*, which Arthur Miller directed, SFA adopted the 1943 casting choices for the play, meaning that Ralph Bell and Lew Gilbert performed the "audience plant" roles of the Man Who Knows and Distressed Man. Subsequent performances of the play between 1944 and 1946 were more flexible regarding sex in casting the audience plants.

28. Marguerite Higgins, "Dramas Bring Issues of Day Home to Women: Program Sponsored by Stage for Action Challenges Audiences to Meet Crisis on Home Front with Courage and Decision," *New York Herald Tribune*, May 21, 1944, C7.

29. Ibid.

30. Almanac of Policy Issues, "Child Care," http://www.policyalmanac .org/social_welfare/archive/child_care.shtml, accessed August 5, 2009.

31. Arthur Miller, *That They May Win* (1948), Stage for Action Collection, series XCIX, folder 7, 1.

32. In the 1944 version of *That They May Win*, Ina is described as "a young woman, now working in a factory. She is dressed in her ordinary go-to-work clothes." Miller, *That They May Win* [1944?], 1.

33. Walton, *Henry Wallace, Harry Truman, and the Cold War*, vii.

34. Miller, *That They May Win* (1948), 8. The "President you got in on a default" jab references Vice President Harry S. Truman's rise to president on April 12, 1945, following the death of Franklin Delano Roosevelt.

35. Ibid., 7.

36. Ibid., 8.

37. "Wallace Gets Fired," *Life*, September 30, 1946, 42.

38. Gaer, *First Round*, 60.

39. For the complete list of the Simple Propositions set forth by the PAC and their full explanations, see ibid., 57–60.

40. They later changed their name to the Congress of Industrial Organizations.

41. Sabato, *PAC Power*, 5.

42. Foreman, "Statement of the National Citizens Political Action Committee," 473.

43. Stage for Action promotional pamphlet, J. B. Matthews Papers.

44. "Stage Group Is Seeking Plays," *Pittsburgh Courier*, December 29, 1945, 22.

45. NC-PAC, "Catalog: The School of Political Action Techniques," June 1946, 13, Printed Ephemera Collection on Organizations, PE036, box 61, Tamiment Library and Robert F. Wagner Labor Archives, New York University.

46. Joseph H. Short, "Bayer's Ballot Box Ballad Makes Debut as Vote Getter," *Baltimore Sun*, June 29, 1946, 1.

47. Ibid.

48. Ibid., 2.

49. Ibid.

50. Bert McCord, "News of the Theater: Castings to Get Under Way," *New York Herald Tribune*, June 9, 1945, 8.

51. Jane Lawson, "Stage for Action," *New Masses*, March 12, 1946, 30.

52. Foreman, "Statement of the National Citizens Political Action Committee," 474.

53. "NCPAC Official Sees Possibility of Third Party," *Modesto (Calif.) Bee and News Herald*, June 29, 1946, 2.

54. Les Pine and Anita Short, "Joseph McGinnical, Cynical Pinnacle, Opus II," 4, Stage for Action Collection, MS99, series XLIX, box 1, folder 8.

55. Ibid.

56. Denning, *Cultural Front*, 123.

57. Pine and Short, "Joseph McGinnical," 2.

58. Wallace, *Sixty Million Jobs*, 4–5.

59. Ibid., 6. The emphasis is in the original text.

60. Ibid., 83.

61. John Morton Blum, editor's note, in Wallace, *Price of Vision*, 425.

62. Kleinman, *World of Hope*, 241.

63. Wallace, *Price of Vision*, 282.

64. Ibid., 255n.

65. Ibid., 255.

66. Pine and Short, "Joseph McGinnical," 7.

67. Flit was a popular brand of insecticide used for killing flies and mosquitoes.

68. Pine and Short, "Joseph McGinnical," 16.

69. The subheading is drawn from Charlie King's 1978 "Taft-Hartley Song," made famous by Peggy Seeger on her album *From Where I Stand* and also included in *The Bottom Line*, a satirical revue about Reaganomics first produced by the Labor Theater in 1982.

70. Miller, *That They May Win* (1948), 6.

71. Lee, *Truman and Taft-Hartley*, 27.

72. Walton, *Henry Wallace, Harry Truman, and the Cold War*, 275.

73. Yarnell, *Democrats and Progressives*, 29.

74. Ibid., 38–39.

75. Lee, *Truman and Taft-Hartley*, 49.

76. Ibid., 12.

77. Ibid., 62.

78. Ibid., 51–52.

79. For the full list of major changes the Taft-Hartley Act made to U.S. labor policy, see ibid., 75–77.

80. Quoted in Culver and Hyde, *American Dreamer*, 478.

81. Walton, *Henry Wallace, Harry Truman, and the Cold War*, 279.

82. Lee, *Truman and Taft-Hartley*, 153.

83. Formed in 1947 as an outgrowth of the Union for Democratic Action, members of the Americans for Democratic Action were staunchly anticommunist liberals.

84. Peggy Clark, letter of resignation to Stage for Action, box 126, folder 2, Peggy Clark Collection, ML31.C59.

85. In this September 12, 1946, speech at Madison Square Garden, Wallace was openly critical of U.S. foreign policy and asserted that the "get tough with Russia" policy currently in practice with the Truman administration would fail, ultimately leading to another war. For extensive exploration of

the speech and its political impact, see chapter 7 of Kleinman, *World of Hope*, 175–214.

3. You've Still Got a Voice

1. Louis Untermeyer, "Why I Am for Wallace," *New York Star*, October 28, 1948.

2. Quoted in Schrecker, *Many Are the Crimes*, 276.

3. W. A. Hunton, "Letter to the Council on African Affairs, 13 July 1949," Paul and Eslande Robeson Collection, Spingarn Library, Howard University.

4. Ibid.

5. Zieger, *American Workers*, 52.

6. Quoted in Schrecker, *Many Are the Crimes*, 32.

7. "How State Senate Voted on the Anti-racial Bill," *New York Times*, March 6, 1945, 17; "Anti-racial Bill Signed by Dewey," ibid., March 13, 1945, 38; "CIO Urges Albany Pass Job-Bias Bill," ibid., February 8, 1945, 14.

8. "Anti-bias Bill Is Passed, 109-32, by Assembly without Amendment," ibid., March 1, 1945, 1, 16.

9. Chen, *Fifth Freedom*, 104.

10. Committee on Un-American Activities, U.S. House of Representatives, *100 Things You Should Know about Communism*, 9.

11. Wertheim, *Staging the War*, 143.

12. Bunny Kacher, phone interview with author, February 16, 2008.

13. "Christophers Cite Four Songwriters," *New York Times*, May 1, 1953, 19.

14. Charles Polacheck's granddaughter Angeliska has produced a beautiful webpage honoring her grandfather. For more personal information and photos, refer to "Charles Lessing Polacheck R.I.P.," *Angeliska Gazette*, http://www.angeliska.com/2012/02/charles-lessing-polacheck-r-i-p/, accessed May 4, 2013.

15. A few newspaper articles indicate that Arthur Arent co-authored *Skin Deep*; however, the vast majority of records list Polacheck as the sole playwright.

16. Johnson, "One Year in the Deep South," 46.

17. Ibid., 46–47.

18. Ibid., 48.

19. W.H., "News of the Theater: 'Skin Deep' in Rehearsal," *New York Herald Tribune*, March 26, 1945, 10.

20. Johande and Puckett, *Leonard Covello*, 203.

21. Ibid., 2.

22. "Student 'Strikes' Flare into Riots in Harlem Schools," *New York Times*, September 29, 1945, 1–2.

23. Ibid.

24. Quoted in Johande and Puckett, *Leonard Covello*, 205.

25. "Student 'Strikes' Flare into Riots in Harlem Schools," 2.

26. "Negro Councilman Warns Mayor of the Danger of Race Riots Here," *New York Times*, June 25, 1943, 8.

27. "Harlem Is Orderly with Heavy Guard Ready for Trouble," ibid., August 3, 1943, 1.

28. Quoted in Katznelson, *Fear Itself*, 86.

29. Quoted in Anderson, *Eyes Off the Prize*, 64.

30. [Charles Polacheck], *Skin Deep*, Manuscripts, Archives and Rare Books Division, Schomburg Center for Research in Black Culture, New York Public Library, 1.

31. Ibid., 16–17.

32. Sarvis, "Leaders in the Court and Community," 50.

33. "Loyal Order of the Ruptured Duck" refers to an honorable discharge. The lapel pin—which sports an eagle, not a duck—worn by honorably discharged servicemen allowed them to continue wearing their service uniform, despite being discharged from the military, because they were not yet able to afford civilian clothes. It was also a symbol of their service to the country.

34. [Polacheck], *Skin Deep*, 3.

35. Quoted in Singer, "Veteran and Race Relations," 400.

36. [Polacheck], *Skin Deep*, 19.

37. Singer, "Veteran and Race Relations," 408.

38. Ibid.

39. [Polacheck], *Skin Deep*, 5.

40. "News of the Stage: 'Room Service' Purchased by RKO Rather than Warners," *New York Times*, June 16, 1937, 27.

41. J. Williams, *Stage Left*, 239.

42. Bengal, "All Aboard," 500.

43. Ben Bengal, *All Aboard*, in Lieberman, "Best Stage for Action Plays," Billy Rose Theatre Division, New York Public Library for the Performing Arts, 9.

44. Ibid., 10, 11.

45. White, "Civil Rights in Conflict," 122.

46. Ibid.

47. Ibid., 123.

48. Ibid., 124.

49. American Heritage Foundation, *Good Citizen*, 71.

50. Ibid., 43.

51. "B'klyn NAACP Opens Drive for Members," *New York Amsterdam News*, May 3, 1947, 15.

52. "N.A.A.C.P. Mass Membership Rally," ibid., April 26, 1947, 17.

53. Richard Dier, "In the Big City," *Baltimore Afro-American*, March 1, 1947.

54. "Sheldon to Discuss Klan Activities Here," *Jewish Exponent*, March 14, 1947, 5.

55. "Stage for Action Scores Hit at Carnegie Hall," *Worker*, April 7, 1946, 14.

56. Arnold Perl, *Dream Job*, in Lieberman, "Best Stage for Action Plays," 9–10.

57. Ibid., 16.

58. "Arnold Perl Play Listed," *New York Times*, March 25, 1946, 28; Library of Congress Copyright Office, "Dramatic Compositions and Motion Pictures."

59. "The News of Radio: MBS Abandons Its Plan for Dramatization of Civil Rights Report Series," *New York Times*, February 23, 1948, 36.

60. Ibid.

61. Ibid.

62. "Stage For Action Makes Carnegie Hall Debut," *New York Age*, March 9, 1946, 10.

63. Lieberman, "Best Stage for Action Plays," 1.

64. "N.Y. Unity Players Off Good Theatre," *Pittsburgh Courier*, September 3, 1949, 18.

65. "'Naked City' Writer Malvin Wald Dies," *Variety*, March 12, 2008, http://variety.com/2008/film/news/naked-city-writer-malvin-wald-dies -1117982282/, accessed November 8, 2013.

66. Malvin Wald, "Talk In Darkness," Stage for Action Scripts, 13, 1947, John Randolph Papers, WAG255, box 8, folder 15, Tamiment Library and Robert F. Wagner Labor Archives, New York University.

67. Devine, *Henry Wallace's 1948 Presidential Campaign*, 65.

68. American Business Consultants, "Here's Proof of Communist Control of New 'Progressive' Party," *Counterattack*, July 30, 1948, 1.

69. Culver and Hyde, *American Dreamer*, 486.

70. Devine, *Henry Wallace's 1948 Presidential Campaign*, 156.

71. Ibid.

72. Harry S. Truman, "Executive Order 9981, July 26, 1948," Harry S. Truman Library and Museum, http://www.trumanlibrary.org/photos/9981a.jpg, accessed September 10, 2013.

73. Culver and Hyde, *American Dreamer*, 493.

74. Peterson, *African American Theatre Directory*, 15.

75. Mitchell, *Papers of Clarence Mitchell Jr.*, 556.

76. "Radio Held Biased on Negro Problem," *New York Times*, July 10, 1949, 31.

77. "Telegram to Paul Robeson from the Producer and Cast Members at War with the Army," June 18, 1949, Paul and Eslande Robeson Collection.

78. Perucci, *Paul Robeson and the Cold War Performance Complex*, 34.

79. Black, "'New Negro' Performance in Art and Life," 61.

80. Ibid., 67.

4. The People's Voice Must Sound Louder

1. U.S. Government, "Uniting and Strengthening America by Providing Appropriate Tools Required to Intercept and Obstruct Terrorism (USA PATRIOT Act) Act of 2001," Public Law 107–56, October 26, 2001, 2, https://www.gpo.gov/fdsys/pkg/PLAW-107publ56/html/PLAW-107publ56.htm, accessed June 3, 2016.

2. George W. Bush, "Proposal to Create the Department of Homeland Security," Department of Homeland Security, June 2002, http://www.dhs.gov/proposal-create-department-homeland-security, accessed January 5, 2013.

3. Merritt A. Edson, "Power-Hungry Men in Uniform," *Collier's Weekly*, August 27, 1949, 16.

4. Feldman, *Free Expression and Democracy in America*, 430.

5. Unpublished manuscript copy of Lewis Allan's *The Investigators*, 1, Stage for Action Collection, Charles Deering McCormick Library of Special Collections, Northwestern University.

6. Ibid., 2. The Investigators accuse Smith of falsifying his identity and assert his name is undoubtedly something closer to "Stanislavsky Gregorovitch."

7. Baker, "Abel Meeropol," 29.

8. Allan, *The Investigators*, 1.

9. Owen McNally, "Our 'House': Populist WWII Anthem Resonates Anew, Capturing Essence of American Unity," *Hartford Courant*, September 8, 2002, http://articles.courant.com/2002-09-08/entertainment/0209080522_1_tom-brokaw-s-greatest-generation-paul-robeson-lauritz-melchior/5, accessed June 5, 2016.

10. Allan, *The Investigators*, 6.

11. Ibid., 1.

12. Ibid., 6.

13. Musser, "Carl Marzani and Union Films," 131.

14. Hovey would eventually compose the score for SFA-member Arnold Perl's *Tevya and His Daughters*, as well as handle the music direction for Brecht's *Galileo in Hollywood*.

15. Originally called the Let Freedom Ring Company, because the actors involved (including Lenthier as well as Will Geer) were touring Albert Bein's *Let Freedom Ring* to "labor halls from Lawrence, Massachusetts to Camden, New Jersey," the group changed its name following Lenthier's death on the battlefield in Spain; Green, *Wobblies, Pile Butts, and Other Heroes*, 291.

16. Musser, "Carl Marzani and Union Films," 131.

17. American Communications Assn. v. Douds, 339 U.S. 382, 1950.

18. Miller, *Timebends*, 82.

19. Arthur Miller, *You're Next!*, Stage for Action Scripts, 1, 1947, John Randolph Papers, WAG255, box 8, folder 15, Tamiment Library and Robert F. Wagner Labor Archives, New York University.

20. Ibid., 1–2.

21. Ibid., 3.

22. Ibid., 4.

23. Ibid., 5.

24. Ibid., 6.

25. Goodman, *Committee*, 167–68.

26. Henry Winston was chair of the CPUSA from 1966 to 1986 and was integral to the formation of the American Youth Congress, the Southern Negro Youth Congress, and the Abraham Lincoln Brigade. He served in the military during World War II and was one of twelve CPUSA leaders indicted under the Smith Act in 1948. Winston served seven years in prison and continued his work with the CPUSA immediately upon release. He is remembered as an advocate for black causes and especially for his publications *Strategy for a Black Agenda: A Critique of New Theories of Liberation in the United States and Africa* and *Class, Race, and Black Liberation*.

27. Brooklyn Communist Party ad, "Brooklyn Rally," *Daily Worker*, April 3, 1947, 4.

28. Goodman, *Committee*, 226.

29. Quoted in ibid., 392.

30. Ibid., 394.

31. "77 Groups Here Organize for Wallace Drive," *Brooklyn Daily Eagle*, May 11, 1948, 3.

32. "Sydenham Benefit," *New York Amsterdam News*, February 21, 1948, 4. Some of Alexander's major publications include a biography of Marc Chagall, historical novels on the life of Michelangelo, and translations of significant Italian works.

33. Miller, *Timebends*, 231.

34. Henry Raymont, "Translator Gets PEN Club Prize: Sidney Alexander Is Named for Work on Italian Text," *New York Times*, May 16, 1970.

35. "Sidney Alexander, Historian, Novelist and Translator, 87," ibid., December 22, 1999, C26.

36. Selden Rodman, introduction to *The Man on the Queue*, by Sidney Alexander, 4.

37. Miller, *Timebends*, 237.

38. Maurice N. Irvine, "In Good Company," *New York Times*, June 11, 1950, 197.

39. Rodman, introduction, 4.

40. Brown and Hamilakis, *Usable Past*, 1.

41. Kaplan, *Radio and Poetry*, 47.

42. Samuel Sillen, "Subtle Balance: *The Man on the Queue*, by Sidney Alexander," *New Masses*, June 10, 1941, 26.

43. Louis Calta, "Two More Shows May Quit Tonight," *New York Times*, September 18, 1948, 11.

44. Sydenham Hospital plays an important part in the history of racial struggles in New York City. Besides being interracial, it was the first hospital in New York City to hire black doctors and was one of the initial race riot sites following the shooting of a black soldier by a white policeman in August 1943. Lack of funding threatened to shut the hospital down in 1948, but a series of benefits (including SFA's) saved it, and in March 1949 the city took the hospital over in order to preserve its interracial status. Other performance benefits included a jazz concert featuring Duke Ellington, Count Basie, and Billie Holiday. See "Sydenham Seeks Aid to Bar Closing," *New York Times*, March 1, 1948, 20; and "Sydenham to Benefit Tonight," ibid., April 3, 1948, 10.

45. "Bernecker Plans Aid to Sydenham," ibid., March 2, 1948, 26; *House Reports*, "Miscellaneous," 78th Cong., 2nd sess., 179–80 (January 10–December 19, 1944); Mitchell, *Papers of Clarence Mitchell Jr.*, 556; Foner, *Organized Labor and the Black Worker*, 285.

46. Theatrical program for *Salem Story*, March 12–14, 1948, Gene Frankel Collection, Billy Rose Theatre Division, New York Public Library for the Performing Arts; "Sydenham's Needs," *New York Times*, March 5, 1948, 20.

47. "To Present Witchcraft Play," *New York Times*, March 11, 1948, 35. According to Robert Riggs's biography of Leon Kirchner, Alexander approached Kirchner in 1946 to "transform his successful radio play *Salem Story* (1940) into a libretto." Kirchner had previously composed another work based on a text by Alexander. It is unclear at this point why Haufrecht, and not Kirchner, ultimately composed the score for *Salem Story*. See Riggs, *Leon Kirchner*, 28, 162.

48. Stage for Action, "*Salem Story* Press Release" [1948?], J. B. Matthews Papers, David M. Rubenstein Rare Book and Manuscript Library, Duke University.

49. Bert McCord, "News of the Theater: Sydenham Hospital Benefit," *New York Herald Tribune*, March 12, 1948, 19.

50. Alexander was the writer for the June 14, 1943, *Cavalcade of America* program "Make Way for the Lady," and Miller adapted the December 28, 1942, program on Garibaldi and wrote the April 19, 1943, program on Pastor Martin Niemoeller, "Listen for the Sound of Wings." Actor Will Geer, another member of SFA, was a radio performer in each of these programs.

51. Sidney Alexander, *Salem Story*, 6, in Lieberman, "Best Stage for Action Plays," Billy Rose Theatre Division, New York Public Library for the Performing Arts.

52. Perhaps reflecting Alexander's work with the government in Harlem during the 1940s, he changes the ethnicity and race of the servant character in the Parris household between 1940 and 1948. In 1940 the servant is the historically accurate Tituba, a slave from Barbados; in *Salem Story* she becomes a Welsh servant named Hagar. In Alexander's scripts it is Parris's sixteen-year-old daughter, Elizabeth, and not the slave from Barbados, Tituba, who instigates the witchcraft accusations with Abigail Williams (as occurs in Miller's work).

53. This is not to say that *Salem Story* is free from sexuality. There is a line in both *Where Jonathan Came* and *Salem Story* reading, "No husband lies with his wife but Mather lies between" (Alexander, *Salem Story*, 17). According to Milton Kaplan, the only radio station willing to play *Where Jonathan Came* was the noncommercial WNYC. All other stations banned it due to the sex theme. The director of dramatic programs at WNYC was Mitchell Grayson, who would become a member of SFA's board of directors in 1945. See Kaplan, *Radio and Poetry*, 62.

54. Alexander, *Man on the Queue*, 130, 113. Both lines are spoken by Giles Corey.

55. Miller, *Theater Essays of Arthur Miller*, 172–73.

56. Alexander, *Salem Story*, 33. In Alexander's version, this question is put to Martha Corey by Cotton Mather; in Miller's work, the slightly modified phrasing by Judge Hathorne is, "How do you know, then, that you are not a witch?" Miller, *Portable Arthur Miller*, 200.

57. Miller, *Portable Arthur Miller*, 165.

58. Murphy, *Congressional Theatre*, 139.

59. Alexander, *Salem Story*, 32; ellipses in original text. Corey's speech at the end of *Salem Story* is not Alexander's original creation. It is drawn almost verbatim from Henry Wadsworth Longfellow's 1868 short play *Giles Corey of the Salem Farms*. Alexander was something of a Longfellow scholar, though impressed more by the scope of his writing than by the merit, and yet did not hasten to borrow freely from the author. So too with Alexander's play we find an uncredited adaptation of an earlier work.

60. Miller, *Theater Essays of Arthur Miller*, 154.

61. Ibid., 27. See also Miller, *Timebends*, 330.

62. John C. Thirlwall, "Notes on William Carlos Williams as Playwright," in W. Williams, *"Many Loves" and Other Plays*, 435.

63. Starkey, *Devil in Massachusetts*, vi.

64. Arthur Miller, "Are You Now or Were You Ever," *Guardian/Observer*, June 17, 2000.

65. Alexander, *Salem Story*, 29; the emphasis is mine.

66. Miller, *Timebends*, 232–33.

67. Thirlwall, "Notes on William Carlos Williams as Playwright," 435.

68. Fones-Wolf, *Waves of Opposition*, 140.

69. Ibid.

70. Billy James Hargis, report on Stage for Action, Inc., 23, 1946, Billy James Hargis Papers (MC 1412), box 26, file 36, Special Collections, University of Arkansas Libraries.

71. Ibid., 22.

72. Ceplair and Englund, *Inquisition in Hollywood*, 216.

73. Quoted in Riegl, *Historical Grammar of the Visual Arts*, 20.

74. *Hearings before the Committee on Un-American Activities*, 80th Cong., 1st sess., 105 (July 21, 1947) (statement of Walter S. Steele, chairman of the national security committee of the American Coalition of Patriotic, Civic, and Fraternal Societies).

75. Laura Frankel, daughter of Gene Frankel, e-mail message to author, June 10, 2012.

76. In the Paul and Eslande Robeson Collection at Howard University, there is a script for a Progressive Party rally held at Madison Square Garden on October 26, 1948, one week before the presidential election. Paul Robeson was the emcee for the event, and the majority of the participants were either SFA performers, sponsors, or board members, including Jack Gilford (he led a *Schnitzelbank*), the People's Songs Trio and Pete Seeger (People's Songs shared office space with SFA early on, and Seeger recalls performing at some of the group's events), C. B. Baldwin, William S. Gailmor, and Vito Marcantonio.

77. *House Reports*, "Report on the Congress of American Women," 81st Cong., 2nd sess., 8 (October 23, 1949).

78. Quoted in Gannon, *Biographical Dictionary of the Left*, 214.

79. Fast, "Why the Fifth Amendment," 45.

80. Miller, *You're Next!*, 12.

5. A People's Theatre in Every Sense

1. Eisinger, *1940s*, xiv.

2. Ibid., xv.

3. Yarnell, *Democrats and Progressives*, 6, 7.

4. Ibid., 7.

5. Louis N. Ridenour, "A Scientist Turned Playwright," *Milwaukee Journal*, December 26, 1945, 14.

6. Ridenour, "Scientist Fights for Peace," 82.

7. Louis N. Ridenour, "Letter to Robert Adler, 24 November 1946," Louis N. Ridenour Papers, box 8, folder 9—fiction (1945–57, N.D.), Manuscript Division, Library of Congress.

8. Ibid.

9. Robert Oppenheimer, "Letter to Dr. Louis N. Ridenour, 14 May 1943," ibid., box 2, folder 5—general correspondence (1931–47).

10. Robert Adler, "Letter to Dr. Ridenour, 5 April 1946," ibid.

11. Robert Adler, "Letter to Dr. Ridenour, 8 January 1947," ibid.

12. U.S. Copyright Office, *Catalog of Copyright Renewal Records*, 5582.

13. Adler, Bellak, and Ridenour, *Open Secret*, 181–82.

14. Schweber, *In the Shadow of the Bomb*, 4.

15. Ibid., 6.

16. Quoted in ibid., 7.

17. Nuse, *Legislative History of the Atomic Energy Act of 1946*, 8.

18. Ibid., 10.

19. Ibid., 13.

20. Ibid., 1.

21. "American Survey: Political Scientists," *Economist*, February 2, 1946, 178.

22. Ibid.

23. "Momentous Decision," 12.

24. Ibid.

25. Ibid.

26. Adler, Bellak, and Ridenour, *Open Secret*, 178.

27. Ibid., 181.

28. Ibid., 188.

29. Ibid., 184, 189.

30. Ibid., 202.

31. Morrison writes that "the device detonated about half a mile in the air, just above the corner of Third Avenue and East 20th Street, near Gramercy Park. Evidently there had been no target chosen, just Manhattan and its people." In Masters and Way, *One World or None*, 3.

32. Ibid., 3–5.

33. "Eight Scientists Protest Thomas Committee's Methods," *Bulletin of the Atomic Scientists* 4 (October 1948), reprinted in Eisinger, *1940s*, 302.

34. Ibid.

35. Walter Gellhorn, *Security, Loyalty, and Science* (Ithaca: Cornell University Press, 1950), reprinted in Eisinger, *1940s*, 313.

36. Ibid.

37. Joseph Lieberman, "Best Stage for Action Plays," 5, Billy Rose Theatre Division, New York Public Library for the Performing Arts.

38. Shore and Williamson, *Who Are the Weavers*, 81.

39. Allan Keller, "Why Puerto Ricans Leave Home," *Dunkirk (N.Y.) Evening Observer*, November 1, 1947, 1.

40. U.S. Bureau of Labor Statistics, "Consumer Expenditure Survey," 22, http://www.bls.gov/cex/#tables, accessed July 15, 2014.

41. Shore and Williamson, *Who Are the Weavers*, 86.

42. Ibid.

43. Joseph Shore and Scott Graham Williamson, *Who Are the Weavers* [annotated by Maria Piscator], box 139, folder 8, 2, Erwin Piscator Papers, Special Collections Research Center, Southern Illinois University Carbondale.

44. Quoted in Hoernel, "Sugar and Social Change in Oriente, Cuba," 229.

45. Ibid., 239.

46. Meyer, *Vito Marcantonio*, 148.

47. "Larger Parish to Air Puerto Rican Problems," *Brooklyn Daily Eagle*, January 17, 1948, 4.

48. Ayala and Bernabe, *Puerto Rico in the American Century*, 336–37.

49. Schaffer, *Vito Marcantonio*, 142.

50. Ibid., 169.

51. Ibid., 46.

52. Ibid., 212.

53. Ayala and Bernabe, *Puerto Rico in the American Century*, 338.

54. Shore and Williamson, *Who Are the Weavers*, 99.

55. Quoted in Schaffer, *Vito Marcantonio*, 214.

56. Miller, *Theater Essays of Arthur Miller*, 323–24.

57. Cohen, *Rainbow Quest*, 80.

58. Pells, *Liberal Mind in a Conservative Age*, 264.

59. Richard Hofstadter, "The Paranoid Style in American Politics," *Harper's Magazine*, November 1964, 82.

60. Marvin Silbersher, phone interview with author, June 3, 2015; Bunny Kacher, phone interview with author, February 16, 2008.

61. Marcia Haufrecht, phone interview with author, October 1, 2011.

62. Ibid.

63. Hyman, *Staging Strikes*, 142.

64. Himelstein, *Drama Was a Weapon*, 232.

65. Bigsby, *Modern American Drama*, 88.

66. Ibid., 89.

67. Silbersher phone interview.

68. "They Shall Not Die," *Chicago Defender*, May 14, 1949, 16.

69. "Wexley Play to Be Revived," *New York Times*, May 12, 1949, 26.

70. "New Theatre Group to Do Social Plays," *Worker*, April 6, 1947, 14.

71. Ibid.

72. "Program of the New Theatre," *New York Times*, January 23, 1948, 27.

73. Leo Shull, "What about Summer Stock?," *New Masses*, June 18, 1946, 30.

74. American Lincoln Brigade Archives, "Robert Steck," http://www.alba-valb.org/volunteers/robert-steck, accessed April 15, 2014.

75. Barnard Rubin, "Successful Launching of People's Drama: Wexley's 'They Shall Not Die'—A Smash Hit," *Daily Worker*, June 13, 1949, 11.

76. Ibid.

77. "Ban on Play Assailed: Hays Terms Trenton Official's Action 'Unconstitutional,'" *New York Times*, December 27, 1949, 25.

78. "Names Aid Drama School," *Pittsburgh Courier*, April 8, 1950, 20.

79. Brooks Atkinson, "At the Theatre: Arena-Style Acting Presented in Remodeled Garage in Eldridge Street by People's Drama Group," *New York Times*, May 4, 1950, 41.

80. Ibid.

81. Quoted in Jones, *Voices and Silences*, 122; Walter Kerr, "Stage: Masks, Ritual and the Color White," *New York Herald Tribune*, May 14, 1961, D2.

82. Brooks Atkinson, "Theatre: Little Revue: Mr. Zero Plays It Low in 'Once Over Lightly,'" *New York Times*, March 16, 1955, 39.

83. Howard Taubman, "Theatre: Sacco and Vanzetti Drama," ibid., October 15, 1960, 27; "Two Plays to End Runs," ibid., November 12, 1960, 12.

84. John Gassner, "The Theatre Arts," *Forum*, March 1948, 156.

85. Ibid.

86. "Gladys Williams, Star of 'Stage for Action,'" *Chicago Defender*, November 18, 1944, 14.

87. Harry Taylor, "Stage for Action," *New Masses*, January 2, 1945, 29.

88. Stage for Action informational pamphlet, J. B. Matthews Papers, David M. Rubenstein Rare Book and Manuscript Library, Duke University.

Bibliography

Included here are sections for manuscript collections; newspapers, magazines, and periodicals; and books and journals.

Manuscript Collections

Billy James Hargis Papers. Special Collections. University of Arkansas Libraries.

C. B. Baldwin Papers. University of Iowa Libraries. Iowa City, Iowa.

Erwin Piscator Papers. Special Collections Research Center. Southern Illinois University Carbondale.

Gene Frankel Collection. Billy Rose Theatre Division. New York Public Library for the Performing Arts.

Hilda Worthington Smith Papers. Radcliffe Institute for Advanced Study. Harvard University.

J. B. Matthews Papers. David M. Rubenstein Rare Book and Manuscript Library. Duke University.

John Randolph Papers. Tamiment Library and Robert F. Wagner Labor Archives. New York University.

Lieberman, Joseph. "Best Stage for Action Plays." Billy Rose Theatre Division. New York Public Library for the Performing Arts.

Louis N. Ridenour Papers. Manuscript Division. Library of Congress.

Manuscripts, Archives and Rare Books Division. Schomburg Center for Research in Black Culture. New York Public Library.

National Republic Records. Hoover Institution Archives. Stanford University.

Paul and Eslande Robeson Collection. Spingarn Library. Howard University.

Peggy Clark Collection. Music Division. Library of Congress.

Printed Ephemera Collection. Tamiment Library and Robert F. Wagner Labor Archives. New York University.

Stage for Action Collection. Charles Deering McCormick Library of Special Collections. Northwestern University Library.

Newspapers, Magazines, and Periodicals

American Heritage
Baltimore Afro-American
Baltimore Sun
Billboard
Brooklyn Daily Eagle
Chicago Defender
Collier's Weekly
Counterattack
Daily Mail
Daily Worker
Dunkirk (N.Y.) Evening Observer
Economist
Forum
Guardian/Observer
Harper's Magazine
Hartford Courant
Jewish Exponent
Life
Masses and Mainstream
Milwaukee Journal
Modesto (Calif.) Bee and News Herald
New Masses
New York Age
New York Amsterdam News
New Yorker
New York Herald Tribune
New York Post
New York Star
New York Times
Pittsburgh Courier
PM
Theatre Workshop
Times Recorder
Variety
Worker

Books and Journals

Adler, Robert, George Bellak, and Louis N. Ridenour. *Open Secret.* In *The Best One-Act Plays, 1946–1947,* edited by Margaret Mayorga, 177–202. New York: Dodd, Mead, 1947.

Alexander, Sidney. *The Man on the Queue.* Prairie City, Ill.: James A. Decker Press, 1941.

American Heritage Foundation. *Good Citizen: The Rights and Duties of an American.* N.p.: American Heritage Foundation, 1948.

Anderson, Carol Elaine. *Eyes Off the Prize: The United Nations and the African American Struggle for Human Rights, 1944–1955.* Cambridge: Cambridge University Press, 2003.

Arvon, Henri. *Marxist Esthetics.* Ithaca: Cornell University Press, 1970.

Ayala, Cesar J., and Rafael Bernabe. *Puerto Rico in the American Century: A History since 1898.* Chapel Hill: University of North Carolina Press, 2007.

Baker, Nancy Kovaleff. "Abel Meeropol (a.k.a. Lewis Allan): Political Commentator and Social Conscience." *American Music* 20, no. 1 (Spring 2002): 25–79.

Bengal, Ben. "All Aboard." *Theatre Arts,* September 1944, 500–504.

Bigsby, C. W. E. *Modern American Drama, 1945–2000.* Cambridge: Cambridge University Press, 2000.

Black, Cheryl. "'New Negro' Performance in Art and Life: Fredi Washington and the Theatrical Columns of *The People's Voice,* 1943–47." *Theatre History Studies* 24 (June 2004): 57–72.

Bohn, Thomas William. *An Historical and Descriptive Analysis of the "Why We Fight" Series.* New York: Arno Press, 1977.

Brown, K. S., and Yannis Hamilakis, eds. *The Usable Past: Greek Metahistories.* Lanham, Md.: Lexington Books, 2003.

Ceplair, Larry, and Steven Englund. *The Inquisition in Hollywood: Politics in the Film Community, 1930–1960.* Berkeley: University of California Press, 1983.

Chadakoff, Rochelle, ed. *Eleanor Roosevelt's My Day: Her Acclaimed Columns, 1936–1945.* New York: Pharos Books, 1989.

Chen, Anthony S. *The Fifth Freedom: Jobs, Politics, and Civil Rights in the United States, 1941–1972.* Princeton: Princeton University Press, 2009.

Cohen, Ronald D. *Rainbow Quest: The Folk Music Revival and American Society, 1940–1970.* Amherst: University of Massachusetts Press, 2002.

Committee on Un-American Activities, U.S. House of Representatives. *100 Things You Should Know about Communism.* Washington: U.S. House of Representatives, 1949.

Culver, John C., and John Hyde. *American Dreamer: The Life and Times of Henry A. Wallace*. New York: W. W. Norton, 2000.

Denning, Michael. *The Cultural Front: The Laboring of American Culture in the Twentieth Century*. New York: Verso Books, 1997.

Devine, Thomas W. *Henry Wallace's 1948 Presidential Campaign and the Future of Postwar Liberalism*. Chapel Hill: University of North Carolina Press, 2013.

Du Bois, W. E. B. "Criteria of Negro Art." In *Theatre in Theory 1900–2000: An Anthology*, edited by David Krasner, 165–68. Malden, Mass.: Blackwell, 2008.

Eisinger, Chester E., ed. *The 1940s: Profile of a Nation in Crisis*. New York: Anchor Books, 1969.

Fast, Howard. "Why the Fifth Amendment." *Masses and Mainstream* 7, no. 2 (February 1954): 44–50.

Feldman, Stephen M. *Free Expression and Democracy in America: A History*. Chicago: University of Chicago Press, 2008.

Flanagan, Hallie. Introduction to *Federal Theatre Plays*, edited by Pierre De Rohan, vii–xii. New York: Da Capo Press, 1973.

Foner, Philip Sheldon. *Organized Labor and the Black Worker: 1619–1981*. New York: International, 1976.

Fones-Wolf, Elizabeth A. *Waves of Opposition: Labor and the Struggle for Democratic Radio*. Urbana: University of Illinois Press, 2006.

Foreman, Clark. "Statement of the National Citizens Political Action Committee." *Antioch Review* 4, no. 3 (Autumn 1944): 473–75.

Foster, William Z. "The New World Situation and Our Tasks." In *The Fight against Hitlerism*, by William Z. Foster and Robert Minor, 3–12. New York: Workers Library Publishers, Inc., 1941.

Friedman, Daniel. "Contemporary Theatre for Working-Class Audiences in the United States." In *Theatre for Working-Class Audiences in the United States, 1830–1980*, edited by Bruce A. McConachie and Daniel Friedman, 197–246. Westport, Conn.: Greenwood Press, 1985.

Gaer, Joseph. *The First Round: The Story of the CIO Political Action Committee*. New York: Duell, Sloan and Pearce, 1944.

Gallaway, Lowell Eugene, and Richard K. Vedder. *Out of Work: Unemployment and Government in Twentieth-Century America*. New York: New York University Press, 1997.

Gannon, Francis X. *A Biographical Dictionary of the Left*. Vol. 4. Belmont, Mass.: Western Islands, 1973.

Gassner, John, ed. *Best American Plays, 1945–1951*. New York: Crown, 1952.

———. "The One-Act Play in the Revolutionary Theatre." In *The One-Act Play Today*, edited by William Kozlenko, 243–86. New York: Harcourt, Brace, 1938.

Gilbert, Martin. *The Second World War: A Complete History*. New York: Henry Holt, 1989.

Goodman, Walter. *The Committee: The Extraordinary Career of the House Committee on Un-American Activities*. New York: Farrar, Straus and Giroux, 1968.

Green, Archie. *Wobblies, Pile Butts, and Other Heroes: Laborlore Explorations*. Urbana-Champaign: University of Illinois Press, 1993.

Hill, Christopher. *Lenin and the Russian Revolution*. London: Hodder Stoughton, 1947.

Himelstein, Morgan Y. *Drama Was a Weapon: The Left-Wing Theatre in New York, 1929–1941*. New Brunswick: Rutgers University Press, 1963.

"Historical/Biographical Note." *Guide to the National Council of American Soviet Friendship Records*. Tamiment Library and Robert F. Wagner Labor Archives, New York University. http://dlib.nyu.edu/findingaids /html/tamwag/tam_134/bioghist.html. Last modified June 2014.

Hoernel, Robert B. "Sugar and Social Change in Oriente, Cuba, 1898–1946." *Journal of Latin American Studies* 8, no. 2 (1976): 215–49.

Hyman, Colette A. *Staging Strikes: Workers' Theatre and the American Labor Movement*. Philadelphia: Temple University Press, 1997.

Johande, Michael C., and John L. Puckett. *Leonard Covello and the Making of Benjamin Franklin High School*. Philadelphia: Temple University Press, 2006.

Johnpoll, Bernard K. *A Documentary History of the Communist Party of the United States*. Vol. 7. Westport, Conn.: Greenwood Press, 1994.

Johnson, Oakley C. "One Year in the Deep South: A Documentary of Seventeen Years Earlier." *Journal of Human Relations* 12, no. 1 (1964): 34–49.

Jones, James Earl. *Voices and Silences*. 2nd ed. Pompton Plains, N.J.: Limelight Editions, 2002.

Kaplan, Milton Allen. *Radio and Poetry*. New York: Columbia University Press, 1949.

Katznelson, Ira. *Fear Itself: The New Deal and the Origins of Our Time*. New York: Liveright, 2013.

Kleinman, Mark L. *A World of Hope, a World of Fear: Henry A. Wallace, Reinhold Niebuhr, and American Liberalism*. Columbus: Ohio State University Press, 2000.

Kushner, Tony, Linda Frye Burnham, Doug Paterson, Archon Fung, John O'Neal, Roberta Uno, Holly Hughes et al. "How Do You Make Social Change?" *Theater* 31, no. 3 (Fall 2001): 62–93.

Landy, Robert J., and David T. Montgomery. *Theatre for Change: Education, Social Action and Therapy.* New York: Palgrave Macmillan, 2012.

Lee, R. Alton. *Truman and Taft-Hartley: A Question of Mandate.* Lexington: University of Kentucky Press, 1966.

Library of Congress Copyright Office. "Dramatic Compositions and Motion Pictures." *Catalog of Copyright Entries* 19 (1946): 150.

Lieberman, Robbie. *"My Song Is My Weapon": People's Songs, American Communism, and the Politics of Culture, 1930–50.* Music in American Life. Urbana: University of Illinois Press, 1989.

Mally, Lynn. "The Americanization of the Soviet Living Newspaper." *The Carl Beck Papers in Russian and East European Studies* 1903 (February 2008): 1–40.

———. "Inside a Communist Front: A Post–Cold War Analysis of the New Theatre League." *American Communist History* 6, no. 1 (2007): 65–95.

Marx, Karl. "Production and Consumption." In *Marxism and Art: Writings in Aesthetics and Criticism*, edited by Berel Lang and Forrest Williams, 31–38. New York: David McKay, 1972.

Masters, Dexter, and Katharine Way, eds. *One World or None.* New York: Whittlesey House, 1946.

Mayorga, Margaret, ed. *The Best One-Act Plays of 1944.* New York: Dodd, Mead and Company, 1945.

McDermott, Douglas. "The Workers' Laboratory Theatre: Archetype and Example." In *Theatre for Working-Class Audiences in the United States, 1830–1980*, edited by Bruce A. McConachie and Daniel Friedman, 121–54. Westport, Conn.: Greenwood Press, 1985.

Meyer, Gerald. *Vito Marcantonio: Radical Politician, 1902–1954.* Albany: State University of New York Press, 1989.

Miller, Arthur. *Arthur Miller: Collected Plays 1944–1961.* New York: Library of America, 2006.

———. "Concerning the Boom." *International Theatre Annual* 1 (1956): 85–88.

———. *The Portable Arthur Miller.* New York: Penguin Classics, 2003.

———. *That They May Win.* In *The Best One-Act Plays of 1944*, edited by Margaret Mayorga, 45–59. New York: Dodd, Mead and Company, 1945.

———. *The Theater Essays of Arthur Miller.* Edited by Robert A. Martin and Steven R. Centola. New York: Da Capo Press, 1996.

———. *Timebends: A Life.* New York: Penguin Books, 1995.

Mitchell, Clarence, Jr. *The Papers of Clarence Mitchell Jr., Volume 1: 1942–1943.* Athens: Ohio University Press, 2005.

"Momentous Decision: Senate Committee Prepares Domestic Bill." *Bulletin of the Atomic Scientists of Chicago* 1, no. 6 (March 1946): 1, 12.

Muray-Irizarry, Néstor. *Rafael Ríos-Rey: The First Puerto Rican Muralist.* Ponce, P.R.: Casa Paoli, 2003.

Murphy, Brenda. *Congressional Theatre: Dramatizing McCarthyism on Stage, Film, and Television.* Cambridge: Cambridge University Press, 2003.

Musser, Charles. "Carl Marzani and Union Films: Making Left-Wing Documentaries during the Cold War, 1946–53." *The Moving Image: The Journal of the Association of Moving Image Archivists* 9, no. 1 (Spring 2009): 104–60.

Nuse, James D. *Legislative History of the Atomic Energy Act of 1946, Public Law 585, 79th Congress.* Washington, D.C.: U.S. Atomic Energy Commission, 1965.

Pells, Richard H. *The Liberal Mind in a Conservative Age.* Hanover, N.H.: Wesleyan University Press, 1989.

Perucci, Tony. *Paul Robeson and the Cold War Performance Complex: Race, Madness, Activism.* Ann Arbor: University of Michigan Press, 2012.

Peterson, Bernard L., Jr. *The African American Theatre Directory, 1816–1960.* New York: Greenwood Press, 1997.

Ridenour, Louis. "The Scientist Fights for Peace." *Atlantic Monthly,* May 1947, 80–83.

Riegl, Alois. *Historical Grammar of the Visual Arts.* Translated by Jacqueline E. Jung. New York: Zone Books, 2004.

Riggs, Robert. *Leon Kirchner: Composer, Performer, and Teacher.* Rochester: University of Rochester Press, 2010.

Rodman, Selden. Introduction to *The Man on the Queue,* by Sidney Alexander, 2–4. Prairie City, Ill.: James A. Decker Press, 1941.

Rolland, Romain. "The People's Theatre." In *Theatre in Theory 1900–2000: An Anthology,* edited by David Krasner, 61–63. Malden, Mass.: Blackwell, 2008.

Saal, Ilka. *New Deal Theater: The Vernacular Tradition in American Political Theater.* New York: Palgrave Macmillan, 2007.

Sabato, Larry J. *PAC Power: Inside the World of Political Action Committees.* New York: W. W. Norton, 1984.

Samuel, Raphael, Ewan MacColl, and Stuart Cosgrove, eds. *Theatres of the Left, 1880–1935: Workers' Theatre Movements in Britain and America.* Boston: Routledge and Kegan Paul, 1985.

Sarvis, Will. "Leaders in the Court and Community: Z. Alexander Looby, Avon N. Williams, Jr., and the Legal Fight for Civil Rights in Tennessee, 1940–1970." *Journal of African American History* 88, no. 1 (Winter 2003): 42–58.

Satterfield, Jay. *"The World's Best Books": Taste, Culture, and the Modern Library.* Amherst: University of Massachusetts Press, 2010.

Schaffer, Alan. *Vito Marcantonio, Radical in Congress.* Syracuse: Syracuse University Press, 1966.

Schrecker, Ellen. *Many Are the Crimes: McCarthyism in America.* Princeton: Princeton University Press, 1998.

Schweber, S. S. *In the Shadow of the Bomb: Bethe, Oppenheimer, and the Moral Responsibility of the Scientist.* Princeton: Princeton University Press, 2000.

Seeger, Peggy. Vocal performance of "Taft-Hartley Song." By Charlie King. *From Where I Stand: Topical Songs from America and England.* Folkways Records FW 8563, 1982, compact disc.

Shore, Joseph, and Scott Graham Williamson. *Who Are the Weavers.* In *The Best One-Act Plays, 1947–1948*, edited by Margaret Mayorga, 77–100. New York: Dodd, Mead, 1948.

Singer, Henry A. "The Veteran and Race Relations." *Journal of Educational Sociology* 21, no. 7 (March 1948): 397–408.

Starkey, Marion L. *The Devil in Massachusetts: A Modern Inquiry into the Salem Witch Trials.* New York: Alfred A. Knopf, 1949.

Sugrue, Thomas J. *The Origins of the Urban Crisis: Race and Inequality in Postwar Detroit.* Princeton: Princeton University Press, 1996.

U.S. Copyright Office. *The Catalog of Copyright Renewal Records.* Whitefish, Mont.: Kessinger, 2007.

Wald, Alan M. *American Night: The Literary Left in the Era of the Cold War.* Chapel Hill: University of North Carolina Press, 2012.

———. *Exiles from a Future Time: The Forging of the Mid-Twentieth-Century Literary Left.* Chapel Hill: University of North Carolina Press, 2002.

———. *Trinity of Passion: The Literary Left and the Anti-Fascist Crusade.* Chapel Hill: University of North Carolina Press, 2007.

Wallace, Henry A. *The Price of Vision: The Diary of Henry A. Wallace, 1942–1946.* Edited by John Morton Blum. Boston: Houghton Mifflin, 1973.

———. *Sixty Million Jobs.* New York: Simon and Schuster, 1945.

Walton, Richard J. *Henry Wallace, Harry Truman, and the Cold War.* New York: Viking, 1976.

Weigand, Kate. *Red Feminism: American Communism and the Making of Women's Liberation.* Baltimore: Johns Hopkins University Press, 2001.

Wertheim, Albert. *Staging the War: American Drama and World War II.* Bloomington: Indiana University Press, 2004.

White, John. "Civil Rights in Conflict: The 'Birmingham Plan' and the Freedom Train, 1947." *Alabama Review* 52, no. 2 (April 1999): 121–41.

Williams, Jay. *Stage Left: An Engrossing Account of the Radical Theatre Movement in America.* New York: Scribner's, 1974.

Williams, William Carlos. *"Many Loves" and Other Plays: The Collected Plays of William Carlos Williams.* New York: New Directions, 1965.

Wolf, Friedrich. "Art Is a Weapon!" In *The Weimar Republic Sourcebook,* edited by Anton Kaes, Martin Jay, and Edward Dimendberg, 230–31. Berkeley: University of California Press, 1994.

Yarnell, Allen. *Democrats and Progressives: The 1948 Presidential Election as a Test of Postwar Liberalism.* Berkeley: University of California Press, 1974.

Zieger, Robert H. *American Workers, American Unions.* Baltimore: Johns Hopkins University Press, 1994.

Index

Page numbers in italics indicate illustrations.

CHRYSTYNA DAIL is an assistant professor of theatre history at Ithaca College. Her essays and reviews have appeared in the *Journal of American Drama and Theatre, Theatre History Studies, Arthur Miller Journal, Theatre Journal, Performing Arts Resources,* and the edited collection *Working in the Wings: New Perspectives on Theatre History and Labor.*

Theater in the Americas

The goal of the series is to publish a wide range of scholarship on theater and performance, defining theater in its broadest terms and including subjects that encompass all of the Americas.

The series focuses on the performance and production of theater and theater artists and practitioners but welcomes studies of dramatic literature as well. Meant to be inclusive, the series invites studies of traditional, experimental, and ethnic forms of theater; celebrations, festivals, and rituals that perform culture; and acts of civil disobedience that are performative in nature. We publish studies of theater and performance activities of all cultural groups within the Americas, including biographies of individuals, histories of theater companies, studies of cultural traditions, and collections of plays.

Queries and Submissions
Scott Magelssen, Editor
magelss@uw.edu

Founder and Editor, Robert A. Schanke, 2000–2014